W9-BNT-617

High class hijinks and low-down murder—
Praise for the previous
DEBUTANTE DROPOUT MYSTERIES
by SUSAN McBRIDE

"I'll read anything by Susan McBride."
Charlaine Harris

"Kick off your Manolos and skip the cocktail hour
to curl up with Andy Kendricks,
her socialite mother, and her blue blood buddies."
Nancy Martin

"A wonderful new series with a character
who is feisty without being snotty,
witty but not a smart-aleck,
and just plain likeable . . .
Andy Kendricks's [next] appearance
can't come soon enough."
January magazine

"Susan McBride creates a wonderfully determined
and clever sleuth who is willing to peel off
the white gloves and don a Wonderbra
in pursuit of the bad guys. And for this,
all mystery readers should applaud."
Jerrilyn Farmer

"Susan McBride kept me laughing all the way
through this delicious romp of a mystery."
Tess Gerritsen

Books by Susan McBride

THE LONE STAR LONELY HEARTS CLUB
THE GOOD GIRL'S GUIDE TO MURDER
BLUE BLOOD

SUSAN McBRIDE

The Lone Star
LONELY HEARTS
Club

A DEBUTANTE DROPOUT MYSTERY

AVON BOOKS
An Imprint of HarperCollinsPublishers

AVON BOOKS
An Imprint of HarperCollins*Publishers*
10 East 53rd Street
New York, New York 10022-5299

Copyright © 2006 by Susan McBride
ISBN-13: 978-0-06-056408-7
ISBN-10: 0-06-056408-3
www.avonmystery.com

First Avon Books paperback printing: February 2006

Avon Trademark Reg. U.S. Pat. Off. and in Other Countries, Marca Registrada, Hecho en U.S.A.
HarperCollins® is a registered trademark of HarperCollins Publishers Inc.

Printed in the U.S.A.

10 9 8 7 6 5 4 3 2 1

This book is dedicated to mothers and daughters
everywhere.
And to the memory of my grandma,
Helen Meisel,
who just wanted a hand to hold.

Acknowledgments

Again, thanks to Robin Waldron, M.D., for answering my crazy questions; also to pharmacist Ethel Neal for confirming that my method of murder was not too far-fetched for fiction.

I've said this before, but it's worth repeating: working with Sarah Durand is an absolute joy. I'm also extremely fortunate to have found my way to Andrea Cirillo and Maggie Kelly this past year. Here's to many fun and fruitful days ahead!

To the rest of my friends and family who keep me smiling even when things get nuts. If not for you, I would have to be medicated. (I'm kidding. Sort of.)

"It is never too late to be what you might have been."
—George Eliot

The Lone Star
LONELY HEARTS
Club

Chapter 1

Getting old was murder.

Make no mistake about it.

Sarah Lee Sewell tugged on the loose skin of her cheeks and frowned at the mirror, wondering if it wasn't time she got a little nip and tuck. Every woman her age in Dallas—and not a few of the men—had been doing it for years. But, as long as Eldon had been alive, Sarah Lee hadn't put too much stock in her faded appearance.

"I love you for what's inside, honey pie, not for the gift-wrapping"—his blue eyes had twinkled as they'd looked her up and down—"though I've got no complaints about that, either."

The smile that formed on her lips at the memory fast died, and she sighed at her tired reflection.

"Oh, Eldon," she said, to no one but herself. "How I miss you."

She missed his wit.

Missed his scent, of tweed and pipe tobacco.

Missed having a hand to hold. That, most of all.

After five decades of marriage, two years seemed a long time to go without the touch of a man. Maybe some women could stand it, but Sarah Lee couldn't. It was a slow death in itself, like being starved or suffocated. Even cats needed to be stroked now and then.

Sarah Lee was only human.

Which was why she'd gone and done what she had, something she never in her wildest dreams imagined she'd do and still wasn't too all-fired sure about.

She'd started dating.

She hadn't told any of her friends what she was up to and wasn't certain she'd stick it out, but she'd promised herself she'd give it a decent shot before she chucked the idea as pure insanity.

She'd been out to dinner twice already with several different gentlemen, the conversation pleasant if not a little awkward. They had asked if they might call on her again, and Sarah Lee hadn't objected. Though getting used to being courted at this point in her life gave her butterflies as big as B-2 bombers.

She fumbled with a silver tube of lipstick, swiping her thin mouth one last time with a well-used crimson. Then she pinched her cheeks and nodded, knowing she'd done the best she could with what she had.

Which is when her legs began to tremble.

Dear God, why on earth was she doing this?

Because you're lonely, a tiny voice reminded her. *Because Eldon's been gone for years, and you don't like to be alone.*

It wasn't even sex. She merely wanted to be held in the snug circle of a man's arms. Was that such a terrible thing?

She sighed and steadied herself against the marble counter.

Before her recent outings, the last real "date" she'd been on was back in high school, and her suitor had been a sixteen-year-old Highland Park football star named Eldon Sewell. Sarah Lee had been top of her class at Ursuline Academy, smart enough to know a catch when she'd hooked him. At eighteen, they'd married, living in off-campus housing in Fort Worth as they'd worked their way through TCU, building a foundation that had lasted "till death do us part." They'd still be together if that damned cancer hadn't chewed Eldon's life away from the inside out.

She'd never been with anyone before him, nor since. Not in the biblical sense. Which made her something of a freak in these fast and loose times, didn't it? She was an eight-track tape in a digital era, and the way her friends kept dying off, pretty soon they'd all be extinct.

You're morbid, Sarah Lee, she thought and laughed at herself.

But death scared her far less than the dating game she'd been playing.

She patted her hair, styled in the same teased and sprayed coif she'd worn for too many years, and she figured it was time for a change. She was a different person than she'd been: more self-assured and assertive.

Maybe she'd try that fellow at the Plaza Park Salon about whom her terribly chic friend Cissy Kendricks had been raving lately. She'd get his name when she saw Cissy Wednesday at bridge, because it wouldn't be appropriate to inquire at the church service for Bebe Kent the next morning.

Ah, poor Bebe.

With bent fingers, she reached for her brush.

The doorbell chimed.

Startled, the brush dropped from her hand, clattering into the bowl of the sink, and she turned toward the hallway, her heart zigzagging in her chest, it beat so loudly.

Who could that be? she wondered, because she'd arranged to meet her date at the restaurant, as she'd done with the two before him. A neutral spot, because she didn't want strangers in her home, not at night when she was by herself, despite the relative security of her surroundings.

Probably just a neighbor, or one of the staff come to sweet-talk her into submission. You'd think for all she'd paid to live in this highbrow retirement home, Housekeeping could come more than twice a week, her toilets would flush properly, and they could keep the damned squirrels out of her attic. No matter if it was the director herself, panting like a puppy dog and begging to please, Sarah Lee wasn't letting her in. They could discuss her complaints at *her* convenience or she surely would drag in her lawyer.

Oh, dear, she realized, smoothing the hem of her dress. She had to leave in fifteen minutes flat if she wanted to be on time for the dinner reservation.

She took a deep breath and shut off the bathroom light as she stepped into the hallway.

The bell chimed again.

"Coming," she trilled and hurried toward the noise, passing the photographs of herself and Eldon hanging on the walls, not seeing them, too curious about the visitor who waited for her on the other side of the door. She seriously hoped it wasn't her date, to whom she'd stated quite plainly that she preferred to drive herself; but some men of her generation found the idea an affront to their chivalry.

Pulse skipping, she put an eye to the peephole and squinted.

Hmmm.

This put her in a pickle.

She unlocked the door and pulled it wide. "Well, goodness, I wasn't expecting to see you." She stared at the visitor who stood on her welcome mat, unsure of how to handle things except to put on a polite face and mind her manners. "Oh, dear, I can only spare a minute or two." She forced a smile and stepped back, making way. "But, please, won't you come in?"

It was the last question Sarah Lee Sewell would ever ask.

Chapter 2

I only had one funeral dress.

My closet wasn't exactly equipped for death.

If I'd been the proper Dallas debutante my mother had reared me to be, I would've owned uncountable black outfits, enough styles to accommodate any social occasion, from cocktail parties to gallery openings to saying *sayonara* to the dearly departed.

But I wasn't a debutante, much less a proper one.

I'd never debuted at all, much to Mother's everlasting chagrin. She'd blamed it on my grief over my father's death when I was eighteen, a sudden stroke of temporary insanity, while I regarded my refusal to "come out" (and I'm talking socially) as finally coming to my senses. Defying Cissy Blevins Kendricks over something so important to her—and so meaningless to me—felt like the unveiling of the real Andy Kendricks. I'd been born-again, only not in any religious sense. It had more to do with my desire to be a regular human being, regardless of how desperately Cissy wanted me to follow in her Ferragamo-heeled footsteps.

I would no more be a society maven—like her—than a brain surgeon or a rocket scientist. It just wasn't in the cards, no matter how she tried to stack the deck. I cherished my independence after growing up alongside far too many Stepford children who seemed perfectly willing to follow the rules, such as they were, so as not to be disenfranchised by their wealthy parents. Any acts of rebellion on their part were carefully exorcised in the bars and on the beaches of Cabo on spring break.

Thank God my father had encouraged my free spirit. Unfortunately, it had taken his death to release it completely. I'd spent the better part of the last decade channeling his strength in order to beat back my mother's attempts to corrupt me with invitations to the city's most exclusive grand openings and galas, or the latest from Escada or Fendi.

So far, I'd done a passable job resisting.

Despite Cissy's best efforts, she'd failed to turn me into a fashion plate, though my brain was still wired to recognize a Pucci when I saw one. I'd been a deb-in-training from the moment I'd left the womb, and those lessons were ones I couldn't shake from my system, not unless I developed amnesia or had a lobotomy (and I wasn't planning to do either).

Regardless of Cissy's influence, these days I was more about comfort than couture. I'm sure the salesladies at Chanel in Highland Park Village would shudder and shoo me out the door were I to walk in wearing my uniform of paint-spattered jeans and faded SAVE THE RAINFOREST T-shirt. While my perfectly put-together pearl-wearing mother had them salivating like Pavlov's dogs the moment she set off the door chime. I didn't doubt they had the digits on her Platinum MasterCard memorized. They had her number, regardless.

There was little chance of my winding up beside Cissy on the *Park Cities Press*'s annual "best-dressed" list. My tastes didn't go much beyond bargain hunting at vintage and resale shops, when I did shop at all.

A fashionista, I was not. I was an artist and web designer, doing lots of pro bono work, primarily for underfunded charities. Most days I lived in sweatpants and wrinkled button-downs left behind by Brian Malone, my current squeeze who happened to be an attorney. Though dating a man with a steady job and clean-cut appearance wasn't my norm, Malone made my heart skip in a way that no free-spirited poet-cum-bartender had before him. And he never complained about the sorry state of my wardrobe, which scored huge points in his favor.

Particularly because he had good cause to complain, I decided, clearheadedly taking in the contents of my small walk-in closet, which more closely resembled donations to the Goodwill bin than the racks at Saks. Full of well-worn jeans, cotton T-shirts, and sneakers, everything—or most of it—made of natural fibers, none branded with a high-class label.

There were times, despite myself, when I wanted to call my Fairy Clothes-Mother to wave her magic wand and fix me up.

Then I'd come to my senses.

I hesitated but briefly before I plucked out a hanger with the only suitable funereal garment I possessed. The curved arms held a lightweight black knit that had served me well since the first time I'd worn it, at my graduation from art school in Chicago. I'd barely had cause to don it since.

I expected my mother to wince when she saw it, but she wouldn't dare criticize, not at the memorial service of a dear friend and certainly not inside the walls of Highland Park Presbyterian where God could hear her. Besides, she was profoundly brokenhearted. As good as she was at maintaining an air of decorum, no matter how rough a situation, the loss of her old chum had her seriously choked up.

"I can't *believe* she's gone, Andrea." Her ever-charming drawl had bordered on a broken-up wail when she'd phoned with the news the previous day. "Bebe was *only* seventy-three, and she was healthy as a horse except for the usual things . . . a touch of high blood pressure, seasonal allergies, certainly nothing fatal. I can hardly think of a day when she was sick. Good heavens, she got her flu shots every year like clockwork, and I've never seen anyone take so much vitamin C. It's a wonder she wasn't orange."

Cissy had recently turned sixty, so Bebe had but a slim decade on her. No wonder she was so shaken, and her audible grief had me so tongue-tied I hadn't known what to say beyond the pathetic and inept, "I'm so sorry for your loss."

"I just *don't* understand. She did yoga and water aerobics three days a week and used her treadmill during *Oprah*. She finished the Susan Komen Walk in June in a hundred-degree heat and didn't stop *once*. No," my mother had protested, and I'd imagined the perfect oval of her face crumpled with desolation. "It doesn't make sense."

But people died all the time, right? Dropped dead for no apparent reason other than a heart that stopped ticking. And once you crossed seventy, you were fair game, I supposed. Heck, every time you stepped off the curb, you were taking your chances.

"You'll go with me to her service, won't you, sweetie? I don't think I could *bear* to do this alone."

Alone?

Unless the fire code prevented it, she'd be surrounded by four or five hundred of her and Bebe's closest comrades.

"What about Sandy?" I piped up timidly, because Sandy Beck had been with my family for ages and still lived in the house on Beverly Drive, taking care of Mother and the mansion with the efficiency of Martha Stewart and the demeanor of Gandhi. She was, beyond all else, a calming force, and that's what Cissy needed most.

Until I remembered that Sandy didn't "do" funerals, neither did she read the obits in the *Dallas Morning News*. Unlike most of us, Sandy Beck didn't like to dwell on negatives.

Damn her.

I wish I'd adopted the "no-funerals" policy my-self right after Daddy died. Could be that I didn't appreciate the closure offered by the tradition and ceremony, but sad hymns and eulogies twisted my guts like a pretzel. I wondered if there was such a thing as funeral phobia. If so, I had it in spades.

"Andrea, please, won't you go?"

Mother's honey-smooth drawl could sound so tragic when it suited her. If SMU had offered a course in Emotional Blackmail, my mother would've aced it. (Heck, she could *teach* it.)

Despite how thoroughly I wanted to decline this particular invitation, my heart wasn't nearly black enough to refuse Mother's plea. Before I could stop the words from flowing off my tongue, I'd told her, "All right. You can count on me."

Well, she didn't ask for my shoulder to lean on very often. Okay, almost never.

And, much as I hated to admit it, it felt pretty good to be needed. I tried to dwell on that instead of the knot of anxiety curled in my belly like the world's largest ball of twine.

"*Poor, poor Bebe,*" she'd said and sighed the most doleful sigh. "I'll miss her terribly. She was the best bridge partner I ever had."

Beatrice "Bebe" Kent wasn't anyone I'd known well, beyond polite "hellos" every so often when I was growing up on Beverly Drive in "the bubble" of Highland Park. She'd been a high-ranking member of Cissy's expansive circle of blue blood friends who'd never met a fundraiser or civic or-ganization they didn't like. Her obit in the *Dallas Morning News* merited nearly half a page and read

like a "what's what" of A-list clubs and philan-
thropies: past president of the Junior League of
Dallas; board member of the Dallas Art Museum;
chairwoman of the Crystal Charity Ball; life member of the Brook Hollow Golf Club, Dallas Country Club, the Dallas Woman's Club, the Dallas
Garden Club, the Park Cities Historical Society,
and on and on, ad infinitum. She'd been the *trés*
wealthy widow of Homer Kent, a much-adored
oil magnate after whom a rather large wing of
Presbyterian Hospital had been named. But, most
importantly, Bebe had been a graduate of Southern Methodist University and an active alumna of
Pi Beta Phi.

My mother's sorority.

In Cissy's eyes, Bebe was a shining example of
Texas womanhood, of living one's life right. Or,
rather, *properly.*

Part of me wondered if one of the reasons
Mother had asked me to accompany her to Bebe's
memorial had less to do with needing my support
than Bebe's legacy serving as an example that it
wasn't too late for me to change my tune and embrace my trust fund with open arms.

I had no such delusions.

Seeing the hordes of Bebe's nearest and dearest
fill the pews, all garbed in the latest somber hues
from New York or Paris, would only serve to remind me that Mother's world wasn't one I wished
to inhabit, not in this lifetime. She had a galaxy of
upper crust chums always flitting around her, like
stars bright with bling surrounding the sun.

So it seemed only right that I be the Black Hole
in her solar system.

Someone had to do it.

Particularly since she was like the Hubble telescope in my Milky Way: not always functioning the way I wished she would and constantly keeping an eye on me, despite a view that was so often distorted.

Cissy had an opinion on everything, from my hair—"sweetie, if you'd just let Roberto give it some shape, you wouldn't have to wear it in a ponytail everyday"—to my car—"Jeeps are for teenaged boys, darling, so don't you think it's time to get something with four doors and a trunk?"—to my love life—"I do like Mr. Malone, very much, I'm just worried he's takin' advantage of you. Don't you know that men won't buy the cow when they can get the milk for free?"

To misquote that famous Valley Girl, Moon Unit Zappa, "Gag me with a silver spoon."

Scowling, I tugged the dress over my head, getting caught inside the stretchy fabric and batting at it, feeling trapped in more ways than one.

Though fighting was useless.

It was *so* true that you could pick your nose, but not your family. I was living proof.

Didn't matter from which angle I viewed it. Plain and simple, I was stuck.

With a grunt, I finally pushed my head through the neckline, feeling like a diver coming up for air.

The static electricity set my hair to standing on end, and I cursed in a very unladylike fashion as I put a little spit in my palms and tried to smooth it down.

Hopeless, I tell you.

I looked like Alfalfa in drag.

Though it could've been worse. On rainy days, my hair leaned toward the finger-in-socket 'do made famous by the brilliant but aesthetically disinclined Al Einstein. I could forget ever being a Breck girl.

Ah, to heck with it, I thought and grabbed a clip from my bureau, pulling the rat's nest of brown into a ponytail.

I realized I was grinding my teeth and forcibly relaxed my jaw, letting out a slow breath. My dentist had threatened me with a plastic mouthpiece if I didn't shake the bad habit, as I was apparently making mincemeat of my molars and bicuspids. But it was my instinctive response to anxiety. That and a stiff neck.

Which is why Malone had bought me a book called *Stress and the Single Girl*. It had plenty of chapters on dealing with a controlling mother, among other nerve-wracking scenarios like being held hostage or getting caught in traffic.

"You're going to have to cope with Cissy for the rest of your life . . . or hers, anyway," he'd said, as if I needed reminding. "So, unless you want to end up a toothless middle-aged woman with high blood pressure, you'd better learn how to shrug her off."

Shrug off Mother?

That was rather like asking someone infected to "shrug off" malaria.

The book had gone untouched for weeks. But I'd reluctantly begun to thumb through it the night before and had gotten so far as attempting the first of the "Six Simple Ways to Lower Your

Stress Quotient," which advised that I "embrace high anxiety moments with a wide grin or belly laugh."

Though I wasn't sure if any semisane person would ever "embrace high anxiety," I figured there was no time like the present. So I let loose a loud, "*ha ha ha!*" before I turned away from my reflection in the mirror.

Geez, I felt better already.

Not.

On my hands and knees, I located my black slides beneath the unmade bed and slipped them on to my bare feet. Mother might have a cow that I wasn't wearing pantyhose, but early September in Dallas generally meant temperatures in the low nineties. Not even threats at gunpoint would get me to put on a pair of L'eggs when it was that warm. Heat and nylons were completely incompatible.

Retrieving my purse and car keys, I gave my place a quick once-over on my way toward the door, checking the kitchen to make sure I hadn't left the stove on and seeing if the red light was blinking on my CallerID, in case I'd missed someone while I was in the shower, like a client or a road-tripping boyfriend (I hadn't).

It wasn't yet nine o'clock, though the air outside already felt like a sauna set on well done. The sky stretched blue as far as the eye could see, not a single smear of white to soften the pervasive yellow sunbeams. Even as I headed toward my Jeep, I felt a trickle of sweat wend its way down my back, and my armpits grew sticky.

One thing was for sure, I thought, as I climbed

into the Wrangler and started the car with one hand while rolling down a window with the other, Dallas was no place for sissies.

Nope, the sissies moved to the Hill Country.

Driving south on Hillcrest, I left the radio off, staring at the cars on the street ahead of me, wondering if any of them were headed to a funeral on this cloudless Saturday morning and wishing I weren't. Malone had gone out of town to do more prep work for a case—all the way to Galveston for an entire weekend—and I suddenly regretted my decision not to go with him. Just the thought of a choir singing "Amazing Grace" (which, of course, they would) tied a knot in my belly. Not that I didn't find the hymn quite touching, but its touch felt more like a punch in the belly. It brought back such vivid memories of the day we buried my daddy. The darkest day I've ever had, so far, and it pained me, in any small way, to repeat it.

Didn't seem to matter that it had happened a dozen years before. Moments like that stayed fresh in a person's mind. It still made my heart ache to think of it.

I wondered if Cissy felt the same, every time she heard "Amazing Grace" or "Jesus Loves Me" or the oft-repeated psalm about "earth to earth, ashes to ashes, dust to dust." Did she mourn my father all over again?

Sometimes I forgot the fact that I wasn't the only one who'd lost a best friend, a cheerleader and moral compass. I'd never discussed with Cissy how she felt, if she still suffered much. My mother wasn't keen on opening up, at least not to me. Was it because she chose not to, or because I hadn't given her the opportunity?

Oh, boy.

I was waxing philosophical, a sure sign that this was all too much. I felt positively maudlin. Death wasn't a comfortable subject for anyone, was it? Except, perhaps, for casket salesmen and morticians.

I sniffled and wiped a sleeve beneath my eyes, decidedly blue despite the sunshine around me.

How I hated funerals.

I had the strongest urge to turn around, go back home, and crawl under the covers.

But bailing on Mother wasn't an option. I couldn't let her down, not in this type of situation and certainly not on this particular morning.

So I gripped the steering wheel tighter, catching a glimpse of my eyes in the rearview mirror. My squint rumpled my forehead into deep lines of worry, and, out of nowhere, I heard the whisper of Cissy's voice, admonishing, *"Don't frown, Andrea darlin', or you'll cause wrinkles. Then it's Botox for the rest of your life, and I know how you hate needles."*

Nothing like my mother's beauty tips to cheer me up.

I switched on the radio, hitting buttons until I stumbled upon the guitar-driven chorus of "Jump," one of my favorite Van Halen oldies. I turned it up as loud as I could stand it, leaving no room for the emotions that threatened to climb from my chest into my throat or out my tear ducts.

Another fifteen minutes of retro rock and roll, and my spirits felt mildly buoyed as I descended into University Park, home to my parents' alma mater, SMU. The church sat just west of the campus on University Boulevard, wedged between that street, Park Lane, and McFarlin. As I circled the block, hitting a gridlock of limos and Mercedes sedans, I felt my gaze drawn to the place where I'd been baptized, where Mother and Daddy had married: an imposing structure of red brick and stone with a steeple that pointed the way to Kingdom Come through a sky bluer than the Danube.

I remembered coming to Sunday school when I was a kid, learning the Lord's Prayer and finding it pretty cool that God had "art in heaven." I imagined that He colored the sunsets with finger paint. A rather clever theory for a five-year-old, I figured.

After a pass around the block and no sign of an empty spot on the streets, I left my Jeep in the spare lot at city hall and took the church shuttle over with a half-dozen other latecomers, all garbed in black like a murder of crows.

I wedged myself between a white-haired man in a wool suit that looked far too hot for the tail end of summer and a woman wearing a wide-brimmed hat that knocked into the side of my head every time she turned hers. Rather than rip it off her, I leaned toward the man on my left, who ignored me entirely and stared out the window.

With a *thump*, the shuttle driver slammed the door, shutting the lot of us in, the air heavy with perfume and cologne, sweat and silence. I felt like I was headed to camp with a group of wealthy strangers all muttering a prayer that one day HPPC would adopt valet parking.

The trip was thankfully brief, and I trailed the pack from the van, through the church doors to the sanctuary where the service had already started, from the sound of things.

I tugged at the knit of my dress, wishing I'd worn a slip (did I even *own* a slip?), feeling oddly self-conscious as I lagged behind the others, hoping Mother wouldn't be ticked that I was a few minutes behind schedule.

Like a bad omen, the lilting notes of "Amazing Grace" swelled over me as I stepped inside the nave, and I sucked in a deep breath, trying hard to ignore the lump in my throat. I hugged my purse to my chest and glanced around me, focusing on the task at hand and wondering how on earth I'd find Cissy in the endless sea of black shoulders that yawned before me. I tried to spot my mother's blond head, but every crown not topped with white or gray was blond—or hidden by a hat— making my mission truly impossible. So many bodies packed the pews. Folks stood in the far aisles and against the back wall.

My daddy's service had likewise filled the church to overflowing. Mother and I had been overwhelmed with flowers, cards, and charitable contributions from those whose lives he'd touched. It had seemed the whole world had mourned alongside us.

I pursed my lips, mulling over my own funeral someday; sure it would not be standing room only. There certainly wouldn't be so many in attendance that they'd run out of parking spaces. Maybe dozens, if I were lucky.

I'd always told myself that it was better to have a handful of close friends than a million acquaintances, and I firmly believed it.

Still, a part of me envied Bebe Kent and my father, for having so many who missed them that the close-packed church had looked like a sold-out Yo-Yo Ma concert.

My eyes strayed to the gargantuan columns standing sentinel on either side of the spacious hall and to the rows of mourners endlessly flowing toward the pulpit. Floral arrangements abounded, surrounding a portrait of the late Mrs. Kent, raised on an easel. Beyond stood the full choir in dark robes with white V-necks. Climbing high above was tier after tier of pipes for the organ, looking very much like a ladder to heaven, if not a stairway.

I hung back, not sure of what to do. Perhaps, it wouldn't be a bad idea just to stick to the rear, near the doors, in case I couldn't get through the service and needed to excuse myself.

A young man approached, hands full of programs. An usher, I guessed, with a gold cross-shaped pin glinting on his dark lapel. I turned my palm up; but rather than slap a program into it, he sidled over to ask, "Are you Andrea Kendricks?"

I nodded, hoping my forehead wasn't blinking LAPSED PRESBYTERIAN in bright neon and he wasn't the religion police, come to arrest me for missing too many Sundays to count.

"Come with me," he said, though I merely saw

his mouth move. The amplified voice of the choir and pump of the pipe organ filled my ears, drowning out all but the nervous thump of my heart.

The fellow took my arm, leading me forward, down the aisle where I'd once, long ago, imagined my daddy would walk me one day, when I was a bride.

So much for childhood dreams.

I had rarely been back in the church since Daddy's funeral, and I was almost afraid that lightning would strike. But it didn't.

I kept my gaze fixed ahead, at the portrait of Bebe, and, for an instant, I saw instead my father's polished mahogany casket, blanketed with blood-red roses from my mother's garden. I could almost smell the too-sweet scent of them, cutting off my breath, making me sick to my stomach.

The passing faces blurred in my peripheral vision. I feared for a moment that we might keep going, straight up to the pulpit, before the usher stopped at the third row from the front, handing me over to a woman dressed in subdued charcoal-gray Chanel.

Cissy.

My mother reached for my hand and drew me into the pew, beside her. Even as I sat down, she didn't let go. Merely hung on more tightly.

As the final strains of "Amazing Grace" rang out like the chime of a bell, resonating in the air and in my skull, I glanced into my mother's eyes and saw her tears. Emotion bubbled inside me like Old Faithful, threatening to erupt.

Despite my best intentions, I began to weep.

For a woman I'd barely known.

For my daddy.

And for the irreparable hole in my heart that even time could never heal.

Chapter 3

It was nearly eleven o'clock when the service ended, sad hymns sung, psalms read, and eulogies rendered.

My body sagged against the pew, drained in every sense.

It astounded me, the number of people who'd gotten up to gush about the generosity of Bebe Kent. No wonder the woman never had children with all the foundations she'd run and fundraisers she'd chaired. She wouldn't have had time for them.

Which made me consider Cissy's choice to bear a child—me—when she'd always been as devoted to philanthropy as her buddy Bea. As the story went, she'd had to leave in the middle of a thousand-dollar-a-plate dinner for the Leukemia Society at the Anatole in order to deliver. My birth, as I'd often been reminded, had lasted hour upon excruciating hour and had been unbearably painful, un-numbed by aspirin or an epidural.

I would never call Cissy a hands-off mother—because she'd always been a huge presence in my life—but she had needed help raising me due to her busy social agenda. She wouldn't have been able to do all the things she did if Sandy Beck hadn't been there to dress and feed me, take me to the pediatrician, or drop me off at school when my mother—or Daddy—couldn't. Still, I knew I'd been lucky to grow up with married parents who had truly loved each other and who'd wrapped me tightly in their protective cocoon. I'd known too many kids who were the products of bitter divorces and extended stepfamilies that didn't in any way resemble the saccharine Brady Bunch save for the sibling rivalry. (*"Marcia, Marcia, Marcia!* How come *she* got a brand-new BMW Roadster when I'm stuck with Mummy's old Jaguar XJS? You must love *her* better!"*)

I glanced sideways at Mother, at her perfect profile, the gray pearls at her throat, not a hair out of place, and it amazed me to realize I had pieces of her inside me, genes that defined me as permanently hers (for better or for worse). At this stage of my life, I was only starting to recognize how much of myself came from her and my father: expressions I caught in the mirror, words that emerged from my mouth that sounded awfully familiar, quirks I swore I'd never inherit in a million years.

I might not be a carbon copy of either, but I couldn't deny where I came from, despite my yen to be different.

I stared at Bebe's portrait as the pews cleared, and I wondered if she'd missed out, despite all the good deeds she'd done through the years. It certainly had to be an incredible feeling to have your name on the side of a building, but bricks and mortar didn't share your DNA.

Because, once you were gone, you were gone.

And wasn't the point to leave behind more than a memory?

"You okay, sweetheart?" Cissy said and brushed a loose strand of hair from my face. "You look so sad."

"We're at a funeral," I murmured. "Sad is part of the dress code."

But she wasn't buying it. "What is it, Andrea?"

I wasn't about to tell her what I'd been thinking about, namely procreation, continuing the thread of life, passing on your bad habits to another generation. Babies was a subject I didn't voluntarily broach with my mother, not with my thirty-first birthday looming so near, and her itching for me to tie the knot and bear her a grandchild while she was still spry enough to shop till she dropped and shower the kid with unnecessary things.

"I'm really missing Daddy today," I admitted instead, because it was true, and a little "hic" caught in my throat.

She made a soft "hmm" sound and touched her forehead to mine, brushing noses.

"I miss him, too," she said. "Today and every day." She pressed a dry kiss to my cheek and passed over her handkerchief. "Now wipe your eyes and blow your nose, before we say our goodbyes."

I did as she asked, feeling a little better after.

Mother laced her fingers with mine, holding onto my hand and tugging me along with her as she paid her respects to Bebe's sole surviving relatives: two cousins from London who slipped Cissy their calling cards and admitted having to dash off to a lunch meeting with Bebe's lawyers before catching an evening flight back to Heathrow.

Then Mummy Dearest was off to the races, working the narthex of the church like a thoroughbred, greeting friends with air kisses and shared condolences.

I saw more than a few familiar faces, girls I'd gone to school with, now grown women with husbands and children; soccer moms who carpooled in their fuel-inefficient Hummers, lunched at Café Pacific in Highland Park Village, and bronzed year-round at Palm Beach Tan. Not exactly my crowd, though Cissy made sure I politely addressed each, keeping me in line with an occasional well-placed elbow to the ribs. Part of her still dreamed I'd end up chums with them someday, pushing strollers around NorthPark Mall and doing car pool to Hockaday or St. Mark's Academy.

Not that there was anything particularly *wrong* with either of those things—if that's what floated one's boat—but it's not what I wanted. If I never had to worry about choosing silver patterns from Reed & Barton, I'd be perfectly content.

"Don't ever burn your bridges, darlin'," she whispered in my ear. "You never know when you're gonna need to get over the water."

"If that should ever come up, I'm counting on you to pull some strings so I can walk across," I whispered back.

Mother gave me one of those "what am I going to do with you?" looks that felt strangely reassuring.

I needed no such encouragement to exchange warm hellos with a pal of mine, Janet Graham, society columnist for the *Park Cities Press*, the colorful rag that covered posh Highland Park and neighboring University Park, mostly boasting stories about the designer duds Mrs. Hoity-Toity wore at this gala or that, whose pedigreed daughter was marrying which pedigreed son, and other such vital tidbits.

"Would chat, but can't," Janet confessed, as she was on the clock for the paper and had to skedaddle. She had her bright orange-red hair trapped beneath a black cloche hat, and her olive-green pantsuit was vintage 1940s. It was almost shocking to see her looking so subdued, when she usually wore clothes bright enough to glow in the dark.

Janet also had on a pair of black-framed glasses—nearly identical to those Katie Couric sported during her more serious morning show interviews. Out of sheer quirkiness, Janet had adopted that particular affectation and donned hers when she wrote her more serious features. So I'd venture to guess her ode to Bebe would be far more solemn than her last column, "The ABCs of Dallas Society," starting with "A is for Ashton Bradford, the most eligible bachelor in Big D!"

When there appeared to be no one left that Cissy and I hadn't addressed, including the minister, the choir director, and the coat-check girl, we were finally able to pull an Elvis and leave the building.

Normally, I would have slipped out as soon as the fat lady warbled—or, in this case, a very thin, dark woman with a Met-worthy contralto—but I didn't want to desert my mother until she was ready. Sitting beside her, passing back and forth her increasingly soggy linen kerchief, had been the closest to a bonding moment that we'd shared since Daddy had passed away. The child in me wanted to milk it for as long as it would last.

I was hoping for another five minutes.

As we descended the steps toward the sidewalk, a blast of a car horn drew my attention to the street.

The mass exodus of mourners had turned into a bottleneck on University Boulevard, horns honking as waiting limos held up traffic. I recognized the Bentley that had once belonged to my Paw Paw double-parked, smack in the midst of the congestion. Though I couldn't see his face beyond the tinted glass, I knew Fredrik sat behind the wheel. He was Mother's part-time driver, a young married man whose wife had a high-powered PR job in the city. He played Mr. Mom when he wasn't hauling Cissy around on days when she didn't feel like handling her champagne-hued Lexus or my father's boat-sized, perfectly preserved Cadillac Brougham that rarely left the garage.

Cissy waved at Fred, giving him a finger—not *the* finger—and letting him know she'd be another minute.

"Well, I guess this is where I exit stage left," I said and summoned a smile, squeezing her hand, proud of her for having made no cracks whatsoever about my unfashionable dress, lack of pantyhose, missing slip, or bad hair.

I was proud of myself, too, for surviving the

long morning and all the memories it had dredged up, for lending my mother support when she'd needed it, and for avoiding any public arguments. It was definitely one for the books.

"I'm parked in the lot off Vassar," I told her, as I untangled our fingers, though she seemed reluctant to let go. "I think I'll grab a bite somewhere and then head home."

I'd promised myself a stop at Bubba's at Snider Plaza before I drove back to North Dallas. I had my mind set on slipping into one of their old-fashioned booths and clogging my arteries with their legendary fried chicken and mashed potatoes. I might've invited Cissy along, but I knew how much she liked getting her fingers greasy. (About as much as she liked watching NASCAR or shopping at the Dollar Tree. Ha!)

"I'm really sorry about Bebe." I breathed the words against her hair as I leaned in for a hug, inhaling the cloud of Joy that always clung to her. Then I pulled away. "I'll see you later, okay? You call if you need me."

She caught my wrist, something close to panic in her eyes. "But, sweetie, you're coming along, aren't you? They'll have something for you to nibble on there, and I really don't want to go alone."

What was this "alone" business again? As if that had ever bothered her before. I'd always thought of my mother rather like Amelia Earhart, never afraid to fly solo. Clinging just wasn't her style. So what was with the death grip she had on me? Her fingers wrapped around my wrist like a manacle.

Obviously, I wasn't going to Bubba's, not unless I

aimed to drag her. "All right. I give. Go with you where?"

She sighed. "I explained it on the phone."

"No, you didn't."

"Don't be obstinate, Andrea."

Obstinate?

The "bonding moment" I'd alluded to earlier? Scratch that.

"What are you talking about, Mother?" My eyelid twitched. "I'm completely clueless."

As I was so often when it came to our relationship.

"Let's not discuss it here." She glanced at the street, where Fredrik continued to hold up traffic. He gestured to her through the opened window, begging her to hurry. "We can talk in the car, on the way."

"On the way to where?"

Embrace your high anxiety moments with a wide grin or belly laugh, I reminded myself, before I thought, "Screw that."

Why did she always do this? Rope me into things without explaining them, so that I was too befuddled to protest?

Wherever it was she meant to take me, it wasn't to Bebe's interment. I knew the burial had been private, for family only (meaning, the pair of English cousins) and longtime staff, held the previous morning at the Sparkman Hillcrest Memorial Park where Bebe would slumber forever beside her beloved Homer and at least several generations of Kents before them. That's where my daddy had been buried, along with most of Dallas's favorite sons and daughters: Greer Garson,

Mary Kay Ash, Mo Connolly, Mickey Mantle, and, may he rest in peace, Tom Landry (who, it was rumored, went to heaven with his hat on).

"Mother, *spill*," I begged, putting my foot down, literally, and nearly stepped on her Chanel-shod toes. "Or I'm catching the van to my Jeep right this minute."

"There's a special reception, and the Wednesday bridge girls will be there. I'm sure I mentioned it." She frowned, and I noticed her brow didn't crease. Not a single tiny wrinkle. "Didn't I?"

"Um, no."

I would've made a crack about Old Timer's Disease, but après Bebe's service didn't seem an appropriate moment.

On any other day, I would've assumed Cissy was playing innocent; but she did appear genuinely baffled, which raised my guilt to another level entirely (sort of like the terror alert going from orange to red—or was it red to orange?). One of her best friends had just gone boots up, and she probably felt as though the Grim Reaper was stalking her like the paparazzi after J-Lo. She had every excuse to be absentminded.

Geez, Louise, I chastised, giving myself twenty lashes. When had I become so cynical? Where was my compassion?

I reached deep down to unearth the kinder, gentler me. It had to be there, somewhere, lodged between my usual extremes of "I'm a happy camper" to "you're on my last nerve, jerk!"

"Er, you know, maybe I did forget," I volunteered, and her face softened, looking almost grateful. "Can you tell me the plans again?"

"There's a small reception at Belle Meade immediately following the memorial at the church," she said, as if that would clear things up. "I promised to be there, and I hoped you'd come, too."

I had never even heard of Belle Meade, but then I was constantly out of the social loop. It sounded like a swanky country club where four hundred mourners could comfortably mingle, eating cucumber sandwiches and drinking sweet tea while everyone chatted about how beautiful the service had been and how much they'd miss Bebe.

My nose felt raw from blowing it into Cissy's linen kerchief, and my stomach cried for Bubba's. My feet barked, and I wanted out of this dress (it was starting to itch).

As hard as it was to say no to Mother sometimes, I'd done my duty. It was time for an honorable discharge. I didn't want to go anywhere but home.

"I wish I could, really," I lied and wrenched my arm free of hers so I could dig for my keys in my purse. "But I've got, er, plans."

Before she asked why—and because my only excuse was a yen for a deep-fried lunch and a yearning to put on Malone's much-washed St. Louis Cardinals T-shirt and while away the afternoon, working on an abstract painting I'd started a few days before—I flashed a tired smile, said, "Okay, love you, bye-bye," and started walking.

I'd taken no more than two steps before she tossed out a verbal lasso that roped me faster than a three-legged calf.

"Oh, but, sugar, Annabelle's *expectin'* you. She's excited as could be about seeing you again. How long's it been? Since before you deserted your

mother and ran off to that art school in the Mid-
west?" My back turned, I froze, waiting for her to
finish. "It'd be a real shame if you didn't recon-
nect. Friendships are so very precious. A girl
never knows when a day could be her last," she
added, laying it on thicker than her Laura Mercier
mascara.

Good grief, I thought, before the realization of
what she'd said truly hit me, smack in the solar
plexus.

Annabelle?

I only knew one girl with that name: a chubby
brunette with freckles who seemed forever on the
verge of tears. We'd both been shipped off to
Camp Longhorn for four straight summers, during those awkward years leading up to puberty.
She was always screwing up, crapping out on activities and forgetting to say "please, sir" and
"thank you, ma'am," which left her with few of
the precious merits we accumulated as chips on
our shower rods and used to buy goodies from the
camp store, like silver James Avery charms and
nylon backpacks. Needless to say, I'd slipped her a
few of mine to keep her from bawling.

She endlessly complained, about the heat, the
bugs, the competitions. She'd earned a host of
nicknames for her actions—or, rather, inaction—
like "Dumb Belle" and "Ding Dong Belle." Those
were the kinder ones. The rest, uttered behind her
back, ridiculed her weight, not her tendency to
flake out. It wasn't part of the Camp Longhorn
spirit to belittle a camper, but that didn't stop it
from happening.

We'd both played wallflowers at the Thursday

night dances—I was gawky and thin, and she was bigger than most of the boys—so neither of us was very popular with the opposite sex. When we got a little older—say, closing in on twelve—she used to fake menstrual cramps so often to get out of activities that someone had once filled her bunk with Midol.

Naw, it couldn't be her. *Could it?*

"Annabelle Meade from Camp Longhorn?" I voiced the name aloud, sure I was mistaken.

"That's right, sugar. She's done so well for herself, despite everything. Just wait till you see her. She looks fabulous for a girl of her proportions."

That coming from a woman who thought a size eight was tipping the scales.

"You won't recognize her. She's come a long way from the child who used to throw a tantrum when her au pair picked her up from boarding school and plunked her on the charter bus for Austin."

So it *was* that Annabelle Meade.

Wow. It had been ages.

I turned around, sure that I was making a mistake by not flying like a bat out of hell toward the shuttle. But, Mother had piqued my curiosity, just as she'd intended. Much as I liked to believe she didn't understand me, she knew me too damned well.

"So, this place holding the reception belongs to Annabelle? Why didn't you tell me sooner?"

"If you'd only read the paper once in a while, sugar, you'd know all about it. Janet Graham did a huge feature on it for the *PCP.*"

By "PCP," she didn't mean angel dust. She meant the *Park Cities Press*, where Janet Graham helmed the prominent "Society" section. The *Wall Street Journal*, it wasn't, but it didn't pretend to be.

"Your old camp friend swooped in from the Hill Country and purchased a piece of prime real estate on Forest Lane a while back. That's where she built Belle Meade. She opened its doors six months ago, and already has a full house and a waiting list a mile long."

Opened its doors? Full house? Waiting list?

Did Annabelle operate an orphanage? A homeless shelter? Was she the new Mayflower Madam?

Why hadn't I heard a peep about this before?

"What is it, exactly?"

"Belle Meade's a very lovely retirement community," Mother said in a hushed voice and smoothed her skirt.

Ah. I squinted. "An old folks' home?"

"My word, Andrea, get with the program. No one calls them that!" She sniffed, defensive, looking at me like she wanted to wash my mouth out with soap. "It's for mature adults who don't want the trouble of maintaining their own property, and it's beautifully done. Annabelle modeled this one after the first Belle Meade, which she debuted in Austin a few years back. She told me she flew down Jimmy Miller from Chicago to do the interior design for both." She sucked in her cheeks and added, "He did Oprah's penthouse, you know, and her farm in Indiana."

Call me slow, but I was getting the picture.

"So it's not like the depressing place where we

visited Meemaw?" I asked, conjuring up the medicinal smell, the fluorescent-lit hallways and frowning nursing staff, every one of whom I'd nicknamed Nurse Ratched. Though, admittedly, toward the end, Meemaw was rather wretched herself.

"Oh, heavens, not even close." Mother tugged at a gray-pearl earring. "Your Meemaw needed constant nursing supervision before she passed on, and that was eons ago, practically the dark ages. Belle Meade doesn't have a skilled nursing unit. It's for independent and assisted living only."

"So, if you get really sick, they ship you off to somewhere like Meemaw's Hellhole of Jell-O?" Well, that's what I'd used to call it.

"Really, Andrea, you're impossible." Cissy stared down her nose at me. An astonishing feat, considering we were at eye-level. "Living at Belle Meade is rather like staying at the Four Seasons, with three squares a day and a doctor on-call."

Hush my mouth.

That was lavish praise indeed, coming from Her Highness of Highland Park, Queen of Good Taste, and Staunch Defender of the Uppity.

"Sounds nice," I offered, sensing a trap being set, and I was the hapless mouse.

"Well, you'll see for yourself," she drawled, toying with the rings on her fingers, paying particular attention to her wedding band. "Annabelle claims to have spared no expense, and I believe her, though they're still working out some kinks. Dallasites are so particular, you know. We're used to being spoiled." She shrugged dismissively.

"But the dining hall is scrumptious, and Annabelle hired away a chef from the Mansion so it's as good as eating out anywhere in town."

Uh-huh, sure it was.

I eyed her skeptically, and a crow cawed from a tree nearby, seeming to echo my cynicism. This Xanadu for the Medicare crowd sounded too good to be true, and Mother was talking like its marketing director.

"There's also a full-service spa that does divine seaweed wraps. And, of course, there's a crack medical staff on the premises, and they have nearly as many yoga and Pilates classes as the Cooper Clinic."

"Sounds *très* posh," I remarked, figuring it must've cost a bundle to build, and not a small price to live there. If such a place had existed when my Meemaw was still around, she would've signed up faster than you could say "Geritol."

"It's very comfortable, indeed," Mother concurred and smiled primly.

Holy cow.

A bell went off in my head.

How come Cissy knew so much about this place? Was it just because Annabelle ran it, or because she'd been doing some research for herself?

Was this something my mother had been considering? Selling her and Daddy's house and moving into a luxury resort for the senior set? How else could she speak so fondly of the seaweed wraps and the dining room décor?

Oh, fudge.

My stomach pitched.

I imagined the elegant 1920s stucco on Beverly

where I'd grown up with a "For Sale" sign posted on the front lawn. I tried to picture losing it and all the memories it held of my daddy and my childhood, and I swayed, the warm air suddenly seeming exceedingly hard to breathe. "You're not thinking of moving?"

"No, Andrea, I've no plans to live there," she pooh-poohed, and I gulped with relief, my heart returning to its rightful spot in my chest. "But I have several friends who do. Mostly widows who're tired of the responsibility of a big house and grounds, what's left of their families all grown up or gone." She ticked off a name on her finger. "Sarah Lee Sewell got herself a townhouse like Bebe's a few months back, and she's joined our weekly bridge group, though"—her voice trailed off, and she sucked in her cheeks.

"Though what?" I prodded.

She shook her head. "I didn't see her at the church this morning, and I'd expected her. Hmm, perhaps she had a migraine and stayed in bed." She cocked her head. "Oh, well, that's why Annabelle is having the reception. It'll give everyone who knew Bea a chance to say goodbye, particularly those who didn't get to the memorial service, and I'm sure there were plenty."

There was something more to this, I could tell. The way she fiddled with the clasp on her pocketbook and didn't meet my eyes.

But I didn't push. Whatever it was, I was sure I'd find out when she was ready to confess.

"Oh, dear, there's a policeman headin' toward the Bentley. If we don't go now, he'll give Fredrik a ticket. So are you comin' with your mother or running off on me again?"

I thought of the carbohydrate-packed grub at Bubba's that I wouldn't be eating for lunch, and still I caved. "All right, I'll go."

"Marvelous." Cissy looked pleased as champagne punch. She took my hand and led me along as she had all morning.

Ah, well. Doing my dutiful daughter routine for a few hours more surely wouldn't kill me, would it?

Chapter 4

I perched on the edge of the leather bench in the back of the Bentley, strangely eager to see Belle Meade and my long-lost camp comrade who'd built this alleged Shangri-la for seniors.

Although it was rather difficult to imagine that the wannabe Greta Garbo with whom I'd shared a cabin—"*I just . . . boo hoo . . . want to be alone*"— had turned into the Donald Trump of old folks' homes . . . excuse me, independent retirement living.

Mother's babble about Annabelle's miraculous transformation reminded me of the lesson I'd learned on my first trip to Tiffany those many moons ago, about how an iridescent pearl grew from a tiny, irritating grain of sand. Annabelle had been quite irritating herself when she hadn't gotten her way. She was an only child with older parents who hadn't seemed at all involved with their late-life offspring. I'd never even met them, and she'd never talked about them much.

I shrugged, because one never knew, right? The

schoolyard bully could grow up to be an opera singer, or the neighborhood klutz, a prima ballerina. And look at Bill Gates. A total geek who'd grown up to be . . . well, a billionaire total geek.

Like Doris Day used to sing, "*Qué será, será . . .* whatever will be, will be."

Which was not a bad mantra, actually.

I listened as Mother gave Fredrik directions to our destination, which apparently sat off Forest Lane, west of Preston Road, a spot I recalled used to have a sprawling antiques mall in the middle and a consignment store on the corner. As we came closer, I pressed my nose against the window, my mouth open and breath steaming up the glass. The antiques mall and consignment shop had vanished. So had the surrounding parking lot.

Instead, tall perfectly trimmed hedges served as a privacy fence, stretching along the entire block. We passed yards and yards of green before we reached an opening and entered through a pair of enormous rock slabs topped with huge carriage lanterns.

Very Stonehenge chic.

Juxtaposed with the Fred Flintstone posts was a very contemporary pair of raised cameras focused on the drive and a discreet sign that let visitors know Big Brother was watching.

But where was the sign announcing, BELLE MEADE: LUXURY LIVING FOR THE GOLDEN YEARS or something to that effect? I'd half-expected a Times Square-worthy billboard or Las Vegas-style neon lights after Mother's glowing descriptions. There wasn't anything of the sort, not in plain sight.

Maybe it wasn't actually a retirement community for well-to-do widows and widowers. Maybe it was really an insane asylum for women who'd cochaired one Big Steer Ball too many and had gone over the edge.

If that were the case, I'd have to book a room for Cissy.

Ha ha. Sometimes I cracked myself up.

"Is somethin' funny?" my mother asked, and I realized I'd chuckled out loud. Maybe I was taking that stress book too seriously. Or else I was becoming delirious from the lack of food in my belly.

"Not a thing," I said and closed my mouth, still staring out the window.

Mature trees that must've cost a bundle to transplant bowed above a lengthy brick drive that made for slow going, but didn't give me whiplash the way speed bumps would have. Beyond the tunnel of branches, I could see an enormous pillared mansion, and I felt as though I'd been transported to Twelve Oaks from *Gone With the Wind*. I could easily picture us arriving for a barbecue with Ashley and Melanie Wilkes.

Fredrik slowed the car further as we reached a security checkpoint beside which was parked a golf cart with BELLE MEADE painted on its side in scripted letters. *Hmm, how fast could that baby go in a chase? Five miles per hour? Ten?*

A white-haired fellow in a tan uniform ducked his head out the window to nod us through, which made me wonder if all chauffeur-driven Bentleys were allowed to pass, or if they had Mother's license plate recorded in their system.

"I believe that was Bob," Cissy murmured. "Or was it Sam? I can't keep them straight."

So they had real-live security guards on duty? I was already impressed, and we were just on the driveway.

It stunned me to think that this was something Annabelle Meade had created, after establishing another such site in Austin, according to Mother.

Nope, it hardly seemed possible; but then I hadn't seen her in years. After our camp days, for a while, there'd been an occasional phone call or letter before we'd left our respective prep schools and headed in different directions (she, to the University of Texas in Austin, and I to Columbia College in Chicago). The last time I'd actually laid eyes on her, we'd barely been teenagers, and we'd hardly discussed our ambitions for the future much beyond the end of camp. She must've changed a lot from the insecure girl I'd known, and I realized I was looking forward to our impromptu reunion, for curiosity's sake, if nothing else.

My daddy used to say that life was a circle, and that seemed to fit in this case. The death of my mother's lifelong friend was about to lead to my reacquaintance with my former Camp Longhorn cabinmate.

But then despair and joy were just flipsides of the same coin, right? (No, not another of my father's sayings. I'd plucked that gem from the broken belly of a fortune cookie when Malone and I had ordered takeout a few nights back.)

Mother started pointing things out as we approached the pillared façade: the wing on the right that housed the salon, spa, and gym, and the streets lined with minimansions to the left, which she informed me were private townhouses with attached garages. The landscaping was lush, lots of flowering shrubs and plantings that doubtless required a team of green thumbs to tend.

"Bebe could let down her guard here," Cissy remarked, and I shifted my gaze to her, watching the play of emotion on her face. "After living alone for years, albeit with a devoted staff, she loved being in the midst of a community like this. She was enjoying herself, truly coming into her own without Homer. Now she's gone, and it isn't fair." She expelled a weighty sigh and sagged against the leather seat. "It was too soon for her, Andrea," she said, and I noticed the faint track of her tears in the powder dusted on her cheeks. "Much too soon. I wasn't ready to give her up yet."

"We're never ready, are we?" I asked, remembering how unprepared I'd been when Daddy had his fatal heart attack.

She pursed her lips before she answered. "No," she said, "we never are."

Beneath the swept-back blond of her hair, the perfect oval of her face seemed to crumple. I'd never thought of my mother as "old" before. Maybe *old-fashioned*, but never any of those awful words to describe someone who qualified for the senior discount, like "past her prime" or "dried up" or "out to pasture." She was prettier than I'd ever be, always so perfectly made-up, so expertly coiffed, so stylishly dressed.

Timeless.

That was the word for her. She was my comic book Wonder Woman come to life—or the Highland Park version, anyway—using her diamond tennis bracelets to ward off bullets and her Gucci belt to shackle her enemies. I'd always imagined she'd live forever. Despite how she drove me nuts sometimes, I wished she would stick around, as long as I was here. I couldn't imagine my life without her, though I told myself she was ornery enough to make it to a hundred, piece of cake.

But, in the filtered light of the tinted windows, she looked worn out.

My chest hurt to see it.

"You've still got me," I said and nudged her, wanting to cheer her up—and maybe myself, just a little.

For an instant, a spark flickered in her eyes. "Thank God for that," she drawled and lay her cool palm flush against my cheek. It was as close to spilling her guts as Cissy ever got. Her way of telling me she loved me.

I closed my eyes.

Suddenly, I was five years old, stuck in the backseat of the Bentley between Mother and Daddy, their thighs pressed against mine, so that I was in my own private cocoon, so safe and adored.

The Bentley's wheels rolled to a stop, gently rocking us. She dropped her hand away, and I opened my eyes, the moment lost.

Mother waited as Fredrik came around to open her door; then she accepted his proffered hand and gracefully slid out.

Wanting to leave my hands free for some two-fisted eating, I left my handbag on the floor mat, scooted across the seat and disembarked, standing on the drive as Fredrik shut the door. He tipped his cap—Mother liked him to wear it—before he got back into the Bentley and moved it to a shady spot where he'd stay until Mother beckoned.

Though I didn't see any other Bentleys clogging the drive, I figured that, at the very least, Belle Meade had a fleet of Town Cars to haul around the chi-chi residents to the shopping malls or Symphony Hall. Across the brick road, the sun glinted off cars neatly parked in a row marked for visitors.

"Andrea?"

Mother's voice tugged at me, like a leash on a puppy.

She was already ascending the front steps, and I caught up with her, taking in my surroundings, the pillars that stood like grinning teeth, holding up the portico as we passed beneath. Unlike in the Old South, however, the architecture of Belle Meade had modern conventions that flowed into the setting seamlessly, like wheelchair ramps that sloped gently toward alternate entrances and artfully designed metal rails for support.

Cissy appeared to know where she was going, so I followed on her heels, sticking behind her as she approached an enormous door painted a shiny black like the window shutters. I noticed a tiny camera placed above the doorframe, aimed right at us and doubtless beaming our images to a carefully watched monitor.

At the threshold, Mother paused and rummaged in her handbag and emerged with what looked like a credit card. Only she used it to slide through a mechanism beside the jamb in the fashion of a hotel key. Within seconds, a light flashed green, and I heard the lock click free.

"Where'd you get that?" I asked her.

"It's Bebe's spare," she said and tucked it back into her purse. "She put me on her list of regular visitors, which just made things so much easier, since we play bridge every Wednesday"—she caught herself, and her already faltering smile vanished. "Since we *played* bridge every Wednesday," she corrected and drew in a steadying breath. Then she palmed the brass handle to push the door inward.

The faint strains of music floated toward us, too faint to make out more than the bass line, and I picked up the murmur of voices as well, from somewhere down the hall, not so far away.

As I turned to shut the door, there came the quick taps of shoes on marble, before they stopped abruptly.

"Ah, bless your heart, Cissy Kendricks, there you are!"

The squeal reverberated through the terra cotta–colored cavern of the foyer, but I couldn't see much beyond the glass-topped table and its centerpiece of wildflowers, obscuring my vision like Shaquille O'Neal with his arms spread. I glanced up to the Austrian chandelier that was every bit as large as the floral arrangement and produced so bright a light I found myself blinking, like I'd stared into the sun itself.

I caught the blur as a body rushed toward us, and a rush of jasmine-scented air swept past as a curvy woman in navy swallowed my mother in a bear hug. Not exactly the delicate air-kisses Cissy's friends practiced.

"Oh, it's awful, just awful," the woman cried,

the words partially muffled as she hunched over to bury her head in Mother's shoulder.

"There, there, dear. I know it's going to be hard without Bebe, but we will survive," Cissy reassured her, a small hand patting a broad blue shoulder, before she deftly detangled herself and stepped a safe distance back. "We just have to pull ourselves together. *N'est-ce pa*?"

"Yes, yes, you're right, of course. I'll try not to be so weepy." The woman wagged her chin and composed herself, fussing at her hair and smoothing the lapels of her jacket.

Boy, I thought, watching her, *Mother wasn't lying about AB coming into her own.*

Annabelle Meade had grown up indeed, her ample figure no longer confined by ill-fitting cotton camp shorts and T-shirts. I'd wager the tailored linen suit she wore—and the pointy-toed pumps—had cost a pretty penny and fit her shapely form like a kid glove.

Her brown eyes and pug nose were exactly as I remembered, though her glossy dark hair had expensive streaks in it. Her tentative mouth, painted fire engine red, quivered as she finally realized I was there, standing in the shadow of my mother.

I smiled at her, gave a wiggle of my fingers.

"Oh, my gosh!" Her pupils widened, and her mouth fell open as pale pink hands fluttered to her face.

"Hi, Annabelle," I said.

"Great balls of fire!" She came at me like a running bull in Pamplona, catching me in the same tight bear hug she'd given my mother; only she drew me off my feet for an instant before she set me down again and back-tracked so she could look at me and shake her head. "I'm not hallucinating, am I? It's really you, Sparky, isn't it?"

"Sparky?" my mother repeated, eyebrows arching.

Yipes. That was definitely a memory I'd suppressed.

Does a person ever get too old to blush?

My guess would be "no," because my cheeks flamed like I'd swallowed a jalapeno pepper.

I opened my mouth to respond, but not-so-shy-anymore Annabelle Meade beat me to the punch, explaining in a rush, "Well, bless her heart, they were on about the fifteenth verse of 'Kumbaya,' after we'd climbed up the darned hillside and it was late and dark, so it's no wonder Andy was so tired she nodded off and toppled over toward the campfire. Her ponytail went up like a sparkler, and Counselor Dave had to dump his canteen on her head to put it out. Remember that, Andy?"

Oy.

I winced, thinking, *how could I ever forget?*

"Uh, yeah, a little." Truly, amnesia was highly underrated.

"Well, isn't that interesting." Cissy frowned, tapping a finger against her cheek. "Andrea, sweetie, didn't you tell me that Cinda Lou Mitchell spit gum in your hair, and the counselor had to cut it out with pruning shears? So that I made her mother drag her over to our house and apologize once you were both home, though the poor girl swore she'd done nothing wrong."

Why did her disapproving tone still get to me?

Wasn't that something you were supposed to out-grow before you hit thirty?

"For Pete's sake, I was ten years old"—I started to defend myself, but Annabelle cut me off again.

"Really, Cissy, don't be such a stickler. Who cares about a little fib? I don't know what I would've done without your daughter all those years." She clasped her hands between her breasts, and her dimpled chin trembled. "She was a lifesaver, truly. I tried and tried, but I never felt like I fit in. If it wasn't for Sparky, I would've never gone back to face my fears, and I wouldn't have made one of the best friends I've ever had in my whole life."

Me?

My cheeks warmed, and I felt suddenly immea-surably guilty, for losing touch and for not realiz-ing the importance she'd placed on our friendship, as we'd grown up and away.

"Closest pal" wasn't a title I'd done much to earn, except for giving Annabelle whichever bunk she preferred and sharing my bug spray with her for four years straight. I'd always divided Sandy Beck's care packages with her, since she'd never received any of her own. Annabelle Meade was the only girl I'd known who'd actually cried when she had to *leave* camp, rather than weeping from homesickness after arriving. What I recalled most was that she'd been a terrific storyteller, making up fantastical tales shared via whispers in the dark. I'd imagined she'd become a novelist or a playwright, not a nursing-home magnate.

"You put more stock in me than I did, Annabelle," I told her, and her mouth broke into a goofy grin.

"Stop that!" She clapped me on the shoulder, hard enough to sting. "Quit being so modest, you silly goose. We were blood sisters, right? Pricked our pinkies and promised loyalty through thick and thin. The only soul I trust more than you is my guardian angel."

Pricking pinkies to pledge our sisterhood?

I think not.

The sight of blood made me woozy.

That scene sounded right out of a movie, and I decided Annabelle the Storyteller had reshaped some camp memories to better suit her, because her real life had been so much more unpleasant. I couldn't blame her a bit. She'd put up with a lot, that's for sure, pretending she didn't know that I'd become her bunkmate because no one else had wanted to sleep in the lower berth beneath her sagging cot; ignoring the muffled "oinks" when she'd passed, always refusing to rat out the offenders. Preferring to keep the pain tucked inside, even when I'd suggested nefarious pranks to get them back, like tossing all their underwear in the lake or putting frogs in their beds.

We'd shared a sense of being lost and out of place amidst the children of privilege who had all seemed cast from a mold, superficially perfect.

"Camp was a long time ago," I said, hoping to shift the subject onto something more pleasant for us both.

But Annabelle hadn't finished with me yet. "You haven't changed much, have you? Still wear that same old ponytail and you've only got on a smidge more makeup than you did when we were twelve. I'll bet your heart's every bit as big as it was back then, too, am I right? I'll wager she's still picking up strays and taking them home, isn't she, Miss Cissy?"

She turned to wink at my mother, who assured her that I was, noting that the latest "stray" added to my collection was a Yankee lawyer from Missouri.

"Oh, my, is that so?" Annabelle said with a wink. "Why didn't you bring him with you, Sparky, so I could take a peek? I'll bet he's cute."

"As a bug in a rug," Cissy said, with a saccharine-sweetness to her voice that made me wince, particularly since I was fully aware of her disapproval at how close Malone and I had gotten without the benefits of holy matrimony.

Mind you, she's the one who'd thrown us together, but now she wished she could keep us an arm's length apart—or at least rig me up with a chastity belt—until wedding bells pealed. As soon as "I do's" were exchanged, Brian would be one of her favorite people in the world again. But that wasn't going to happen, not anytime soon, no matter how she looked down her nose at our "arrangement."

My nosy neighbor Penny George—one of her church buddies—had spied Malone's red Acura coupe parked in front of my condo overnight early on and had generously passed the news along to Cissy. If I got the "why buy the cow when you can get the milk for free" lecture one more time, I was gonna do more than moo.

"He's in the middle of a big case"—I sent a warning look at Mother and turned the tables on

Annabelle—"what about you? Did you settle down, get married?" I didn't see a ring on her finger.

"Oh, heavens, no." She twirled a strand of hair, an old habit she obviously hadn't broken. "Been too busy these past years, building a company."

"I still can't believe it. Have you really been in town for months, AB? When did you first bump into Mother? Why didn't you call me?"

Annabelle glanced at Cissy. "I ran into your mama a few weeks ago, actually. I'd been going back and forth a lot to Austin. Transitioning, you know. And I was usually busy in the office when she came on Wednesdays for her bridge group. But I took a breather and wandered over to the recreation room, and my eyes nearly fell out of my head when I saw her. She looked exactly as I remembered."

"Oh, go on," Cissy said, a glutton for flattery if ever there was one.

"It was like coming home, truly. I asked about you, Andy, and she gave me your number. But things have been crazy around here, getting everything up and running, settling the residents in, and then losing Bebe like that." She kept twisting the hair until it tangled. She uncaught herself and dropped her hand.

"It's all right," I said, not wanting to make her feel worse. Besides, I'd been busy, too, designing Web sites for fun (and nonprofit) and grabbing time with Malone whenever he wasn't buried in briefs at Abramawitz, Reynolds, Goldberg, and Hunt, better known around these parts as ARGH.

"Why don't you show Andrea around Belle Meade, Annabelle?" my mother suggested, and I looked at my old camp comrade expectantly.

I was actually dying to get the scoop on why she'd come back to Dallas to build and run a swanky retirement facility. I recalled that her parents had lived on one of the lakes near Austin, which is why she'd gone to school at UT, to be near home after years away in boarding school and a smorgasbord of camps during summer breaks.

"Well, goodness' sakes, I'd love to give you the grand tour, Sparky . . . in a little bit, all right? First, let's head into the dining room, shall we? That's where we're holding the reception in honor of Miss Bebe. Some of the folks couldn't make the memorial service this morning. It's not easy for all of 'em to get around," she remarked, herding us through the foyer, toward the sound of music. "But they surely loved Mrs. Kent, and they wanted to put together a fitting tribute for her. I'd like to think it's just what she would've wanted . . . especially since she left us such detailed instructions, which we followed to the letter."

Ah, now that sounded like something my mother would do. Leave me explicit directions on how to arrange her send-off, from start to finish, as well as how to live my life each day thereafter.

Cissy took that moment to clear her throat gently, and I braced myself. Mother's throat clearings were often a warning sign in the vein of a tornado siren; a portent of bad things to come, like breaking a mirror or stepping on a crack.

All hands on deck! Lower the rowboats! Grab your life vests!

"Speaking of Bebe," she began, benignly enough, "I have a few questions about what happened, if you don't mind."

We had passed a pair of elevators with polished gold doors and walked down a hallway lined with wrought-iron sconces that illuminated gilt-framed oils of landscapes and seascapes.

Annabelle didn't slow down, merely inquired over her shoulder. "What kind of questions?"

"How exactly did she die?" Cissy asked without further preamble, the directness of it apparently catching Annabelle off guard. She stopped in midstep, swayed, and paused before a large painting of a shipwreck.

The music seemed louder where we stood, and I could hear the murmur of voices, the clinking of silverware, so I figured the dining room wasn't much farther. My stomach must've heard as well and started grumbling.

Annabelle hesitated, gnawing on her bottom lip a moment before she answered my mother. "When she didn't show for her water aerobics class on Thursday morning, I called to check on her, but got her voice mail. I didn't think too much of it, knowing what a busy woman Bebe was, until she missed lunch as well, and she never misses the Niçoise salad. It's one of Chef Jean's specialties."

"Go on," Mother prompted.

Annabelle fidgeted, fussing with the oil, straightening a corner that didn't appear to be crooked. "Well, I tried calling again to no avail, and I got worried. I was heading over when I was paged by Elvira from Housekeeping." The pitch of her voice fell. "Elvira was babbling that she hadn't known Mrs. Kent was home and had let herself in, not aware that anything was wrong, until she went up to the master bedroom and found her. It must've happened in her sleep, because she never rang her panic button.

"Oh, dear." She pressed fingertips to forehead, as if to clear her mind of an unpleasant image. Then she went on, more slowly. "I got over there as fast as I could. Bebe was lying in bed, neat as could be, with her eyes closed and in a lovely nightgown with lace trim on the neck and sleeves. I immediately phoned our doctor—Arnold Finch, you'll meet him at the reception, Andy. There wasn't a thing he could've done. Our Bebe had gone quietly while she dreamed."

"You found her on Thursday, you say," Mother repeated, shaking her head. "I don't understand because she was absolutely fine at bridge on Wednesday. No complaints about anything except the bad cards we were dealt and needing a refill of her allergy prescription because the mold count was up."

"That's how it happens so often, without a warning to anyone." Annabelle wrung her hands. "Just nature running its course and us powerless to change it."

"But she looked well, except for the ragweed . . ."

"Looks can be deceiving, Miss Cissy,"

Annabelle snapped; then seemed to realize her bad manners. She sighed. "I'm sorry, but this isn't easy to discuss. I wish we could've done something for Bebe, I really do. But the Man Upstairs must've called her back so she could be with her beloved Homer again."

Mother didn't seem at all convinced, if the hard set of her jaw was any indication. "So you discovered her on Thursday, and she was buried on Friday."

"Yes, those were her own instructions, to be interred beside Homer in a speedy fashion."

"So speedy that no type of . . . physical examination was done," Mother said delicately, and Annabelle shook her head. "If that's the case, how can anyone know for sure that what happened to Bebe *was* entirely natural?"

"Dr. Finch made that determination, of course, and our security team found no signs of foul play, no indication of a forced entry. Nothing in the house was disturbed or appeared to be missing."

Security team, I mused, as in the white-haired Bob and his cohort Sam? Were they certified in crime-scene investigation by AAA or the AARP? I wondered.

"What if they missed something subtle?" Mother pressed. "Were blood tests run? Did she have a fatal disease? Was it salmonella or food poisoning?"

"It was cardiac arrest, Miss Cissy. Her heart just stopped beating, that's what Dr. Finch said." Annabelle reached for Mother's hand, clasping it hard enough to make Cissy flinch. "Please, don't do this. It doesn't help Bebe any for us to ponder why she left us. Just accept it, and let's move forward. She would've wanted that."

Not for the first time since we'd run into her, tears sprang to Annabelle's eyes, glistening on her lashes, and she sniffed as she let go of Cissy's hand. "Let's not talk about this anymore, shall we? I'm sure y'all are hungry, and Chef Jean has laid out quite a spread. Let's go enjoy ourselves. Bebe would've expected it."

With that, she pivoted and strode forward, up the hallway, not waiting to see if we followed, obviously sure that we would. Or maybe hoping we wouldn't.

I took a couple steps forward, hesitated, and turned around.

Mother hadn't budged an inch.

She snapped open her purse and removed her compact, popping it wide and glancing at herself in the tiny mirror, snatching out the powder puff and blotting at her cheeks a little too ferociously.

I walked back to her.

"It can't be," she murmured. "It's absurd, really. I heard what Annabelle said, but I'm not at all convinced."

"What's wrong?" A knot of worry gripped my chest. Cissy was taking Bebe Kent's death awfully hard, it seemed, as if she were looking for someone to blame or a way to find fault. Like she needed to point the finger at something or someone before she could put her grief to rest.

She clamped the compact shut and shoved it back inside her tiny bag. Her jaw betrayed a vague tremor as she looked me squarely in the eye and proclaimed, "Beatrice Kent was one of my dearest friends for thirty years, and I knew things about her that even her doctor didn't."

Oh, boy. I crossed my arms. "Like what, Mother?"

"If Annabelle found Bebe lying in her bed, neatly tucked in and wearing a frothy nightgown, then something funny's afoot."

Something funny's afoot?

Are you kidding me? She sounded like Angela Lansbury in an old episode of *Murder, She Wrote*, and I would've laughed except she looked so dad-blamed serious.

"What's so strange about that?"

Didn't lots of older folks pass away peacefully in their sleep? It sounded pretty reasonable and not a bad way to go if the Big Guy was pushing your punch card.

A spark lit her eyes, and she raised her chin, the very image of defiant. "Bebe never wore a night-gown to bed, not unless she was visitin' friends or had overnight guests. She once told me that she'd slept in the buff for as long as she'd been alive. Naked as the day she was born. Homer used to joke that he made her keep a robe at the foot of the bed just in case there was a fire and she had to jump out a window. Don't you get it?"

Get it? I was trying hard to erase the mental image of a bare-nekked Bebe dangling from a windowsill.

"Someone must've done this to her, don't you see?" Cissy insisted and tugged at my sleeve. "It's like someone's sending me a sign, and I've got to follow the arrow, sugar, wherever it takes me."

"What arrow?" Oh, man, I wasn't in the mood for one of her conspiracy theories. Not even close. "See *what*?"

She blinked, bemused by my lack of empathy. So she slowed her drawl to halftime, as if I were a dimwit with an IQ to match my hardly significant bra size. "It couldn't have happened the way Annabelle said it did. Bebe wouldn't have gone to bed in anything but her birthday suit, not in her own home. Unless . . ."

"Unless what?" I asked, on cue, fighting the urge to groan.

"Someone else must've been there, and who-ever it was must've wanted it to look like she'd gone peacefully, only she was pushed." As if I didn't get what she meant, she drew a finger across her throat.

Her words made me dizzy. What was she say-ing? That someone shut off Bebe's lights—permanently—dressed her in a pretty nightgown, then covered up by neatly tucking her into bed?

Ah, geez.

If only Mother were a drinker, I could write this one off.

Instead, I took a deep breath, wishing I'd gone to Bubba's for fried chicken.

Here Cissy was, talking murder, and we hadn't even had lunch yet.

Chapter 5

 "Mother, promise you won't mention this to anyone else, okay? Let's keep it between us for now, our little secret, please?"

Oliver Stone had nothing on Cissy.

She and her clubby *compadres* had a fondness for coming up with flaky conspiracy theories to pass the time between bridge hands, cake and coffee. Though usually silly beyond belief, once in a while they'd concoct a real doozy that had a pinch of merit. Like the idea that e-mails were a plot to eliminate the writing of proper thank-you notes. I'll bet the Cranes—that's the stationery Cranes—wouldn't disagree.

"But, Andrea, how can we keep such a thing secret if there's a killer on the lam?" she said matter-of-factly. "Shouldn't people *know* so they can protect themselves? What if he should strike again?"

Protect themselves?

I figured the folks who lived here had more protection than some mob families. There were cameras at the end of the drive, at the front door of the "manor house," as it was apparently called, and probably elsewhere on the grounds. They had Bob and Sam on patrol, and magnetic key cards to gain admittance to the main building. Did Mother want the residents to take up arms, like aging Rambos jacked-up on Centrum Silver?

"Andrea, are you listenin' to me? Don't I have a responsibility to share what I know is the truth?"

I gnawed on my bottom lip, wanting to choose my words carefully. There were plenty of times when Mother and I debated politics or fashion, but wrangling over a touchy subject like murder left me feeling terribly ill equipped.

"Consider this, okay?" *Oh, my, where to begin?* "If there was any proof at all that an actual psycho attacked Beatrice Kent, I'm sure Annabelle would have been the first to inform all the residents." *And call in the National Guard.* "But there isn't any evidence, you see? If there were signs of an intruder, the security people would've summoned the police. If Bebe hadn't gone naturally, the staff doctor would've flagged it. So if you go around insinuating that a homicidal maniac dressed Bebe in her nightgown and tucked her into bed after doing away with her, you'll totally freak everyone out, particularly Annabelle, who's clearly still shaken."

Mother seemed to be paying attention, so I pressed on. "You're grieving for your friend, I know, and it's hard to think straight when your heart is broken. But, you have to accept that Bebe's gone, and you can't bring her back. You need to let go. Don't read more into things and make it worse. It's not good for you. You'll make yourself sick. So, pretty please, drop it," I begged, all but down on my knees.

Besides, if Cissy ran around the reception, crying "murder," one of the white coats might decide to zip her up in an unfashionable wraparound jacket with extralong sleeves, tossing in a free trip to the local hospital psych ward as a bonus gift, which might interfere with the busy fundraising season ahead.

"Are you finished?" she asked.

"Are you?"

"For the moment," she said, hardly reassuring me, and resumed walking, past the shipwreck painting and toward the door that Annabelle had slipped through a moment before.

"Hey, hold on!" I had to do a little jig around her, stopping her just before the entrance to the dining hall. I held out my arms like a traffic cop, blocking her way, unwilling to go any farther unless she agreed. It had been a trying enough day already, and it wasn't quite noon.

I hadn't exactly gotten the go-sign from her that I'd needed, and I certainly didn't want her to cause a scene at the reception, simply because she was on serious emotional overload and her mind was playing games with her common sense. Even in lesser moments, Mother tended toward the dramatic, making molehills into Greek tragedies; this morning, she'd cranked her paranoia into high gear.

And people told me that I had a vivid imagination.

Clearly, it was inherited.

"Promise me you'll behave?" I asked again

when she didn't respond, merely skewered me with a piercing stare, her lips pulled taut. "Did you hear me, Mother? If you don't swear you'll put the kibosh on your *Twilight Zone* scenario about how Bebe died, I'll march you out the front door and have Fredrik drive you home right this minute."

"And will you count to ten in French and give me a time-out?"

"*Mu-ther.* Stop kidding around."

"Don't worry, Sparky, I'll play nice," she said dryly, shifting her gaze toward the dining room doors.

I was tempted to check her hands to see if she were crossing her fingers.

Why didn't I believe her?

"All right." I let out a breath, still uneasy, because my instincts were screaming that I should march her back out the front door and get her home pronto.

Bebe's death had obviously discombobulated Cissy more than I'd imagined, and it troubled me, even scared me a little. She'd lost lifelong friends before, and it had knocked her for a loop each time; but she had never reacted like this. Never insisted one of them was liquidated.

If she didn't regroup in a couple days, I might have to call Dr. Cooper and make an appointment for a physical. I didn't want her making herself sick.

"Stick with me, will you, please?" I implored and caught her elbow as she brushed past me, heading toward the French doors. I wanted to keep her within shouting distance until we could leave. "We'll only stay long enough for you to see the rest of your bridge buddies and get something to eat"—at least, I was getting something to eat— "then we're out of here. Annabelle can give me a tour some other day."

"For heaven's sake, Andrea, I'll stay as long as I want to stay. I'm not a child, I'm your mother."

As if I could ever forget.

She brushed off my grasp. "And would you please stop talking to me this way. It's condescending."

"It's for your own good," I told her, and I meant it. She was behaving like a sixty-year-old with adult ADD.

"My," she drawled, "but that sounds awfully familiar."

"I'm just concerned about you."

"Why on earth?" Her brows arched, and she gave her hair a toss, though her blond coif barely shifted. "Darling, I'm perfectly fine."

"Are you sure?"

"Well"—she tugged on the cuffs of her jacket— "maybe I'm a wee bit tired after everything. This hasn't been easy."

Ah, there it was. She'd admitted all wasn't right with her world. As long as I'd known her, she'd rarely confessed to any weakness, so this was encouraging. Perhaps she even realized how paranoid she was behaving.

Still, my brain was already making plans to accompany her back to the house on Beverly, feed her a Valium (or two), and put her down for an afternoon nap, leaving her under Sandy Beck's watchful eye thereafter. I figured it'd just take some time for her to feel like herself again and get this silly idea of murder out of her system.

Murder.

The word prickled my short hairs.

I rubbed the tight tendons at the back of my neck, telling myself the very thought was preposterous.

Bebe Kent had been a serious player on the Dallas social scene for far too many years. Surely if there'd been any sign of foul play when Annabelle had discovered the woman in bed, dead to the world, she would've called the police. The doctor wouldn't have signed the death certificate if everything wasn't kosher, would he?

Uh-uh. No way. No how.

This wasn't a TV show for the Lifetime cable channel. No physician in his right mind, in the real world, would risk losing his license—or going to prison—by falsifying information on a legal document, I consoled myself, nor would Annabelle conspire to commit any kind of crime that would put her reputation and her business on the line. Not unless she was aiming for professional suicide.

Somehow those thoughts reassured me.

Mother cleared her throat ever so delicately, drawing me back to our conversation. "Am I allowed to go, Warden," she asked, "or do I need a pardon from the governor?"

And she considered *me* the smart aleck in the family?

"Be my guest," I said, and stepped aside so she could walk past me, through the French doors. I was right behind her as she entered the dining room.

The zippy sound of swing swept through me, something along the lines of "Boogie Woogie Bugle Boy," with Andrews Sisters harmonies and a bopping melody that had me itching to snap my fingers and tap my toes.

Not your typical mourning music, I mused. It certainly wasn't Mozart's *Requiem*, but what did I know about postmemorial service etiquette? Considering my motto was "color outside the lines," it was hardly my place to comment. I'd once joked to Malone that I wanted my own will to have a clause requiring that the entire song list of Def Leppard's *Hysteria* be played at my send-off. But that kind of thing went right along with my debutante-dropout image, so it would hardly be shocking.

This reception was a tribute to the venerable Mrs. Beatrice Kent, so hearing swing seemed out of place. I would've expected something moody and baroque, like Handel or Beethoven. Maybe even Elvis singing "Are You Lonesome Tonight?" Though Willie Nelson's version would've worked, too (hey, this was Texas—country music *was* our blues).

"Does anyone need a refill of bubbly?" a high-pitched voice asked, rising above the music.

Champagne?

Okay, that did it. Suddenly, I was the one who felt totally discombobulated. I'd expected an air of solemnity at this reception, with lots of sober faces, like at the church, but I was way, way off.

Belle Meade's tribute to Bebe was something else entirely.

I glanced around, having pictured black wreaths over mirrors, even black crepe paper dripping from the ceiling, sort of like Halloween without the orange.

But there was nothing somber about the dining room with its bright yellow drapes, Chinese patterned wallpaper, and blazing chandeliers that touched light upon silver place settings at the dozens of linen-clothed tables. Mirrors with carved gilded frames hung everywhere, adding the illusion of more space, so it felt as big as a ballroom. Wildflowers like the ones in the foyer, only scaled down from supersized, served as centerpieces for the tables and anchored the tremendous buffet set up smack in the midst of it all.

Color photographs of the woman I'd seen in the portrait at Highland Park Presby had been blown up and tacked to the walls, so that Beatrice Kent's smiling countenance surrounded me, every which way I turned.

It was Bebe-palooza.

Out of nowhere, I heard laughter erupt from the buzz of voices, and my antennae went up. I had flashes of that *Mary Tyler Moore Show* episode where Mary has a laughing jag at the funeral of Chuckles the Clown. Well, people grieved in their own fashion, I rationalized, even if that fashion seemed a mite too perky for me.

Unless the group had been reading *Stress and the Single Girl* and had decided to embrace their anxiety with grins and guffaws.

Still. . . .

The Big Band soundtrack. The bubbly. The laughter. The bell-like clink of crystal. The colorful décor.

If I hadn't known better, I would've sworn it

was a birthday party. Only the guest of honor wasn't around to blow out the candles on the cake.

I scanned the dozens present and realized something else: not a person, beyond Mother and myself, was actually wearing black or gray. Annabelle was in navy, but the rest of the Belle Meade folks gathered in the dining hall wore breezy outfits in summer pastels and prints—I saw plenty of Lilly Pulitzer—though no white, of course, as it was after Labor Day and this was Dallas, not Miami. Of the paltry handful of men congregating with the overwhelmingly feminine crowd, one had donned a plaid shirt and kelly-green golf pants, like he'd strolled in off the fairway.

After the solemnity of the morning's service, that seemed . . . I don't know, too festive. Too cheery. Where were the tears? The glum faces?

"Stop looking so disapproving, Andrea," Cissy scolded. "Bebe wanted a bash, not a wake. So that's what she got. She lived a wonderful life, and that's what we promised to celebrate. Now, go on and get some food, while I look for Sarah Lee and say 'hello' to some of the others I know from bridge."

"So long as you tell me where you're going, so I can keep tabs on you."

"Keep tabs on me? Pish!" She sniffed. "Sweetie, I ran your daddy's company for six years after his heart attack, until I sold it to a global giant in pharmaceuticals whose annual profits are larger than most countries' gross national products, and I still sit on the board with some very high-powered gentlemen and hold my own very well, thank you very much."

"I realize that, but . . ."

"Andrea Blevins Kendricks, stop being so over-protective. I can manage my life perfectly well without your direction." She tsk-tsked me. "And I certainly do *not* need a babysitter."

"Can't you please just . . . ?"

"No, I can't. So shoo." She waved me off and glided away to mingle.

I considered stalking, still fearful she'd do something rash before I could stop her. But before I could follow, a slender woman with short friz-zled gray hair and a bright pink pantsuit sidled up and had me cornered.

"You look like you just got your teeth kicked in, sister," she said and winked. She had a dandy set of false lashes. "You grieving over the dearly de-parted, or did you eat one of those raw oysters that Chef Jean's so fond of serving, like they're part of our essential food pyramid?" She leaned toward me, pulling a face like she'd swallowed a bad egg. "They're supposed to aid the libido, you know, but they send me running for the Pepto-Bismol. You looking for a drink of the pink? I don't have any on me." She patted her pockets. "But I could make a run to the pharmacy. It's just a few steps over that way . . ."

"No," I said, stopping her. "I haven't had any oysters, and the only thing I'm looking for is my mo . . ."

"Ooh, speaking of libido"—she cut me off and gestured broadly at the silver-haired dude in the plaid pants. "Hellooo, Henry," she cooed and primped at her wiry pin curls. "How were the greens this morning? Fast, like you, I hope."

The fellow flashed a half-hearted grin and scurried off.

Wish I'd been as quick on my feet.

"Ah, sister." The woman nudged me. "Now, there's a man who still has a hot putter, if you get my drift. If you had the time, I could tell tales about Henry and all the conquests he's made in this ritzy henhouse." She gave a low whistle. "Oh, boy, oh, boy, how the worm has turned since the invention of Viagra and its brethren. My, my, did I say that? The *worm* has turned?" She chortled merrily. "Get it?"

Yo, Dr. Ruth! Too much info.

"Yeah, I get it."

I almost lost my appetite.

I said *almost*.

The buffet smelled damned good, and I was ready to put on the feedbag and test Chef Jean's prowess. If only I could get around Gladys Kravitz here. But the moment I made a move to leave, she threw a body-block, her thin pink-clad form lunging in front of me. I had to give her one thing: she was agile.

"So you were about to say why your pretty puss is looking so sour." She bent closer, and her powdery scent settled over me. "C'mon, you can share it with ol' Mabel Pinkston. I've spent my whole life taking care of people, so it's what I'm good at." The lines in her heavily rouged face deepened, and her eyes rounded with sympathy. "Anything I can help *you* with?"

"It's my mother," I blurted out, before my better judgment could halt the flow of words. "I've lost her . . ."

"Lost her? Bless your heart"—once again, Mabel jumped in before I'd finished—"Beatrice Kent?" Thinly penciled brows arched, and her mouth puckered with distress. She looked me up and down, disconcerted. "And there I was joking around. Forgive me, child, I didn't realize that the woman had a daughter. I didn't think she had anybody left in the world besides her hot-shot lawyers and a couple of long-lost cousins from across the pond who didn't give a hoot or holler about her until she dropped dead."

"Oh, no, Mabel, my mother wasn't Bebe," I assured her and gestured toward the throngs of elegant older folks milling around the vast room. "She's alive and well, though I'm not sure where. But she's definitely not gone for good."

"She isn't?"

"No."

The woman stared at me, momentarily silent, before her pink-glossed lips parted. She threw back her head and laughed soundly, and when she was done, she patted my back with a blue-veined hand.

"My, my, sister, but you had me going there for a minute. So she ditched you, did she? You're visiting, is that it? Does she live here? What's her name?"

"No, she doesn't live here," I said, answering part of her question. "Not yet. But I'm seriously thinking of having her committed somewhere."

Mabel tapped her sagging cheek, clearly pondering my comment. "Getting fruity as a cantaloupe, is she?"

"I'm hoping it's temporary insanity."

She nodded sympathetically. "Tell me about it, sister. Seems some women go through the change and get nutty or, worse, turn mean as a snake. Doesn't take much to get some of 'em riled as a polecat. But, then again, could be what happens when you stick a hundred hungry hens in a closed pen with far too few roosters . . ."

"Got it," I butted in. No more barnyard sex talk, please.

The scent of pork tenderloin called my name.

"Excuse me, Mabel," I said and hoped I was convincing, "but I've really got to find my mum. Sometimes she wanders off where she shouldn't, and she can be a real danger to others, if I'm not around to keep her in line."

Her pink lips puckered. "Is it the Alzheimer's? We don't usually see those kind here. Once the senses start to go, the doctor ships 'em off to skilled nursing. So your mama must be a special case."

"Oh, she's a case, all right," I agreed.

Mabel glanced away, losing interest in me, probably scouting for that hot Henry in his bright green pants.

So I made my escape.

I did a quick check for Cissy, but didn't see hide nor hair of her, so I pushed aside any rising panic—I mean, how far could she get in a gated retirement village—and listened to the pangs of hunger waging war in my stomach.

First things first.

With a smile pasted on my kisser, I maneuvered my way around and through the clusters of merry mourners, not slowing down until I'd reached the elaborate buffet and picked up a plate to fill. Chef

Jean had indeed laid out quite a spread, and it was an effort to keep from drooling as I made my way around, taking a little bit of everything: meats, fruits, pasta salads, and tiny cheesecakes and tortes for dessert. The raw oysters, I bypassed.

Plate stacked, I found a table to myself in the far corner, and I took it, afraid of having to make polite conversation with another living soul before I was so full I couldn't eat another bite.

Only after I'd inhaled every morsel—after I'd pushed away my plate and belched oh-so-discreetly behind my napkin—did I figure it was time to track down Cissy. She'd already been out of my sight for half an hour, and, since pandemonium hadn't struck (that I was aware of), I had to believe she'd kept her promise to ixnay the "Bebe was murdered" nonsense.

The distinct sounds of B.B. King and his guitar Lucille bounced through the air as I left my napkin on the table and wove my way through the happy mourners. Blues, I mused and nodded approvingly. That seemed far more appropriate for après-funeral than the Andrews Sisters.

"Andrea! Yoo-hoo!"

Turning toward the voice, I spotted Annabelle madly gesticulating, urging me to hurry over, halfway across the room. She stood beside a tall man and a tiny woman, both staring in my direction.

I swallowed, praying they weren't part of Belle Meade's security team, come to tell me that Cissy had scrawled RED RUM on the door of Bebe's townhouse in Coco Red lipstick.

As I sidestepped my way through tables and people, I craned my neck, trying to locate my mother, but I didn't see Chanel hide nor salon-blond hair. Where had she disappeared? I tried not to think of it as I continued my progress toward Annabelle and her companions.

No one smiled as I approached—further assuring me that this had something to do with Mother and it wasn't good—which led to an attack of nerves that triggered a round of babbling.

"Well, hey, y'all, I just sampled Chef Jean's wares, and I'd give him a big thumbs-up. Though I was warned to skip his raw oysters. I heard they can clean out your pipes, if you're not careful." I attempted a guffaw, but it emerged as a nervous snort.

Oh, boy, I sounded like Sister Mabel of the Pink Pantsuit.

"Well, goodness, I'll keep that in mind, about the oysters, I mean." Annabelle gazed at me, a funny look on her face. "Um, Andrea Kendricks, I'd like you to meet our staff physician, Dr. Arnold Finch."

She inclined her head toward the tall man with the brooding good looks—I say, "brooding," because he stood frowning at me, dark brows sitting caterpillar-like above mud-brown eyes. I'd guess he was in his forties, with just enough creases in his face to qualify him for middle age, a trace of salt in his pepper hair, which lent a sort of Mr. Rochester quality to him. He had the same disapproving air. Though maybe his tie was too tight, or else he'd had the oysters for lunch and wasn't feeling too cheery at the moment. I liked to give folks the benefit of the doubt when I could.

"Andy's a friend of mine from summer camp," Annabelle went on, by way of introduction.

"A pleasure to meet you, Dr. Finch," I said and stuck out my hand, which he made no attempt to grasp. He kept his own paws clasped behind his back. Could be he had one of those germ fetishes and only liked to touch other people when he was wearing latex.

"I'm sure the pleasure is mine, Miss Kendricks," he uttered without an ounce of sincerity.

All rightee then.

Annabelle nodded at the petite blonde to Finch's left, who didn't appear any more enthusiastic than the good doctor to be making my acquaintance.

"This is Arnie's wife, Patsy. She's our in-house pharmacist and works alongside her hubby. Isn't that just the coziest arrangement?"

Cozy as a pair of possums, cornered and hissing.

"Nice to meet you, Patsy," I said, offering my hand once again—I'm a glutton for punishment—surprised when it wasn't rejected. She grasped it lightly before letting go. Her milquetoast features suddenly bordered on pretty as she gave a slim smile.

"Hello, Andrea. So you know our Annabelle from camp? You'll have to tell us all about that," she chirped. "I'd love to get the dirt on our beloved boss woman."

"The dirt, huh?" I repeated and shook my head at Annabelle, hoping she wouldn't share my long-buried nickname or the sordid "Kumbaya" campfire story with them, much less the made-up bloodletting. "Suffice it to say, neither of us was much of a nature girl. I remember one time when we sat in the same patch of poison ivy on a hike and ended up splitting a bottle of calamine to cover our . . ."

"Assets," Annabelle jumped in, her cheeks flaming to fuchsia.

"Ticks and mosquitoes liked us, too. Guess we were just special." I grinned, and Annabelle gave a shy smile back.

"I'd have to disagree, Miss Kendricks." Dr. Finch hooked his thumbs into his trouser pockets, rocking on his heels in the way that some men did when they were about to pontificate. "When you consider that over 90 percent of people on the planet are allergic to the urushiol oil in poison ivy and sumac plants, it doesn't make you special at all. Just very ordinary."

Well, thank you, Dr. Know-It-All.

I glanced at Annabelle, my tongue itching to re-tort something about 90 percent of the world pop-ulation being allergic to pompous jackasses, but her eyes went wide, and she shook her head, warning me off.

"So you're an expert on poisonous flora, Dr. Finch?" I asked, an innocent enough question.

"No, no, not an expert. Though I am well versed in general medicine, of course. My expertise is geriatrics." He crossed his arms over his chest, puffing out his lower lip. "Which is why Annabelle lured me here from my clinic."

"Arnold has such a deep understanding of the

aging process." Patsy touched her husband's sleeve. "He's devoted his career to prolonging the lives of others. We both have."

Then it was a shame that they couldn't help Bebe Kent so Cissy would still have her friend, not to mention all her marbles, I wanted to say. I opened my mouth, ready to let loose.

As if anticipating my reaction, Annabelle reached for my hand and gave my arm a painful jerk. "Oops, gotta dash. I promised Andy a tour of Belle Meade, so I'll catch up with you later, Patsy . . . Arnold."

Then she dragged me away, past the champagne-sipping, oyster-eating, brightly dressed mourners and out the rear dining room doors to a blissfully empty courtyard.

She closed the French doors snugly behind us, drawing me around wrought-iron furniture toward a fountain with burbling waters that glinted in the midday sun, far away from any prying ears.

"I thought you were gonna clobber him, Sparky," she said with a chuckle, releasing me to unclip a tiny cell phone from her waistband, hidden by her short-sleeved jacket. Palming it, she sank down onto the limestone bench that circled the fountain.

I plunked down next to her, sighing as I settled onto the sun-warmed stone. "He would've had it coming. 'Blah blah blah, it doesn't make you special at all. It makes you very ordinary,' " I mimicked. "How do you stand him? After you finished your undergrad degree, did you take special training in massaging overblown egos?"

"I know, I know, he's a little full of himself,"

she agreed. "But he's good to his patients. The ladies adore him."

"Seriously?"

"He might've flunked cocktail chatter, but he's got a great bedside manner. He's very sweet with them. Gets them to take all their medicine without having to add a spoonful of sugar."

"Go figure." I slipped out of my shoes, setting them on the bench beside me. I stretched my toes on the Mexican tiles, still cool underfoot, while I half-turned to trail a finger in the water. Uncountable pennies glittered underneath the surface, and I thought of all the wishes they must represent.

My gaze wandered around us, beyond the edges of the patio, toward paths that extended through landscaped trees, shrubs, and flowers. Birds twittered, a few fluttering from secluded branches to soar through the sky. It was hard to believe the place sat so close to major intersections. I felt like I was in the country, or at least at a country club.

Beyond the courtyard, I could see a pair of tennis courts and the flag on a golf green, as well as a smattering of outbuildings. Belle Meade didn't look like any retirement facility I'd ever seen.

Heck, *I* wanted to move in. I wondered what the age requirement was, and if they might bend it by a couple decades.

"What're you thinking, Andy?" Annabelle asked, an edge of accusation in her voice. "That I'm crazy to be doing something like this? That I should be happily married, chasing around my little heirs and heiresses? Or maybe designing my

own plus-size clothing line for other fat rich
girls?"

"No, not at all." *Where had that come from?*

"Then what?" Annabelle wiped at the beads of
sweat on her upper lip, her soft face turning suddenly hard, as if a shield had gone up and she'd
readied herself for my attack.

"I'm just stunned," I admitted.

"Oh, sure." Her mouth tightened into a smirk.
"Stunned that I hired an arrogant doctor like
Finch?" She exhaled noisily. "Really, Andy, physi-
cians who think they're God are a dime a dozen.
It's next to impossible to find one who doesn't."

"It's really no shocker that you hired a doctor
with a God complex," I tried to joke and wiped off
my damp finger. "But what I'm amazed at is *you*.
What you've accomplished."

"Never thought a crybaby like me would amount
to much, did you? Well, you're not the only one."

There it was again: the self-deprecation, the ex-
pectation that I'd belittle her achievements. I got a
glimpse of her insecurity creeping out, as it had so
often during summer camp.

I shook my head. "Please, Annabelle. You're
talking to the girl who ripped out her mother's
heart by bailing on my debut. I'm surprised she
hasn't had my ball gown bronzed. Cissy still tells
people I went to Columbia University, in the Ivy
League, not Columbia College, the art school in
Chicago. I turn thirty-one next month, I'm still
not married, heaven help me." I threw up my
arms. "So, let me tell you, I know a thing or two
about blowing expectations."

Annabelle's armor cracked. She sighed and

raised her chin, tossing brown curls over her shoulders. "I'm sorry, Andy. I wasn't thinking. We're both square pegs, aren't we?"

"Square pegs with nice round trust funds."

"And yet, we're almost entirely normal." She wrinkled her nose. "Well, as normal as we can be, all things considered."

"You're right," I agreed. "We could've been the Hilton sisters."

"Ack!"

When we stopped laughing, I nudged her. "We did all right for ourselves, AB," I said. I didn't know how to describe what I was feeling, how proud I was that we'd both overcome our biggest obstacles to achieve something. "I love what I do, but designing Web sites for nonprofits seems small compared to getting a place like Belle Meade built. And not just one, but two."

Her shoulders relaxed, and she nodded vigorously. "Two for now, yes, but would you believe we've got plans for more on the table? We've got tremendous waiting lists for both facilities, and I have more interest from investors than I can handle."

"I can't believe I know a business tycoon."

"Oh, please, they grow like ragweed around here."

"Not the kind who build their dreams from scratch," I told her. "You might've had a head start in the numbers department, but you built this yourself. No one gave you Belle Meade on a silver platter."

"I guess so." She shrugged, shaking dark hair off her shoulders. "It's really wild, Andy, how much I've grown up and learned to direct my own life." Her eyes widened.

I'd never seen Annabelle look as happy as she did right that minute, and I figured it was long overdue.

"With Belle Meade, I finally realized who I was," she admitted, luminous with the sun at her back and the fountain gurgling merrily behind her. "After all the rejection, and my parents always griping that I'd amount to nothing, I've proved them wrong."

"Good for you," I said, remembering her complaints about how hard on her they were and realizing how great it felt to accomplish something on your own, no matter what it was.

"Worst part is"—she cast her gaze down and plucked at the buttons on her jacket—"they never saw any of it."

The news blindsided me. "I'm sorry, Annabelle. I had no idea. When was this?" I wondered, so surprised that Cissy hadn't mentioned it; because I couldn't believe she hadn't heard. Mother's grapevine worked better than Ma Bell ever had and was faster than any Internet connection.

"Before I even started thinking of the first Belle Meade, about six years ago." She exhaled, looking away, her eyes misting. "They were at their lake house in Austin, when it burned to the ground. They were both asleep. The fire investigators eventually ruled it was an accident. They said a burner had been left on the stove, and a potholder or dishtowel must've been lying too close. Their smoke alarms must not have gone off. My father was always forgetting to replace the batteries."

"Oh, geez, I don't know what to say."

What *could* I have said to that?

She turned and gazed directly at me, taking my hand and squeezing. "It's when I decided to do this, Andy. To build a place where people could enjoy life and be safe as they grow older. I wanted to watch over them, so they could live their lives to the fullest, not lacking for anything."

Though she wasn't exactly helping the indigent, her aspirations seemed more admirable than many of the goals I'd heard from girls with whom I'd gone to prep school, most having to do with marrying well and producing sons to carry on the family crest.

"You've done that, Annabelle. I'm sure your parents would be proud to see who you've become."

"Maybe." Her chin trembled. "I feel just horrible about Bebe," she said, swiping her sleeve at the glisten of tears on her lashes. "I wish I could've done something differently, so she'd still be alive today."

"But it wasn't your fault," I reminded her. "It wasn't anyone's fault. You can't stop someone from dying, if it's her time, right?"

"I know," she said and tugged at her jacket, seeming to pull herself together.

"Is Mrs. Kent the first of your residents to"— how could I put this delicately—"check out?"

"No, of course, not." She sniffed. "We've got community members anywhere from sixty years old to Miss Myra Bentwood who just turned ninety-five. If they're too sick for assisted living, we move them to a chronic-care facility near Presbyterian. Which means our rate of loss is relatively

low, but still . . . every once in a while, it happens."
She puffed out her cheeks. "Look, I see where
you're going with this, Andy, but it doesn't make
it any easier to accept. I get to know them so well.
Despite everything, it hurts when I lose a member
of our family."

I watched her as she poured her heart out, wondering if this could really be the same Annabelle
Meade from Camp Longhorn. I remembered the
girl who'd cried herself to sleep, who'd hated
competitions, who'd never liked herself much,
and who'd tried hard to live by the credo of "sticks
and stones may break my bones but names will
never hurt me." (As though that ever worked for
anyone.)

That girl seemed a faint shadow of the woman
who sat beside me on the lip of the limestone
fountain—her fountain, her *everything*.

I suddenly felt very glad that Cissy had twisted
my arm into coming. I liked this Annabelle far better than the younger version I'd known.

A slow smile slipped across my face, and I put
my shoes back on the ground and slid them on,
tugging down my dress as I stood.

Then I extended my hand.

She glanced at me, puzzled. "What?"

"Well, geez, you promised me the grand tour,
right? I want to see the rest of this Disneyland for
the gray hairs."

"Ha ha." She grasped my hand, and I helped
her rise to her feet. "So long as you let me show
you whatever's air-conditioned first," she griped,
and I noticed the perspiration flecking her face.

"Still don't like the heat much, huh?"

"Hate it."

"Bet you don't like bugs any better, either."

She swatted at me. "Hush your mouth, Sparky, or I'll have Arnold Finch give you a *complete* physical."

Annabelle pointed our way down a path that led toward the side of the main building, telling me about their in-house bakery, underground bowling alley, and ice cream parlor—yep, I believe I still had room for a dip of mint chocolate chip— and we were nearly there when the *woo-woo-woo* of a siren burst through the air.

Neither of us moved as the noise grew ever louder.

I grimaced, grinding my teeth, my neck tensing. Sirens were bad news, however you cut it, and I had a bad feeling in my gut about that one.

"What's going on?" I asked, but Annabelle wasn't paying attention, not to me.

She'd yanked her cell phone from her waistband, and turned her head toward the escalating wail, coming from the other side of the main structure.

"The townhouses," she said to herself, and her cell began to chime from the palm of her hand. She quickly flipped it open and drew it to her ear. She only listened for seconds, before she replied, "Thanks, Bill, I'm headed that way," snapped the phone closed, and started running as fast as her straight skirt and high-heeled pumps would allow, which was pretty darned swift, all things considered.

There was trouble, right here in River City.

I kicked off my shoes, left them where they fell, and took off after her.

We cut between a pair of buildings and across a cropped lawn, the siren so loud it seemed on top of us.

Annabelle's hair streamed behind her, and I hiked my dress up to midthigh, trying to keep up. For someone who hadn't liked physical activity as a kid, she could sure book when she had to.

Maybe one of the residents had a heart attack, I thought, *or had slipped in the tub and broken a hip.*

There was nothing to imply that a certain visitor to the grounds had caused a panic or stirred up enough trouble to warrant the police, was there?

Still, as I sprinted behind Annabelle, I had my mind on someone in particular, a guest at the reception who'd been acting odd all morning.

The siren whooped one loud, last time before shutting off.

Dear God, I prayed, my breath rushing hard, my heart beating fast, *whoever's in trouble, please, don't let it be Cissy.*

Chapter 6

We rounded the corner to find a blue-and-white squad car parked smack in front of a pretty brick townhouse with black shutters and trim; perched amidst a row of identical residences, each a mirror of the one beside it.

Birds chirped from red-leaved Japanese maples, potted mums stretched yellow petals toward the sun, and a squirrel scampered across trim squares of grass.

If not for the vehicle with the light-bar rolling on its roof, soundlessly spinning red and blue, things would have appeared serene, even bucolic.

But the sirens had already attracted attention from neighbors, their heads poking past storm doors to see the cause of the commotion. I looked around myself but didn't spot any uniformed officers. The squad car sat empty.

The front door to the house stood wide open, and I had a pretty good idea that the cops hadn't waited to be invited in.

"Great balls of fire, I can't believe this."

Annabelle panted, stopping on the sidewalk and leaning over bended knees to get a second wind. Her prettily made-up face gleamed, slick with sweat, creased with worry. "Oh, God," she moaned, "This can't be happening again."

I wanted to ask what she meant, but someone else started asking the questions.

"What's going on?" a white-haired woman called from the adjacent yard, and Annabelle waved an arm, responding breathlessly, "It's a private matter, Helen, and not your concern. Go on back inside."

But Helen didn't seem convinced.

The woman took a few steps toward her door, but stayed on the stoop with her arms crossed, watching.

I paused behind Annabelle, trying to get my own pulse back to normal, tugging at my dress and hopping from one leg to the other as I checked the soles of my bare feet, which had picked up bits of grass and dirt from our horse race over. Nothing bled, so I brushed off the dirt and waited for Annabelle to right herself.

"Whose house is this?" I asked as I scrambled after her, toward the porch, where I noticed a black metal mailbox hooked over the railing, its contents poking out of the lid.

As soon as she said, "Sarah Lee Sewell," my stomach knotted and my brain went, "Uh-oh."

"Go on and get some food, while I look for Sarah Lee and say 'hello' to some of the others I know from bridge."

Cissy had left the dining room to find Sarah Lee earlier, and now a police car with whirling bubble lights perched in front of the woman's townhouse.

Coincidence?

Sure it was, I told myself. *And "Al Dente" was the weatherman on the* Today Show.

Oh, please, let this be a false alarm, a silly mistake. Please let my mother not have done anything worth a police escort out the gates. Normally, Cissy did everything by the book—that tome being *Amy Vanderbilt's Complete Book of Etiquette.* But I couldn't trust her, not when she'd been acting so weird.

I took a step toward the open doorway, and Annabelle did a half-turn, bracing her palms on the jamb.

"You might want to stay outside. This could get sticky." Streaks of sweat trickled down her temples, and she was clearly uneasy about what awaited us behind yonder walls. "Really, I should do this myself."

"My mother's involved, isn't she?" I asked, but her expression was all the answer I needed. "I'm not staying out here if Cissy's inside."

Annabelle pursed her lips. "Just don't get in the way, Andy, okay?" she said, not answering my question. Then she turned around and went in.

I slowly followed her through the small foyer and into the living room, an enormous space with cathedral ceilings and a stone fireplace with two sofas placed parallel. I stopped by the baby grand piano, resting a hand on the smooth surface, letting Annabelle go ahead. As she'd requested, I hung back.

The officers—two men in blue with radios

squawking from their shoulders—leaned over a woman lying on the far sofa. I couldn't see the face or much of the rest of her. All I could make out were the limp legs, black pumps on stocking feet positioned awkwardly, and my throat tightened as something clicked in my head.

My mother had been wearing stockings and black shoes that looked very much like . . . that.

I tried to swallow, but my mouth was too dry to summon the spit.

Annabelle approached the cops quickly, identifying herself as the facility owner and director and getting closer than I dared.

"She's not breathing?" I heard her ask.

"She hasn't been breathing for a while, ma'am," the shorter of the two cops replied. "I'd say she's been dead for a matter of hours, though I'm no medic. Dispatch said the woman who called said we'd find a DB, and we did."

DB? As in, dead body?

I held onto the piano more tightly, leaning against it, feeling woozy.

"If you could leave her there, Officers, we'll take care of everything," Annabelle assured them, her voice remarkably controlled when I knew that she was frantic. "The doctor is on his way, and so is the head of Belle Meade's security. We won't need your assistance to handle the body. The funeral home will be notified, and they'll transport her remains . . ."

She kept talking, but I'd stopped listening. Instead, I focused on one word and one word only.

Remains.

But whose remains were they?

Where, oh, where had my Cissy gone?

I felt a rising sense of panic. She hadn't been in the dining room nor in the empty courtyard, so it seemed reasonable to figure she'd be here, at Sarah Lee Sewell's.

"... won't need assistance to handle the body ... the funeral home will be notified ..."

I still wasn't sure exactly who was dead—though I had a pretty good guess—and Annabelle hadn't told me a thing besides the situation being "sticky."

Peanut butter was sticky. Scotch tape was sticky. Chewing gum was sticky.

A dead body was something else entirely.

Where the heck was my mother?

My eyes blurred so that I couldn't make out one person from another. I heard a jumble of voices, but they were as muffled as if I were underwater.

Still, I took a few stuttering steps forward, wetting my lips to ask, "Excuse me, Officers, but have you seen a sixty-year-old blond woman in a gray suit?" My voice sounded foreign to my ears, a barely audible croak. "She was wearing black pumps a lot like those and a charcoal gray mourning suit."

The police looked at me, then at each other, before shifting their eyes to glance down at the sofa. "Would you call that gray?" one said to the other. "Or is it more of a purple?"

Oh, God.

I swayed.

"Andy, it's not her." Annabelle hurried over and caught my elbows to steady me. When I ceased wobbling, she turned her back to make a call on her cell.

It's not her, I told myself, and my heart started beating again.

"Cissy?" I warbled, wandering toward the stairs and hollering upward. I'd check out every room upstairs and down if I had to, then I'd start on the neighbors. "Cissy Blevins Kendricks, are you here?"

A hand landed squarely on my shoulder.

"I'm right behind you, sweetie," the familiar voice drawled in my ear, and I spun on a bare heel to face her. Have you ever wanted to smack someone and hug them at once?

"My God, Mother, you nearly gave me a heart attack."

"I'm sorry, sugar." She brushed sweat-sticky hair from my face. "I was in the little girls' room . . . pulling myself together."

"Don't ever do that again."

"Use the powder room?"

"You know what I mean!"

The breath rushed from my lungs, and my knees sagged inward till they knocked. Cissy's arms came around me, and I deeply inhaled the scent of Joy on her skin and ozone-killing spray on her hair.

"I thought that might be you on the sofa, for a moment there," I admitted. "They looked so much like yours."

"The shoes?" she said.

I nodded, queasy, the taste of bile on my tongue.

"Sarah Lee did love a classic pump. Though she was more partial to Coach and Cole Haan. I once tried to get her to buy the prettiest pair of Stuart

Weitzmans to go with a Dior gown, but she found them too strappy. Said her feet felt naked."

Hello, Imelda? I wanted to shake her. "Why didn't you listen and stick with me like I asked? But, no, you had to wander off, looking for trouble. Did you find her . . . like *that*?" I couldn't bring myself to say the word.

"Oh, darlin', I did." Her chin vaguely trembled. "Just like that, only a little more upright. She toppled over sideways when I shook her by the shoulder."

"So the woman with the shoes is . . ."—I couldn't get the rest past my lips.

"Sarah Lee Sewell," she finished with a sigh, the day so full of sighs that surely the quota had been used up.

"How did it happen?" I asked, ever the soul of brevity. "Why did you have to wander off?"

"Because I sensed something wasn't right with Sarah Lee," Mother said, keeping her voice hushed. "She wasn't at church or the reception and her Jag's in the garage. I could see it through the tiny windows. The bell went unanswered, and the door wasn't locked. What else was I to do?" Her tone fell further, calm and oddly flat. She could've been reciting names from her Pi Phi blue book. "I stepped into the foyer and called out, not wanting to frighten her."

She pursed her lips, and I saw the struggle in her eyes, the hesitation before she could finish. "As soon as I entered the living room, there she was. At first, I didn't realize she was . . . gone. I set a hand on her shoulder and shook gently. I was afraid she'd had a stroke or something." Her slim shoulders quivered. "But she was cold, Andrea. Her lips were the palest blue. I knew then. I knew. I put the afghan on her, then I phoned them from the kitchen."

"So *you* called the police," I said, understanding why Annabelle wouldn't answer my question about Cissy's involvement in this . . . incident.

"I had to, sugar. You know I did after what went on with Bebe."

Me? What the hell did I know, except that Sarah Lee Sewell was the second of my mother's friends to die in a matter of days?

Was it fate? God's plan?

Or, as Mother seemed to believe, as fishy as mackerel?

I had no clue about the reason—medical or metaphysical—and I didn't need an answer, didn't want one, not when my heart raced so fast I couldn't breathe fast enough to keep up with its pounding.

How would my mother deal with two successive blows so close together?

She was stronger than she looked, I'd discovered that a while back, but it still surprised me, how she seemed so in control. For Pete's sake, she appeared far steadier than I felt, and it wasn't me who'd lost another pal.

"Will you be all right?" I said, as if I hadn't asked a million times already.

"I don't know, Andrea"—her ever-smooth drawl cracked—"I'm not sure that I will. Not until I figure out the truth. Because something's very, very wrong here."

Her grasp loosened, and she shifted away, her attention fixed elsewhere, on Annabelle's rising voice in response to the clipped tones of the Dallas police officer telling her they'd stick around until the doctor appeared to pronounce Sarah Lee Sewell dead, as they wanted to be sure no further intervention from the authorities was required.

Annabelle's face had drained of its earlier flush, and I watched as her shaky hands ended a call and dialed another while she paced the spacious room.

"Dr. Finch? Where are you?" she cried into the handset, wandering away from the cops and closer to where Mother and I stood. "Didn't security call you? Please, get over to the Sewell place *now*. We have a slight issue."

A slight issue?

As in, Mrs. Sewell was stone cold on her sofa?

Death was a big damn problem, as far as I was concerned.

My reservoir of calm—if I had such a thing— was seriously depleted after the memorial service that morning, and I wasn't in the mood to laugh in the face of adversity. Not this time. Which may be why my eyelid started twitching.

"Sarah Lee makes two," Cissy murmured, voicing my thoughts exactly. A hand fluttered to her throat. "What if it's the same man?"

The same man? A senior serial killer?

"Don't talk like that, Mother." I hushed her. "No one is whacking your friends for the heck of it. Please, cut the paranoia. I can't take it."

I was in no mood for more blather about murder conspiracies. My head whirled, and spots began to dance before my eyes. I shut them and slowly opened them again.

My gaze fell instantly upon the feet in the black shoes, resting cockeyed on the cushions. Then I saw the afghan, heaped in a sage green puddle on the carpet where it had been tossed aside, likely by the cops.

I imagined my mother draping it over the life-less woman before dialing 911, visualized her waiting alone with the deceased, until the cops had appeared on the scene.

Just thinking about it gave me a serious case of the heebie-jeebies.

I may not have eaten any of Chef Jean's raw oysters, but the contents of my stomach lurched regardless.

"Excuse me," I murmured into my hand, before I ran out the door and lost my lunch behind the azaleas.

When I stopped heaving and could finally stand up again, I wiped a hand across my mouth and slowly turned to find that a slim crowd had gathered on the sidewalk.

Terrific.

Nothing like tossing your cookies in front of a live audience.

A tall man with black bag in hand slipped through the spectators and barreled forward, brushing past me on his way into the townhouse.

Dr. Finch, I realized, truly not impressed with his curbside manner.

"Are you all right, Miss Kendricks? Maybe you should sit down."

His better half, Patsy, came up beside me, blond

bangs clinging damply to her forehead, as if she'd run from another side of the compound, much as Annabelle and I had minutes earlier.

I couldn't admit that I'd rarely been so close to a dead body before. I was a novice at this kind of thing.

"Must've been the pork," I told her, wetting dry lips. "I'm feeling better now." Besides, I wasn't about to stay out here, much as I wanted to, not with Cissy still inside, itching to tell the cops her theory. "I have to go back in."

Before all hell breaks loose, I left unsaid. As if it hadn't already.

Patsy Finch went in alongside me, and, this time, it was Dr. Finch hovering over poor Sarah Lee Sewell while one of the officers—the stockier of the two with a crew cut—stood nearby, observing.

Patsy gave my arm a pat and left to join them.

I found my mother and Annabelle with the second cop in the kitchen, all three talking at once so that I wished I could've put my fingers to my lips and whistled. Only I'd never mastered the art, nor had I learned to make farting sounds with my armpit (not that I'd want to).

So I settled for a subtle cough. It always worked for Mother.

Not even an eyebrow lifted.

". . . Miss Cissy, you're simply overwrought and don't know what you're saying . . ."

". . . ma'am, what makes you think it's foul play . . ."

". . . if you'd only looked into Bebe's death, perhaps the killer would have been captured and this wouldn't have happened . . ."

I cleared my throat. Loudly.

Still, the voices continued to rise, each trying to outtalk the other, with no sign of abating.

". . . Dr. Finch called Bebe's death 'natural,' and I've no doubt he'll do the same in this case . . ."

". . . if you don't mind my asking, ma'am, did your friend have any enemies that you're aware of . . . ?"

". . . no, Officer, none at all. Nobody didn't like Sarah Lee . . ."

As the verbal battle raged on, I studied my surroundings.

". . . please, Miss Cissy, you're just making this worse for us all . . ."

". . . if the doctor doesn't find the death suspicious, ma'am, and there's no sign of forced entry or intrusion, then we don't have cause to call in the medical examiner . . ."

". . . what if it's a very clever killer who knows not to leave behind a trail of evidence . . ."

An expensive set of copper-bottomed pots dangled from a baker's rack, and I climbed on a wooden chair, helping myself to one and to a large wooden spoon lying in a spoon rest on the countertop.

Like a five-year-old who'd forsaken Fisher-Price for the fun stuff hidden in Mother's cabinets, I wielded the copper pot and banged it with a spoon until the voices stopped and my own ears rang.

But it was worth it.

They shut up.

Three pairs of eyes turned in my direction.

"What's the matter with you?" I asked, speaking far too loudly. "Sarah Lee is lying there in the very next room, and you're squabbling in her kitchen like a bunch of girls . . . no offense, Officer. If that's not bad enough, there's a reception going on in the dining room of Belle Meade to honor Bebe Kent. Can't we act like grown-ups and at least pretend to have some dignity?"

Annabelle blushed and hung her head.

The police officer excused himself, one hand on the baton in his utility belt as he left the kitchen, maybe wishing he could bop me with it for calling him a girl.

"Speaking of dignity," my mother said, frowning, "Andrea darling, where on earth are your shoes? Your feet are filthy, and you're standing on a piece of furniture that doesn't belong to you. For goodness' sake, I taught you better than that."

With all that was going on, she was worried about my dirty feet?

Unbelievable.

I stooped to set the pot and spoon on the counter and carefully stepped down from the chair.

"Mother, let's go." I had a powerful urge to leave this place, sure that hanging around wasn't helping things. We were only in the way. I made myself face Annabelle. "I'm sorry," I told her, "for any trouble we may have caused you."

"Trouble?" Cissy repeated, incredulous. "Don't apologize for me, sweetie. Not when I'm the only one who sees the need to investigate. The police are duty-bound to find out why Sarah Lee and Bebe were killed, but instead"—she flicked slender fingers in the air—"you brush the possibility aside in order to pretend nothing's wrong. These were healthy women, not horses headed to the glue factory. They had plenty of good years left in them, and suddenly they're gone. It's not natural, and I've seen enough to prove it."

"What have you seen, Miss Cissy?" Annabelle asked, her expression bordering on an all-out glare.

"Oh, geez, not the nightgown again," I groaned, which only made my mother's chin nudge higher.

"What nightgown are you talking about?" Annabelle appeared equal parts unnerved and baffled.

"The one Bebe was wearing when you found her," I jumped in before Cissy could offer her silver dollar's worth. "Miss Marple here"—I winged an elbow at Mother—"says that Bebe slept in the buff and that everyone close to her knew it. So she wouldn't have been caught dead in a nightgown . . . except that she was . . . cripes, you know what I mean."

"It's a fact, Andrea, and worth investigating," Cissy argued. "Because the circumstances at Bebe's were as unnatural as what I witnessed here, with Sarah Lee."

"And, pray tell, what unnaturalness did you find on these premises?" Annabelle warbled, looking on the verge of tears. "Was she wearing an outfit from last season? Or the wrong color shoes?"

"No, dear, those black Cole Haan pumps are entirely appropriate for her ensemble. That's not the problem." My mother wandered over to the sink and homed in on glassware drying on a dishtowel.

"Mother?" I called, and she turned around. "What did you see?"

Calm as she could be, she turned around and replied, "What? Oh, yes, the smoking gun and Sarah Lee."

"You found a gun?" Annabelle looked ready to jump out of her skin.

"No, no," Mother countered. "It was her lipstick."

"Her lipstick?" my old campmate and I echoed in tandem.

"Obviously, she had plans for last evening, as she's got on that pretty ensemble from Carolina Herrera's fall collection and Sarah Lee didn't get gussied up to stay home and watch TV." Cissy came back around the granite-topped cooking island. "Only something was off, and I noticed the first moment I laid eyes on her." She paused and tapped a finger against her painted mouth. "Her lipstick," she said. "It was rubbed away almost completely."

That was the smoking gun?

Lord have mercy on us all.

I put my head in my hands.

Could this be real? Or was I trapped in a horrendous nightmare, like Dorothy in Oz? Was an attack of the flying monkeys soon to come?

"I'll get you, my pretties!" echoed through my head.

Annabelle wasn't so slow to react.

"So, Miss Cissy, what you're sayin' is that you believe Bebe was murdered because she'd gone to bed in a nightgown . . . and Sarah Lee must've suf-

fered the same fate because her lip rouge was
smeared off and she was dressed for a night on the
town? Have I got that down pat?"

Cissy's slim shoulders stiffened at Annabelle's
tone. "Sarah Lee was *always* meticulous with her
make-up. She would *never* leave the house without
her lipstick intact. Someone was here when she
died, just as I know someone was there with Bebe.
Scoff all you want, but it's the truth . . ."

"*Mother*," I said, more sharply than I should
have. The day had begun with a funeral and had
only gone downhill from there. My patience had
worn thinner than dental floss. "Hush, *please*."

"Ah, so that's the way it is?" Cissy tossed her
head. "I'm the elephant in the room, am I? Just
pretend I'm a crazy old lady and disregard what
comes out of my mouth? If my own mother had
demanded my attention, I'd have given it in an instant. That's the difference between our generations. Mine respects age and wisdom. I'm sorry to
say, I don't think yours respects much of anything
at all except flat tummies."

I bit my tongue, so I wouldn't interrupt her
tirade. Better to let her rattle on until she sput-
tered out.

She picked up her purse and wagged it at me.
"I'll wait for *you* in the car, young lady. As for you,
Annabelle, I'm sorely disappointed. I thought you
had more sense than this, but I guess I was
wrong." She tucked the bag beneath her arm. Her
eyes snapped from Annabelle to me, then back to
Annabelle. "For now, *adieu*. But I haven't finished
with you yet."

Annabelle's face clouded up like a thunderstorm.

I chewed on the inside of my cheek, waiting until Mother had exited the kitchen before I said again, "I'm really sorry. I had no earthly idea she'd be affected like this. She's practically hallucinating."

"It's all right, really," Annabelle said, but I'm not sure she meant it. "Grief does strange things to people, and lashing out is a normal defense mechanism. But I do think you should take her home." She walked up and caught my hands in hers. "It really was good to see you, Andy, and Cissy again, too, despite everything. Please, don't be a stranger. I want to finish that tour I promised you. Some other time, then?"

"Sure, another time," I agreed.

She began to twirl a thick strand of hair around her finger, spinning and spinning, until her digit was entirely wrapped up in the coil.

"You sure you're all right?" I asked.

She furiously untangled finger from hair, her chin trembling so I expected the water works to start any minute. "Can't anything go right for me?" she finally exploded, fists clenched at her sides.

Mindful of the opened archway between the kitchen and living room, I marched her quickly into the butler's pantry and closed the door.

"Annabelle, for goodness' sake, what's really going on?" I thought of her remark outside: *"Oh, God, it's happening again."* Something was eating at her, and it wasn't just Sarah Lee and Bebe's deaths.

She jerked away from me in the narrow space

and covered her face with her hands. "It's bad *mojo*, Andy. It follows me wherever I go. I can't get away from it," she mumbled through her fingers.

"What are you talking about, bad *mojo*? Things have been going so well for you. You told me so yourself."

She peeled her hands away and looked at me. Tears streaked her cheeks, coming thick and fast, taking clumps of black mascara down with them. "It started when my parents died."

"Six years ago at their lake house," I said. "But that wasn't your fault any more than this is."

"What I didn't tell you, Andy, was that I was there the day it happened. I had dinner with them both, and it turned into a row, as usual. I can still hear the screaming in my head. God, they could be vicious." She slumped against the slim cupboards. "The last words I uttered that night before I ran out, slamming the door, were that I hated them. Despised them to the core. 'I wish you'd die!' I told them both." Tears splattered on her blue jacket. "The next morning, they were dead."

I hardly knew what to say to that. "My gosh, Annabelle," was all I could come up with, because I couldn't imagine having to live with that kind of memory. That kind of guilt.

"There was a drawn-out investigation of the fire. Something about the pattern of how it spread. They thought for a while it might be arson, and they considered us all suspects."

"Us all? Meaning you?" I stared at her, shaking my head.

"Yes, me, and Emmy and Franklin . . . the couple who cared for my parents, and the house and grounds." She sniffled. "They raked us over the coals for months, the fire inspector, the police, and the insurance company, until they ruled it accidental. It was horrible, Andy, the worst time of my life. I barely survived."

She didn't elaborate, but I guessed what she meant.

"I couldn't bear to go through anything like that again." She wrung her hands. "I couldn't. It would kill me."

"Annabelle, stop, don't think about this now," I said quietly. "You have enough to handle without dwelling on the past."

"You're right," she agreed and swallowed, hard. I could see the lump go down her throat. "I've got to call the funeral home and pull Sarah Lee's file with all her postmortem instructions." Lines of worry cut into her cheeks and brow. "Then I'll have to inform the residents, and they haven't even had time to get over losing Mrs. Kent. I know Sarah Lee has next of kin somewhere out of state, an older sister, I think, though I can't remember her name. Damn it. Why can't I ever get things right? I'm such a stupid, stupid cow!"

Before she said another word, I wrapped my arms around her, feeling her shake and hearing a low, keening sound come from somewhere deep inside. I patted her back, waiting for the tears to come; but she suddenly stiffened and stepped out of the circle of my arms. She opened the pantry door and strode into the kitchen.

I followed as she walked toward the sink, yanked a paper towel from a roll on the counter, and began to mop up her tear-streaked face.

She tossed the wadded-up towel into the sink and stood for a moment, gripping the stainless-steel lip, gazing out the window. "I have to hold myself together. There's too much at stake. My whole life . . . Belle Meade . . . everything."

I went over to where she stood, saw a pair of ceramic mugs drying on a dishtowel, and filled one with cold water from the tap.

"Here." I held it out to her. "Sip on this. You'll feel better."

"Please, Andy," she said, tucking her arms across her chest, pushing the glass away, "please, just leave."

If I could've felt crummier, I wasn't sure how.

I dumped the water in the sink and set the cup back on the dishtowel. With only a glance at Annabelle's blue back, I shuffled out of the kitchen and passed through the living room to see the police officers had gone. Someone had covered Sarah Lee Sewell with the sage blanket, though it didn't quite reach her black shoes.

Dr. Finch and Patsy stood near the fireplace, huddled together in conversation, pausing only when they realized I was there.

Patsy nodded at me, but Finch scowled and looked out the nearest window.

I didn't feel it was appropriate to wave, so I kept walking, to the foyer and out the door.

The Bentley purred at the end of the sidewalk.

Behind its dark windows, I knew Mother was waiting. If I could've walked any slower, I'd have stood still.

Fredrik appeared in a flash as I neared the car,

sailing around the hood to open my door. I murmured my thanks and crawled inside.

Cissy tipped her face so I caught her expression in the glimpse of sunlight that swam inside before Fredrik shut me in.

On her Coco Red lips sat an odd little grin.

"What's the matter with you? Just what are you up to?" I said, the first thing that popped into my mind.

"For heaven's sake, but you're on a tear today," she replied, "accusing me of everything but nabbing the cat."

"Did you take a cat?" I checked the area around me, expecting to spot something furry.

She rolled her eyes. "That was a joke, Andrea."

Mother was joking? Since when? Did hell freeze over, and I'd missed the announcement on CNN?

I scowled, but it didn't seem to bother her a bit.

The Bentley swayed as Fredrik pulled away from the curb and headed away from the row of townhouses, nearly sideswiping the security guard's golf cart as it rolled up the street, too late to do anything helpful.

"Poor Annabelle," my mother murmured. "She has no one to count on, no one to give her advice, and she could use a steady influence. She's still such an emotionally delicate creature. I wish she'd listened to me. I was so close to Bebe and Sarah Lee. I could help her figure this out, if only she'd let me."

"No more about your theories, please." I pressed my fingers against my throbbing temples, on the verge of a serious headache. "You've done enough already."

"Done what? I haven't done a thing . . . yet," she said, but her hand moved over something beside her, pulling it close to her skirt.

I lowered my hands from my head and turned deliberately toward her, edging near enough that I could reach for whatever it was she was trying to cover up—something rolled up and secured with a rubber band.

"What are you hiding?"

"I'm not hiding anything."

It wasn't much of a struggle to tug it away from her. Maybe she'd wanted that all along.

She sat primly, hands in her lap, not saying a word as I unwrapped the bundle to find several catalogues, a copy of *Texas Monthly*, and assorted bills, letters, and junk mail addressed to one Sarah Lee Sewell.

I blinked a couple of times, rubbed my eyes to be sure I'd read right. Then I pictured the mailbox on the railing of Sarah Lee's porch, its contents keeping the lid from closing, and I cringed when I realized what she'd done.

"You took her mail," I blurted out.

I couldn't believe it.

My blue-blooded, champion fundraising, card-carrying socialite mother was a thief.

Great balls of fire, indeed! I felt like I had stolen diamonds in my lap.

"So I picked up Sarah's mail from her box? She won't be reading it anytime soon, will she, sugar?"

"It's still a crime," I reminded her.

Her eyes narrowed. "So is murder, and you don't seem to care about that."

I stared at her, sputtering with frustration, wondering if she'd gone completely mad, or if I was the one who'd lost her mind.

She leaned over and began plucking each piece of mail from where it spilled across my thighs and the leather bench. "Oh, don't be so judgmental, Andrea, not when it's all for a very good reason."

There was a good reason for snatching a dead woman's mail?

"If no one else intends to look for more evidence"—she sighed—"well, then, it's up to me, isn't it? I owe it to Bebe and to Sarah."

"More evidence?" I peeled back my fingers to stare at her. "Evidence of what? No one suspects foul play but you. Nightgowns and lipstick," I muttered. "Please, tell me you're going to drop this. You're not seriously going to push this issue, are you? You're not going to call Anna Dean?"

Anna Dean was the police chief of Highland Park. She and Mother were well acquainted, and not just because of Mother's ample donations to the Widows and Orphans Fund. Cissy had once been on the receiving end of Anna Dean's questions in a homicide investigation.

"No, I won't get Chief Dean involved. It isn't her jurisdiction."

Phew. I let myself breathe again. Maybe I was a tad too hasty.

"But I'm quite serious, Andrea. Obviously, Annabelle and her staff want to whitewash what's happened, and I can't blame them a bit. Their license to operate could be in jeopardy, not to mention what bad publicity could do to Belle Meade, here and in Austin, as well as to any future investments." Her eyebrows peaked. "Oh, yes, I know about her plans for expansion. But I can't let that worry me, and I won't stop until I know what the truth really is. So if you don't like it, then leave me be. I'm a grown woman, and I can do as I please without my daughter telling me differently."

Ding, ding, ding! Round One to Cissy Blevins Kendricks!

"That's settled then." She snapped the rubber band in its place, around her pilfered goodies. "Though you seem to have forgotten one thing"— she started, but I cut her off in a flash.

"I've forgotten what? That you've gone bonkers? The truth is that an elderly woman passed away quietly in her own home, but for some unfathomable reason you want to believe she didn't die naturally. Instead, you've convinced yourself that there's a homicidal maniac knocking off bridge players at an old folks' home."

"Retirement village."

"Whatever!" The words exploded from my mouth before I could stop them. "So I'm supposed to forget that you basically insulted an old acquaintance of mine because she wouldn't take your accusations seriously? Is that what you're saying?"

Round Two. The challenger comes out swinging!

"No," she said softly. "It's not."

"Oh, really?" I was breathing hard after my diatribe, clenching my fists against the leather seat and grinding my teeth—yes, grinding them, dammit—as I waited. "So set me straight then, Mother. What one thing have I forgotten?"

"Other than your manners?" She smoothed her gray skirt and replied quite calmly, "Your *shoes*, Andrea darling. You forgot your shoes . . ."

"My shoes?" I'd left them in the courtyard when Annabelle had taken off running after the sirens. I could never have chased her in slides.

". . . and your feet are simply filthy, so keep them squarely on the mat, if you would, please."

Ouch, that had to hurt! The Debutante Dropout takes a right jab to the kisser, and the fight goes to Her Highness of Highland Park in a unanimous decision!

I caught Fredrik's smile in the rearview mirror.

Somehow, I refrained from banging my head against the window or throwing myself out of the Bentley into a busy lane of traffic.

Chapter 7

Fredrik dropped me off at the church overflow lot, where my Jeep baked in the sun, its dusty windows and bird-poop-ravaged body looking nearly as hot and miserable as I felt. Some helpful soul had even scrawled WASH ME in the film on the rear window. I didn't bother to smudge it off.

Sweat turned my skin slick as I sat in the driver's seat for a few minutes after, the side windows open wide and the warm AC blowing while I dialed Sandy Beck on my cell phone.

Mother had promised that, once snug at home, she'd get a bite to eat and have a brandy or a Valium—but not both at once—then she'd trot herself upstairs for a nap. Only I wasn't convinced she'd made those assurances because she'd *meant* them, or if she were just trying to pacify me.

I also needed to fill Sandy in on the day's events—what had really transpired, not Mother's sure-to-be glossed-over version. Someone had to keep tabs on Cissy, and Sandy was my best bet, since she'd basically been doing that for longer than I'd been alive.

"I'm sorry I wasn't there, Andy," she said, right off the bat, when I described the memorial service and how despondent Mother was at losing Bebe Kent. "But I'm not one for funerals, and Cissy so appreciated that you were going with her. I figured it would be good for both of you."

Good for us? I wondered. Sort of like brussels sprouts and penicillin?

I next laid out what had happened at Belle Meade, most notably Mother's discovering the recently deceased Sarah Lee Sewell, pilfering Mrs. Sewell's mailbox, and declaring her intention to play Hercule Poirot, intent on unmasking a killer. When I was done, there was such a delayed silence on the other end that I thought I'd lost the connection.

"You still there?" I asked.

"My word." Sandy's astonishment spoke volumes. "Cissy honestly believes her friends were murdered?"

"Unfortunately, she's convinced herself of it. She figures the acts were committed by someone crazed enough to dress Bebe in her nightgown and tuck her into bed last Wednesday, then hop over to Sarah Lee's on Friday evening and wipe off her lipstick before doing her in."

"Should I call Dr. Cooper?"

Great minds surely do think alike.

I told her not to rule out dragging Mother to her physician for a little tête-à-tête, but advised her to wait until morning. I had a strong inkling Cissy's grief had more to do with a need to fix blame, rather than anything physical. My hope was that, after a good night's rest, she'd again see reality through her rose-colored couture sunglasses and would likely even be embarrassed by what she'd done and said.

Sandy soothed my fears as only she could, giving assurances that she'd take care of things as she always did. I had utter faith she would. She'd handled plenty of boo-boos and tears in my growing-up years, and she'd never let me down. Nor had she ever let down Mother.

"Call if she needs me, okay? Whatever the hour," I said, hearing her assent before I disconnected.

Then I started the Jeep and drove back to North Dallas, shoeless as the day I was born. The first thing I did when I walked through my door was to pull the black dress over my head and toss it to the floor.

Wearing only my bra and panties, I staggered to my unmade bed and climbed in, not bothering to check my voice mail despite a blinking light on my CallerID, indicating I had messages. I did detour briefly to the bathroom to take care of urgent business. But I left my feet unwashed, partly in protest because Mother had made such a big stinking deal about them; but mostly because I had zero energy left to suds up a washcloth.

Though pangs of hunger shot through my belly, I felt too wiped out to eat. Besides, Malone wasn't around to crack open a can of chicken noodle or whip up a grilled cheese, something he was good at doing when I needed a little TLC.

Emotional exhaustion overwhelmed me. Everything had been too much, and I was spent like a beggar's last nickel. Cissy wasn't the only one who needed a siesta.

The arms of my alarm clock pointed at just past three, when I rolled over onto Malone's side of the bed and lay my head upon his pillow. I closed my eyes, breathing in the scent of him and thinking I'd drift off just long enough to wipe the earlier part of the day from my memory. Kind of like hypnosis. When I awakened, it would be like nothing had happened, and I could move on with my life. No worries about Mother, Belle Meade, or murder.

Though I tried to relax, pieces of the day flickered through my tired head: Bebe Kent's face grinning at me from the blow-ups in the yellow dining hall, my ears filling with the howl of the police siren, seeing Sarah Lee Sewell's lifeless legs on the floral chintz, Mother insisting that her pals had been exterminated before their expiration dates, and Annabelle's tale of the fire that killed her parents.

Why wasn't there a remote to switch my brain off?

Groaning, I drew a pillow atop my head and pressed down with my forearm, as if that would squash the images (as well as my hair). I concentrated on the thud of my heartbeat, like the constant, gentle pats of a palm against a drum skin.

Slowly, I began to drift in and out of a fog, shallow and dreamless.

I didn't rouse again until the sun had withdrawn its yellow fingers from between the slats of the shutters and the purple glow of twilight had replaced the bright of day, casting shadows across my room.

The phone trilled, high-pitched and angry, refusing to be ignored.

I reached over to the bedside table and grabbed hold of the handset, saying "Hello?" as I drew myself up against the headboard, more groggy than awake.

"Andrea, I'm so glad I found you! You have to fix this mess!" Annabelle squawked in my ear at such a rapid-fire clip that I couldn't keep up with her. All my muddled mind could catch were sporadic phrases, like, "I can't believe it," "gone too far," "this is beyond crazy," and "meeting here tomorrow."

"Hold on," I begged and switched the phone to the other ear, using my free hand to turn on the lamp. Squinting as my eyes adjusted to the glow, I yawned and got my bearings. My mouth tasted fouler than foul, and I itched to brush my teeth. I rubbed a finger across them, which hardly made me feel minty-fresh but would do until I could gather the momentum to cover the ten feet between my bed and the bathroom.

"Andy? Are you there? Are you listening to me?"

My first coherent thought was about the shoes I'd left lying on the patio at Belle Meade, though I wasn't sure why they'd be the cause of such concern unless someone had tripped over them and broken an ankle.

"Um, you want me to come pick up my slides tomorrow morning?" I offered, hoping that would placate her. "I'm really sorry, AB, but I just completely forgot about them. There was too much going on."

"No, no, no!" She puffed into the phone. "I

don't care about your shoes, don't you get it? It's your mother, Andrea. She's obsessing over Bebe and Sarah Lee, and you have to make her stop!"

That got my attention. "What are you talking about?"

"Look, you know I love Miss Cissy dearly, but she's going to ruin everything if she doesn't cool it. I'd hate to have to get a restraining order or have her arrested for trespassing."

Arrested? Restraining order?

As Malone liked to say, "Whoa."

I was fully alert, my pulse jumping like a hyperactive kid on a trampoline.

Uh-oh, I thought, and swallowed hard. Did Annabelle know about the stolen mail? Or had Cissy done something worse that I wasn't privy to, like when she'd wandered out of my eyesight?

"Er, what are you referring to, exactly?" I proceeded cautiously. "What has Mother done that's so disastrous? Oh, wait, you mean her telling the cop that she wanted an investigation? Because, I was there, Annabelle, and his eyes were practically rolling out of his head. The guy thought she was an escapee from the booby hatch."

"Hell's bells, it's not what she told the cop! It's worse than that."

"Could you be more specific?"

Annabelle cried: "Your mother called Margery Flax before I ever had a chance to phone the poor woman and give her the news myself."

I cringed as I asked, "Who is Margery Flax?"

"Great balls of fire, Andy! She's Sarah Lee Sewell's eighty-year-old sister from South Dakota. Her only surviving kin."

"Ah." I wasn't sure what was so wrong about Cissy getting in touch with this woman, except it meant Mother went home and started dialing rather than taking a nap, as she'd promised. So I decided to tread carefully, wondering aloud, "And that's a bad thing, because . . . ?"

"Because she convinced Mrs. Flax to call Dr. Finch and request that an autopsy be performed on Sarah Lee!" Annabelle's voice rose precariously. "Apparently, Cissy told the poor woman that Mrs. Sewell might not have gone to meet her Maker willingly. She practically insinuated that we were involved in a cover-up!"

If I hadn't thrown up earlier, I might've done it then. My stomach twisted in a painful knot. "She didn't."

"Oh, yes, she did."

Good grief.

I groaned and chastised myself for leaving Mother alone for a single minute, what with the state she was in. That had been a miscalculation on my part, and now Annabelle was paying for it.

"So, do you have to have it done now? The autopsy?" I asked, chewing on a cuticle.

"Only if I can't convince Margery otherwise. And I might have a shot, if you can restrain Miss Cissy." Annabelle sighed. "Margery's already contacted the funeral home and asked them to hold on to her sister's remains and delay cremation until this gets settled. Dr. Finch has signed the death certificate, so this is prolonging the inevitable and making things harder on everyone."

"I'll have a talk with her, okay?" It was all I

could promise, because I realized my mother's actions were well beyond my control.

"Please, Andy, make it fast. I'm just afraid that, if Cissy gets herself too riled up over this, she'll make good on her threats to contact the local media, the regulatory commission, AARP, the Gray Panthers, the Junior League, and anyone else who'll listen."

Yowza.

"She said that?"

"That was only a partial list." Annabelle sounded truly miserable.

Much as I was tempted, I couldn't lie and tell Annabelle it wouldn't happen. Cissy had contacts all over the city—hell, all across this great big state, in every industry and business—and she could pretty well make life rough for Annabelle if she wanted to.

"Why?" Annabelle moaned. "Why is she doing this?"

Why did my mother do anything?

It was rather like asking why rain was wet.

I scrambled for advice to give; something reassuring that wasn't an outright lie. The best I could come up with on such short notice was my old tried-and-true method of "going with the flow." Sometimes, battling Cissy was akin to flying a kite in a hurricane. Not only would the kite be smashed to smithereens, but you might not come through in one piece, either. So I threw out my pitch: "Maybe you're going about this the wrong way."

"And how's that possible?"

"Well, I'll tell you how, if you've got a couple minutes."

"I'm listening."

I slid my feet off the bed, glancing at my alarm clock. It showed a quarter past six. I wondered what other havoc my mother might've wreaked in the hours while I'd dozed. If she kept this up, we'd need Dr. Phil on retainer. Mother already had the lawyers at Abramawitz, Reynolds, Goldberg, and Hunt at her beck and call.

"Whatever you do, don't tell her 'no,'" I suggested. "It just feeds her fire. You'll make the whole thing worse."

"How can it get worse than her dragging the insurance regulators in and crying murder? Then the police will have to get involved . . . oh, Andy, I couldn't endure another investigation, not after what I went through with my parents." She paused to catch her breath. "The negative publicity alone would totally screw us, even if Cissy doesn't get our license revoked somehow."

Investigation . . . license revoked.

"Play along with her, Annabelle. Say whatever you have to, for now. If you insinuate you're gonna have her arrested for trespassing or served with a restraining order, you're just giving her more ammunition. The more you resist, the more she'll believe she's right."

"So you're saying we should go ahead with an autopsy?" Annabelle's voice quivered. "But Andy, that alone will raise suspicion after Arnold already signed her death papers. I don't think it's possible without getting the medical examiner's office involved."

"Perhaps you won't need to go that far," I said, hoping I was right. "Could Dr. Finch agree to do some blood tests through a private lab? If he checked for poisons or, I don't know, an overdose of Metamucil, I'll bet that would pacify Mother and get her off your back."

"I don't know, Andy." Annabelle didn't sound convinced. "It seems wrong to do anything even slightly invasive when it's completely unnecessary. Sarah Lee died of cardiac arrest . . . her old heart just ceased pumping. Why can't your mother believe that?"

"A blood test seems a small price to pay if it'll get Cissy off your back. Not to mention Margery Fleck."

"Flax," she corrected. "Do you really think that would work? Would it make her stop asking questions about Bebe, too?"

I had no guarantee. But I did know my mother. She was a bulldozer when she put her mind to something.

"Just chill, if you can," I said. "Humor her for now, and when Sarah Lee's tests return negative, Mother will have to accept the fact that she's barking up the wrong tree."

"You think?"

"She'll turn her attention back to her charity work and the fall social circuit. She's got a million parties coming up"—God, I hoped Annabelle was buying this—"as a matter of fact, just the other day she told me about a demolition party being thrown by the mayor's daughter. The woman wants to tear down a perfectly good 1940s ranch house and put up a modern monstrosity that's all glass."

"A demolition party?"

I'd gotten up and was pacing the room, doing semicircular laps around my bed. "Mother said the invitation asked guests to wear dungarees and BYOS."

"Bring your own . . . ?"

"Sledgehammer," I told her. "But hard hats will be provided, along with the wine and hors d'oeuvres."

"Cissy in a hard hat and jeans, whacking a sledgehammer?" Annabelle did sound less pissed. "Would you kill for a picture of that, or what?"

"Can you see it on a Christmas card?"

"Hell's bells, I'd put it on a billboard."

"We could charge pay-for-view."

"On the Home and Garden Channel . . ."

"Or Comedy Central."

Annabelle laughed.

And I breathed a huge sigh of relief, feeling like I'd dodged a bullet, or at least a BB pellet.

"Okay, Sparky, I'll take your advice this time," she said, not laughing anymore. "But I'm not leaving anything to chance. Be here at nine o'clock sharp for my meeting with Cissy. I might need a hand."

"Tomorrow? But that's Sunday." Even God had set it aside as a day of rest, and I considered it one of His better ideas.

"Most of the residents will have headed off to church in the shuttles, so it'll be quiet around here, less chance for anyone to overhear your mother's accusations, or my screams of frustration. And don't even think of bailing on me, Andrea Blevins Kendricks," she groused. "This is way too important."

Were all proper Southern belles trained to use a person's full name when they were ticked?

"Aw, Annabelle, give me a break"—I was really hoping to sleep in after having had to dress up that morning to accompany Cissy to Bebe's service, and, besides, I had some Web site redesigns I wanted to noodle with—"Can't you face Cissy alone? You're a big girl."

"Not that big."

"C'mon. Do I have to?" I whined, because I felt like it.

The dial tone hummed in my ear.

I guess I'd take that as a "yes."

"*Apparently, Cissy told the poor woman that Mrs. Sewell might not have gone to meet her Maker willingly. She practically insinuated that we were involved in a cover-up!*"

Oy vey.

This had to stop.

I hit the reset button, as my first instinct was to call Mother ASAP. Posed to punch the speed-dial to her private line, I changed my mind.

Why confront her over the phone, when she could very well hang up on me (as Annabelle had)? Why not drive on down to Beverly and address her in person, where the very least she could do was kick me out of the house?

Even better, I'd pack an overnight bag, stop at Bubba's on the way, pick myself up the fried chicken I'd missed for lunch, and eat it at Cissy's on her custom-upholstered sofa with my feet propped up on her antique coffee table (so long as she couldn't see me do it) while I watched some cable (which I was too cheap to pay for myself).

Sounded like a finger lickin' good plan. After dinner, I'd settle into my old room and spend the night, have a little mother-daughter slumber party, so I could make sure she didn't do anything else rash before our meeting with Annabelle in the morning.

Having a goal in hand always made me feel better. I'd never been good at treading water.

Water.

As in "soap and"—my synapses crackled, playing their own form of Match Game—which reminded me that my feet were still filthy.

I hung up the phone and shuffled into the bathroom.

Perched on the edge of the bathtub, I turned on the faucet and washed those suckers, scrubbing my skin until all ten little piggies glowed a rosy pink. Never mind the slightly chipped nail polish.

Clean enough to prop on any piece of furniture.

I brushed my teeth and combed my hair for good measure. Slipped on a pair of blue jeans and a Harvard University T-shirt that Brian had given me after shrinking it in the wash.

Which jogged my mind again.

Malone.

Aw, geez. I'd almost forgotten about him with all the madness going on. No doubt, he'd tried to phone while I was gone, as he'd promised to check in from Galveston—and he'd always kept his word. So far.

My CallerID still blinked red, and I hit the button to scroll down the list of three numbers. There was Belle Meade from Annabelle's minutes-ago frantic call. In the second spot was Janet Graham's cell phone, and, last but hardly least, were the familiar digits for Malone.

As independent as I thought I was, my heart did a tiny flutter, and I realized that I missed him. He could always make me feel like things weren't as bad as I made them out to be. And he knew my mother, so he understood why I tended to work myself into a tizzy whenever she was involved.

I didn't bother to listen to the message he'd left, just went ahead and dialed up his number, way too eager to hear his voice.

One ringie-dingie, two ringie-dingies.

As I waited for him to pick up, I stuck my feet into a pair of flip-flops.

Three rings.

I dug out an oversized tote bag from the closet and tossed it on my bed.

Four rings.

Malone, where are you? I thought, and prepared for his brief spiel and the beep before I'd have to leave a voice mail message, which is when I heard a rustling sound and a somewhat startled, "Hello?"

"Oh, boy, are you missing some fun."

"Andy?" He said my name in a near-shout, and I picked up on the noises behind him, other voices and elevator music.

A restaurant? I guessed. I hoped. Better than someone else's hotel room.

"Did I call at a bad time?"

"We're doing a quick dinner before it's back to

work. We've got a boatload of transcripts to go through one more time before some more depos tomorrow. You didn't get my message?"

Well, I had gotten it—or I assumed I had, per my blinking CallerID light—but I hadn't listened to it. Only I didn't tell him that.

"So it is a bad time?" I asked again, wondering who else made up the "we," as in "we're doing dinner."

Not that I was going to pry, since I was the one who'd instituted the "don't ask, don't tell" rule. I just hoped it wasn't that blonde from his office. Allie Price, I recalled, none too fondly, though I hadn't even met her. Merely knew she was an old girlfriend, which meant she had the same ignition quotient as dynamite.

Kaboom.

"You still there, Andy? I can barely hear"—this time, static broke him up—"can I . . . call you later?"

"Later? Yeah, I guess so." I didn't mean to pout, but I'd wanted to talk to him in the worst way. I wanted to get his advice and have him assure me that everything was going to be fine, that my mother hadn't truly flipped her lid and her two friends hadn't been shoved forcibly past the Pearly Gates. "Ring my cell when you can," I told him. "I'll be at Cissy's."

"We must have a worse connection than I thought," he said overloudly, the cacophony buzzing behind him. " 'Cuz I thought you said you'd be at Cissy's."

"Right, I will."

The line crackled. "Damn, my battery's dying,"

I heard him announce, followed by a "hey, you there?" Before he faded into the ether.

Roger, over and out.

I said "goodbye" to dead air and disconnected, dissatisfied in the same way that eating Chinese food left me hungry again fifteen minutes after I finished. How I wished I were the one he was dining with instead of a colleague of his. Preferably, a fat, old, ugly male attorney and not that chit he used to shag.

Why hadn't I gone with him?

Brilliant move, Kendricks.

I kicked myself, figuring I could've avoided this drama with Cissy altogether, though I might've returned to find her in handcuffs. Would that have been worth a sunset walk with Brian on the Galveston beach?

Hmm. That was a tough one.

Dialing in my voice-mail codes, I nodded through Malone's message about being tied up all evening with paperwork, deleting it when I was through. The only thing that bothered me was something he *hadn't* said.

Three little words.

No, not "I love you."

Way too predictable.

Besides, at three months together, that would've sent me running in the opposite direction, and Brian knew it.

What I'd wanted to hear was a simple, "I miss you."

Only he hadn't let that slip.

Which clinched it, I decided. The day had officially sucked.

I tossed the last of my toiletries into the tote bag, doing a final once-over to make sure I hadn't forgotten anything. Which is when my gaze fell on the book Malone had bought me, the one that was supposed to teach me how to lower my stress quotient (as if that could ever happen). I'd already given up trying to laugh my way to low blood pressure, but figured I'd skim through another chapter before I tossed the thing into the trash bin.

So I shoved *Stress and the Single Girl* into my satchel, turned off the lights in the condo, and locked up tight. Not even my next-door-neighbor Charlie was out walking his beagle—nor did I spy Penny George behind her curtains, doing her best covert operative impression—when I crossed to the parking lot and took off in my Jeep for Cissy's neck of the woods.

"Neck of the woods" wasn't a bad way to describe it, when, in fact, I felt a little like I was heading for the crazy witch's house in *Hansel and Gretel*, with the leaking coolant from my Wrangler (I had a wee crack in my radiator) serving as the breadcrumbs, should I end up in the oven and need rescuing by the Texas Rangers. Only Mother never used the oven—I wasn't sure she even knew where the kitchen was—so nix that Grimm comparison.

Maybe I was more like Little Red Riding Hood driving straight toward the big, bad wolf, elegantly dressed in Chanel, of course.

Grandma, what furry skin you have. Did you miss your appointment at electrolysis? And those claws! Tsk, tsk. Couldn't Elizabeth Arden squeeze you in?

An honest-to-gosh smile threatened to crack on my lips, until I nipped that sucker in the bud.

Well, at least I still had my sense of humor.

It was either that or matricide, and I wasn't all that keen on going to prison.

Chapter 8

By the time I got to Mother's house on Beverly Drive in Highland Park, night had soundly fallen. The streetlamps cast a hazy glow as I slowed and turned into the circular drive. Windows gleamed through the dim and warmed the shadowed façade of the familiar two-story stucco as I approached, glancing up through the windshield to see light behind the sheers in Cissy's sitting room.

Good. She was awake.

After I'd filled my belly with the take-out from Bubba's, still warmly tucked in Styrofoam, I meant to have a heart-to-heart with Mother. She definitely had some 'splainin' to do, though I didn't want to come down too hard on her. As upset as I was with her, I knew how much she hurt. In the words of my Paw Paw, "a powerful lot."

I parked smack in front of my old homestead, grabbed my keys, bag, and take-out, and hopped down from the Jeep. The night had cooled the air considerably, and I detected a faint whiff of fall on the breeze, though I knew it would still be months in coming, despite what the calendar said.

A trickle of anxiety ran through me, but I swallowed it down and marched toward the front door and the two whitewashed terracotta lions that guarded it.

I juggled my armload, freeing a hand to push the bell, though, like magic, the door pulled inward.

Sandy Beck didn't look at all surprised to see me, and she hustled me in. "I had a feeling you'd show up," she said, "after I caught your mother on the phone when she should have been resting. Did she call you? I assume she did, as upset as she sounded. The part I overhead, anyway, which wasn't much."

"No, she didn't call, so it wasn't me who upset her this time." I set my bag down on the steps, keeping hold of the foam container, as she shepherded me into the kitchen. "But she probably didn't have a chance to dial me up. She was too busy making trouble for Annabelle, who did happen to phone and nearly chewed my ear off. To make a long story short, Mother and I have an appointment at Belle Meade in the morning at nine, so I figured I'd spend the night."

"You're that worried about Cissy, are you?"

"Yeah," I admitted, and she patted my hand. "I really am."

In a way that I hadn't been since my father died.

It had me rattled then, and it rattled me now.

I tried not to dwell on my own shaky emotions and busied myself, getting my supper ready and wishing I'd brought something for Sandy, although she indicated she'd already eaten and had taken something up to Mother as well.

My one-time babysitter and forever fairy godmother took a seat at the old oak table, while I retrieved a bottled water from the fridge and grabbed utensils from the drawer. Then I sat down with her and proceeded to eat straight from the container, using my fingers to snatch up a crispy-fried chicken breast.

Light-headed with hunger, I buried my teeth in it, chewing and swallowing at a pace that champion eaters at state fairs across the country would surely envy. I'd gotten halfway through my meal before I realized how intently Sandy watched me.

"What?" I mumbled and swiped at the grease on my chin with the back of my hand.

Which prompted her to ask, "Would you like a napkin? Or would that be too civilized? I feel like I'm witnessing a leopard devouring zebra guts on the Learning Channel."

"I can't help it, I'm weak with malnourishment," I got out, after shoving a forkful of mashed potatoes down my throat. I hadn't told her about losing my lunch in Sarah Lee Sewell's azalea bushes.

Sandy got up, went into the butler's pantry, and returned with a pressed napkin.

Linen, of course.

Mother didn't allow paper napkins in her house. A little la-di-dah, sure, but it was good for the environment, so I couldn't fault her for it.

"You are the strangest child," she remarked, sitting down again. But there was such warmth in her voice when she said it, so I took no offense. I knew what she meant, though I preferred to think of myself as charmingly eccentric.

When I'd finished and cleaned up, Sandy leaned back, hands in her lap. The comforting creases in her face puckered with concern.

"So what did she tell you?" I asked.

Sandy shook her head. "Not much. If you hadn't tattled about the stolen mail and her threats to Annabelle, I wouldn't have had any idea what's going on. Once I got her to talk at all, she didn't do much beyond describing everyone she'd seen at the church, what they were wearing, and, of course, who had Botox and who'd gone under the knife for real."

Normally, I'd find that reassuring.

"What do *you* think? You know her better than anyone. Does she strike you as a little . . . off? Compared to the usual, I mean."

She let loose of my hand to tug at her brown cardigan, toying with one of the tiny pearl buttons. "I've gone through loss with your mother before, Andy, and she generally locks up her emotion where no one can see it. She's very private that way. Then she'll throw all her energy into a project, usually a charity fundraiser."

I kept quiet, listening.

"Anyway, I offered to draw her a bath and bring her something to eat, but she waved me off. She told me she was tired and wanted to be alone for a spell. She didn't mention anything about the funeral or what happened afterward, not at first." Sandy paused, and a frown fell over her face. "But you had me worried enough that I fixed a tray with soup and that crusty bread from La Madeleine that she loves. She did sit down at her desk and picked at her food while she filled me in on the memorial service. Then I beat around the bush for a minute, before I got up the nerve to ask a few simple questions, to see if she was thinking straight."

I leaned my arms on the table and waited.

"I said, 'What year is this?' And she said, 'Why, Sandy, old girl, if you've forgotten the date, there's a calendar right here on my desk.'"

I bit my cheek to keep from grinning and had to remind myself this was serious business.

"So next I asked, 'Who's the current president?' She gave me one of those looks and said, 'You know good and well who he is, and I'll take the Fifth rather than remark upon his character, except to say he has a lovely mother.'"

"Oh, boy," I choked out. That was quintessential Cissy.

Sandy shrugged. "I don't know what's going on with her, Andy, but she's perfectly sane."

Or as sane as Mother got.

"Thanks for trying."

She nodded. "She's unexpectedly lost two dear friends, Andy. It's rough on her, and it'll take quite a while for her to get over it. That kind of thing throws even the strongest of us for a loop."

"I'm just so used to her being a steel magnolia." With a spine full of rebar.

"She is, Andy, but she's also human."

"I know."

"Maybe she just needs our love and support,"

Sandy suggested, sage as ever. "Just bear with her, until this passes, like everything else."

That's exactly what I'd advised Annabelle.

Though it didn't make it easier for any of us—or for Mother—in the meantime, did it?

I scooted my chair back, causing a squeal across the floor. "I'm going up," I said, but Sandy grabbed my arm.

"Oh, honey, I'm not sure that's a good idea. She may be sleeping. We shouldn't disturb her."

"She's not asleep. I saw the light on in her sitting room when I drove up."

"Well, all right." Sandy released me, but didn't look any too happy about my plans. "But if she is awake, please don't keep her long."

"Don't get her worked up, you mean." I met her gaze, seeing precisely that warning in her eyes. She was afraid I'd start an argument. Pick a fight. Which might very well happen, if I got on her case about Annabelle. "But I really do need to discuss this situation with her . . ."

"No, not tonight." Sandy's voice was soft, but firm enough that I knew not to contradict her. "Any serious conversation can wait until morning. She's been through plenty today already. Let her be for now, Andy. Let her be."

My mouth opened instinctively, only I didn't have another "but" left in me.

She was right. Which stunk to high heaven. Unlike my mother, I had this primitive urge to get things out in the open, debate a point to death, until I felt some kind of closure.

Obviously, that wasn't going to happen here.

"Okay, you win." I sighed. "I won't bring up

Annabelle or anything else involving Belle Meade or Bebe or Sarah Lee. I'll just go say goodnight, if I may."

"You certainly may." Sandy smiled and cupped my chin in her palm, shaking gently. "That's my good girl," she said, as if I were a child.

Though I guess I was, wasn't I? Forever, no matter how much I grew up. I could be ninety years old, and I'd always be somebody's baby.

I left her there in the kitchen, making those homey noises that took me back to the days when I'd lived within these walls. I heard her humming, the whoosh of water coming on, the clink of dishes as she rinsed them, and the thwacks of cabinet doors and drawers being opened and shut.

The sounds grew softer as I wandered off, toward the front stairwell through a paneled hallway.

Sometimes I forgot how big the house was, after living in such close quarters. My condo wasn't quite a thousand feet, small enough to fit in my mother's living room, but it was plenty large enough for me.

Scooping up my tote bag, I climbed the stairs, the slap of my flip-flops hushed on the Oriental runner, though the wood beneath serenaded me with its familiar groans and creaks.

My free hand slid up the carved banister, the scent of orange polish drawn in with my every breath. I hadn't lived in this house in a dozen years—and had always thought of it as Mother's, not mine, when it came down to it—and still the subtlest nuances of the place clutched at me whenever I came back.

As I emerged on the second floor landing, I

turned my head instinctively toward my father's den, wishing every time I passed that he would be in there, behind his big old desk, that I'd hear the rumble of his voice, calling out, "Is that you, pumpkin?"

If I imagined, I could hear it still.

I pushed my legs onward, toward the room that had been mine. Walking through the opened door, I crossed the silk rug to drop my bag on the bed, not bothering to switch on the light. The moon cast a pale glow through the windowpanes, though I could've worked my way around with my eyes closed and not bumped into a thing. I had every nook and cranny imprinted on my brain.

The room appeared as it had always been: nothing moved, nothing changed. I knew that if I opened the closet door, I'd find the clothing I'd left behind, uniforms for Hockaday and glitzy rags for formal events, including a white Vera Wang gown in its zippered bag. The dress I would have worn at my debut, eternally preserved in plastic.

Instead, I took a deep breath, squared my shoulders and tugged at the hem of my T-shirt, telling myself, "no arguments, no discussions of Belle Meade," as I crossed the hallway to Mother's closed door and knocked gently.

I didn't wait for her summons, but cracked open the door and stuck my head in. The light still burned in the sitting room, and one was on, as well, in the bedroom just beyond the dividing threshold.

Except for the tick-tick of a clock, there was silence. Not a note of Mozart or the canned chatter of the TV.

I went on tiptoe to peer through the graceful arch that separated the rooms of her suite. With only her bedside lamp glowing, I glanced about her antiques-appointed room, seeing no one, at first, and about to call out to her.

Then I spotted her, still dressed in her mourning outfit—or most of it, anyway—curled like a child atop her pearl-pink duvet. It was unusual for her to have fallen asleep with the lights on, considering she always did everything in the proper order and had instructed me endlessly to "hang up your clothes before you rumple them."

"Mother?" I whispered and moved forward, rounding the great posts of her bed.

She had taken off her shoes, which lay discarded on the carpet, and had removed her jacket, draped over the back of a chair. As I crept up to her side of the bed, I noted that she still wore her skirt and silk shell, the gray pearls draped around her neck, several beads of them resting in the hollow at her throat.

Her blond hair fell untidily upon her pillows, and her hands were tucked up beneath her chin into fists.

Despite its soft wattage, the lamp on her night table shone tellingly upon her, revealing what she hid so well in her every waking moment, her human-ness, her vulnerability; all the frailties no one glimpsed when her animation and the strength of her personality overrode any effects of time or heartbreak.

If I had ever seen her so exposed, I could not recall when, and it struck a chord in me, hard and deep.

Let her be, Sandy had told me, and I meant to do just that.

I reached for the tasseled throw at her feet and pulled it from its folds and over her, softly, so as not to wake her.

Bending to the lamp, I glanced once again at her, to the fingers curled tightly beneath her chin, and I saw something there, the glint of silver.

It puzzled me until I looked down at the night-stand and realized something was missing. A scant few seconds passed before I realized what it was: a small Sterling frame that held my father's picture from when he was a young man, hand-some and fresh-scrubbed with a full head of hair.

Oh, Mother.

The sight had me blinking back tears and re-minded me that I was hardly the only one whose day had sucked royally.

I reached for the framed photograph, to remove it, lest she roll onto it in her sleep. But I retracted my hand before I got to it.

Let her have it, if she needed it. Needed him.

Just leave her be.

I shut off the lamp and beat a hasty retreat, flick-ing off the lights in the sitting room as well, before closing Mother's door. I leaned my back against it, my heart beating as if I'd run the fifty-yard dash. I nibbled on my lower lip, something tugging hard at me from inside.

It was a pang right in the middle of my chest, and it wasn't heartburn from my fast-food dinner.

The ache stayed with me as I went back to my old

room to get ready for bed, and I figured it would be with me in the morning . . . and the morning after that, until this craziness was finished.

I wanted things to be back to normal, for Mother to be her old self again. I wanted someone to set things right.

Though I couldn't do anything except worry.

No wonder Mother missed my daddy. He would fix this, if he were here.

But that wasn't going to happen, no matter how hard we both wished it.

So I brushed my teeth and washed my face, removed my contacts, tugged off my jeans, and climbed into the same canopied bed I'd crawled into a million times before (most of them when I wasn't yet old enough to vote). The ruffled spread tickled my chin, so I pushed it down, adjusting the stack of pillows in their lace-trimmed sleeves comfortably behind my back.

The ceiling light off, I used the lamp on the nightstand to read, opening up *Stress and the Single Girl* to the next chapter. I had to hold it so close the pages bumped my nose, as I'd forgotten to pack my glasses.

I thumbed past the second tip for lowering my stress quotient, which involved snapping a rubber band on my wrist whenever I felt anxious. That sounded painful and no better than grinding my teeth. Besides, wasn't that what smokers were supposed to do when they craved a cigarette? It wasn't like I was fighting an addiction to nicotine.

Tip number three seemed tamer, more up my alley.

The gist of it was this: "Take a deep breath and

repeat an empowering statement like 'I feel calm' ten times, until you believe it."

Surely I could handle that.

I set the opened book on my chest, deciding to give it a whirl. I drew enough air into my lungs to fill a flat tire, my inflated rib cage pushing the book into a tent. Then I let it out slowly, bit by bit, telling myself all the while, "I feel calm, I feel calm, I feel calm," and I nearly did.

Until my cell rang, and I jumped out of bed, knocking my self-help tome to the floor as I snatched my phone off the table.

"Oh, thank goodness, it's you," came out of my mouth far too quickly when I spotted Malone's cell phone number on the tiny screen, but I didn't care.

"You're really at your mother's, aren't you?" he asked. "Because I tried the condo first."

"I am."

"My God, what's wrong? And be straight with me, Andy."

Because he knew for damn sure I'd be home otherwise, sleeping in my own bed, even if he wasn't there.

"Um, okay, do you have an hour? I can hardly begin to explain," I said, then proceeded to do just that, spilling everything that had happened since he'd left: the memorial service for Bebe Kent, the oddly cheerful reception at Belle Meade, Cissy finding Sarah Lee, and Mother's fears that her friends had been snuffed prematurely.

When I'd finished, he was so quiet that I thought I'd lost him again.

"You there?" I asked. "Brian, hello?"

"Whoa, Andy." I could imagine him nervously

pushing his glasses up the bridge of his nose. "Is Cissy okay?"

"I'm not sure, and it scares me," I whispered into the receiver. "I think it's too much all at once, you know? A shock to her system and all that."

"I wish I were with you," he said, and I felt another pang in my chest, a variation on the ache I'd felt before. "You need me, and I'm gone until Wednesday."

"What do you mean, Wednesday?"

He was supposed to be back the next day. He'd told me so before he left. Was someone upstairs deliberately messing with my karma? Playing me for kicks? Because it wasn't very funny.

"I'm really sorry, Andy, but things are moving more slowly than we'd hoped. We've had a couple more witnesses just added to the list, which means two more interviews than we'd planned."

"Hey, it's okay. I'll be fine, I promise. You've got plenty of your own to worry about," I insisted, using every iota of strength I had to keep from sounding weepy. I would not make him feel guilty for being away, even if I selfishly needed him here. "So how's the hotel?" I did my best imitation of perky. "Did you get one of those beds with a pillow-top mattress?"

That was enough to get him going, and he loosened up, spending a good ten minutes talking about his trip, telling me mundane details about his room without a view, the lousy dinner with his colleagues, and how his allergies were making his eyes itch.

As long as I heard his voice, I felt calmer than I

would had I snapped a rubber band on my wrist or repeated a silly mantra.

Until we were about to hang up, and he turned the tables on me again, asking pointedly, "Are you sure you're okay? Your mom's not the only one who's got a lot to deal with. You want me to call Abramawitz, see if I can leave early? I could say I had a family emergency . . ."

"No, I'm fine," I lied, feeling tears rush to my eyes. "Stay there and do your job." A job I knew he loved and that I'd promised myself I'd never interfere with. I was not going to ruin his trip, if I could help it.

"You sure?"

"Yes." Another fib. At this rate, I'd have a nose that beat Pinocchio's by a wooden yardstick.

"Um, okay, w-well," he stammered, something he was prone to do when he was rattled. "Uh, good night then."

" 'Night."

I thought he was gone, and I nearly hit "end," when I heard his whispered, "Hey, Andy, you still there?"

"Uh-huh." Barely.

"Yeah, well, um, I . . . I miss you. A lot."

Not the most eloquent of deliveries, and still it made me catch my breath. "Really?"

"R-really."

I'd been waiting to hear those three little words, and, now that I had, I felt suddenly tongue-tied.

"Ditto," I chirped and cringed after I'd said it, realizing how stupid it sounded, earning a soft, "Okay, bye," from the other end.

With a snap, I folded up the phone and stared at it for a long moment—cursing myself for my lack of verbal finesse—before I settled into bed.

Ditto?

Andy Kendricks, I told myself, *you are no Elizabeth Barrett Browning.*

Well, fudge. Who was?

Turning off the lamp, I lay back and stared at the ceiling, a warm flutter spreading through my chest where, minutes before, the pain had been.

Hope flitted in my head, tiny lightning bugs bright against the dark. I could see the brilliant flashes even when I closed my eyes.

Chapter 9

It was the shaking that roused me.

Not the sunlight knifing through the opened drapes or the windows rattling as a plane rumbled through the sky above.

Someone had a hold of my shoulder and relentlessly jiggled, until I peeled open my eyes and grumbled, "All right, I'm up already," half-expecting to see Malone as I squinted to aid my fuzzy vision. But it was Sandy Beck's frowning face that hovered above me, and, even without my contacts, I could see she looked grim.

I scooted into a seated position, sheet tenting above my knees, as Sandy took a step back and rubbed her arms, visibly upset.

"What is it? Is the house on fire or something?" I asked and yawned, scratching at my scalp.

"I thought you were supposed to go with Cissy this morning, isn't that what you told me?" Sandy sounded rattled, something I didn't hear often, if ever.

"Go with Mother?" I repeated, before I remem-

bered where I was and what she was talking about.
"Oh, yeah."

The meeting at Belle Meade with Annabelle at
nine o'clock.

I'd nearly forgotten.

"Your mother's up to something, Andy. I woke
up last night and heard a shuffling above my
room, in the storage area."

"Why would Cissy rummage around in there?"
I asked, blinking and trying to wake myself up.

"I had the same question, so I checked this
morning to see if anything was gone. It was. She'd
removed a suitcase."

"Did she take the Vuitton?" My voice rose in
panic.

"No, honey, just the Tumi Wheel-A-Way."

Thank God. My hand covered my fluttering
heart.

"Then it can't be too bad," I said, because if any
of her "heading to Europe for a month" set of Louis
Vuitton was missing, it could mean that Mother
had planned an extended trip. But if just the Wheel-
A-Way were unaccounted for, it meant a few days
gone, a week max, and that was stretching it. (Seriously, it could barely hold her shoes, her jewelry
case, and her toiletry bag at twenty-six inches.)

"That's not all," Sandy said, and the drawl that
usually soothed me, made me wince.

"What do you mean?"

She fished in her trouser pocket and pulled out a
carefully folded piece of Mother's cream linen stationery. Even the paper gave off her signature
scent of Joy.

"You read it," I told her, not having my "eyes" in.

"It's addressed to me," Sandy started and proceeded to prop a pair of glasses on her nose, worn on a chain around her neck. She cleared her throat and recited: " 'Dearest Sandy, I shall be gone a few days, but will check in occasionally. Please, don't worry. I'll be home soon, I promise. Hold down the fort, please, and tell Andy that, if she can't support her mother in her time of need, she should mind her own bloody business. Most sincerely, Cissy.' "

I pressed a palm against my forehead, more disturbed by the minute. "This is insane," I said.

Sandy tapped the sheet. "There's more." She cleared her throat again. "P.S. I borrowed the Buick, but will bring it back gassed. Feel free to use the Lexus for shopping and errands."

"She took your car?" Sandy drove a Buick Century. Imagining Cissy behind the wheel of a family sedan was rather like picturing Donald Trump flying Southwest Airlines with a paper boarding pass.

Sandy pocketed the note. "I'm not sure what all's going on, but I'm just shy of frantic, Andy." She went to the chair where I'd tossed my clothes and picked them up. "You've got to find her and make her come home." She shoved the wadded jeans and T-shirt in my direction. "And, dear heart, would you please hurry up."

Hurry up?

"But I'll see her at Belle Meade at nine. She's got that appointment with Annabelle."

"Which you're about to miss, if you don't shake a leg." She tapped the face of her watch.

"What time is it?" I reached for the old alarm clock that had been around since my school days, and I drew it close enough to my eyes to discern it was five minutes before the appointed hour. "It can't be," I muttered, setting the clock aside, sure my bad vision betrayed me.

"I should've wakened you earlier, but I didn't realize your mother was gone until I found the note on her pillow when I went to take her coffee at eight-thirty, as she'd requested. I figured she'd be up and dressed by then, only she'd already flown the coop. But maybe that was part of her plan. To dupe us both," Sandy said, wringing her hands. "So I'm not at all sure when she left."

"Did you try her cell?" I asked, ready to reach for mine on the nightstand.

"Of course, I did! But she has it turned off, as usual. It's like she doesn't want to be in touch. Do you think she's run away?"

Run away to where?

To Belle Meade? The retirement village where she believed someone was knocking off her Wednesday bridge group?

Criminy.

"Don't worry," I said, trying to act calm when I'd caught her jitters like cooties. "I'll track her down at Annabelle's office and personally wring her neck."

Sandy held out her armload. "How about you get dressed first? You can't go in a T-shirt and bikini panties. If you got pulled over by the Highland Park Police, you'd have a lot of explaining to do."

"You think?"

The HPPD had, not long ago, arrested and hauled to jail a ninety-seven-year-old woman for an expired registration, so I didn't suppose they'd appreciate a near-naked girl in a Jeep.

I hopped out of bed and snatched my clothes from Sandy's arms, donning them so quickly that I put my shirt on inside out with the tag sticking up at my chin. After a fast readjustment, I made a pit stop in the bathroom to wash up and stick in my contacts so I wouldn't drive the Jeep into a tree.

I started to make the bed, but Sandy stopped me. "I'll do that, Andy. Now *get*."

After I gathered my things and shoved them into the tote bag, she ran me out of the house without so much as a piece of toast in my belly.

Stabbing my key in the Jeep's ignition, I heard my stomach complain about missing the first meal of the day.

What I wouldn't give for a PopTart.

Instead, I chewed on a couple of old Certs, excavated from the bowels of my purse (along with a nickel and a paperclip), grateful that it was Sunday morning and only a smattering of cars were on the road, heading to worship, or maybe hitting a few garage sales.

Mother's house wasn't far from Belle Meade, and, by sailing through a pair of yellow lights, I made it past the Stonehenge-like columns and onto the grounds in what was surely a new land-speed record.

Still, I hated that Cissy had such a big head start.

My foot eased on the accelerator as the Jeep bumped along the brick lane, and I prepared to stop at the guardhouse ahead; but, as I rolled nearer, I could tell no one was there. Perhaps Bob and Sam got Sundays off to golf, or else they'd been summoned elsewhere.

Like to Annabelle's office to physically restrain an irrational, suitcase-wielding society matron?

"I feel calm, I feel calm," I said, again and again, but my pulse didn't slow the slightest, and a vein in my neck started throbbing.

Could a woman under thirty-one (okay, barely) have a heart attack?

Maybe I'd be the first and would end up in the *Guinness Book of World Records* along with the guy who'd stayed awake for seven days straight and the girl who'd hula-hooped for two weeks (I'm assuming with potty breaks).

Sunshine filtered through the trees overhead, and the dappled light danced on the red bricks, as the Jeep picked its way ahead toward the visitors' parking spaces I'd noticed yesterday.

My eyes widened as I pulled in beside a silver Buick with a DON'T MESS WITH TEXAS sticker on the bumper.

Sandy's car.

So Mother *was* here.

A deep breath rushed out of me, as I set the Jeep in Park and scrambled down from the driver's seat, nearly tripping over my own two feet.

Toes clutching at my flip-flops, I sprinted across the drive to the front steps of the pillared main house, flying to the door and grabbing the brass handle, only to realize I couldn't get in without a passkey.

Damn.

Well, I knew Mother hadn't waited to get in, not with Bebe Kent's spare key in her purse.

So I punched the intercom, glancing over my shoulder at the camera mounted above me and giving a big, fake beauty pageant grin.

"Hello?" I crooned. "Anyone there?"

"Andrea!" Annabelle's voice squawked from the speaker a moment after. "Hurry and get in here!"

The intercom snapped off, the tiny light turned green, and the lock clicked open.

Pushing on the brass handle, I shoved my way inside, shut the door behind me, and scurried through the marble-tiled foyer with its ever-present and absurdly large vase of flowers centrally located, heading toward the rear hallway. Which is when I stopped, realizing I didn't know which way to go.

To the right was the dining hall, I remembered, and to the left . . . was a brass plaque on which was printed OFFICE with a little arrow pointing that direction.

All right, so no one would accuse me of having eagle eyes. (And my ophthalmologist could vouch for that.)

My thongs slapped tile as I scurried past doorway after doorway, until I found the one I wanted with ANNABELLE MEADE, DIRECTOR neatly labeled on, yes, another brass plaque beside the jamb. There were even Braille letters beneath, which made me wonder how my own name would look in dots.

I wound my fingers into a fist to knock, only to drop my hand to the doorknob and twist.

Well, it's not like I was unexpected.

I pushed wide the heavy paneled door, stumbling into the room and onto plush carpeting. My gaze flickered over high ceilings, plantation-shuttered windows, and leafy green plants sprouting everywhere from colorful Mexican pottery.

Annabelle looked up from behind her Queen Anne footed desk, practically gulping with relief when she saw me, though she clasped her hands on her desk in a semblance of composure. "Take a seat, if you would," she drawled in a rather clipped manner, like a Southern belle turned drill sergeant. "We've been having a most *interesting* conversation without you."

Well, I couldn't have missed too much, could I? It was barely a quarter past the hour.

Mother's Tumi bag-on-wheels stood beside a wing chair—one of a pair—in which I assumed she sat, its tall back hiding even the top of her head.

First things first, I told myself and steeled my shoulders.

I marched up the aisle between the two chairs, ignoring the empty one to my right and swinging left to give Cissy a piece of my mind for slipping out of the house this morning under my nose and frightening even the unflappable Sandy.

"Mother, how could you scare us like that?"—I began my rant, only to find my words clogging up in my throat like a verbal logjam. "Oh, my gosh," I said, inching my way backward until I bumped into Annabelle's desk and couldn't go any farther. "I'm so sorry, ma'am. But I thought you were someone else."

Egads, what had I done?

I'd screamed at a stranger.

Because the woman in the wing chair wasn't Cissy, unless my mother had been reincarnated into someone totally unrecognizable to me, her only child, the fruit of her loins.

For starters, this gal had inky black hair cut off sharply at the jaw, teased into oblivion, and bangs that sliced straight across her forehead, nearly masking darkly penciled brows. Black cat's-eye glasses with glittering rhinestones at each point sat firmly on a slim nose, distorting the kohl-lined eyes behind the thick lenses. The apples of her cheeks sported way too much rosy blush, and the color on her lips was equally garish, a cross between brown and orange that reminded me of a burnt umber Crayola crayon. Never my favorite color.

Her jewelry was less than subtle, with way too many carats of tinted CZ that looked straight out of the Susan Lucci collection on QVC. (No disrespect intended.)

As if that didn't seal the deal, she wore a warm-up suit, something Cissy wouldn't zip on even if she did work out. This one appeared to be put together with patches of animal prints connected by zigzagging lines of bric-a-brac and glittering with billions of tiny crystals.

Bewildered didn't begin to describe how I felt. If Sandy's car was out front and a suitcase that could be the twin of Mother's Tumi was parked near enough for me to kick it, then where the devil was Cissy?

Was I already two steps behind?

"I apologize," I said again to the woman, then turned to Annabelle. "I didn't mean to interrupt, but I thought you were still meeting with Mother . . ."

"I am."

"You are what?"

"Meeting with your mother."

Okay, I'd lost my mind. It was official.

Annabelle batted her lashes coyly and lifted a hand from the papers on her desk to point at the woman in the wing chair. "Andy Kendricks, this is Miriam Amanda Wallace Ferguson, our newest resident. She'll be moving into Bebe's place for a spell. Though I *do* believe you've met quite a few times before, as a matter of fact."

Er, I didn't think so.

Miriam Amanda Wallace Ferguson?

Why was that name so familiar?

I swung around yet again, keeping a palm flattened on Annabelle's desk because somehow I needed to hang on to it, and I squinted at the stranger I'd been gawking at only moments ago.

Nope, I still didn't know her from Adam.

She smiled at me.

Grandmother, what shiny white teeth you have.

Then a heavily magnified eye winked, and I cocked my head, studying this Miriam woman more carefully and wondering what the heck she had to do with my seemingly absent mummy.

I leaned in a bit nearer.

The subject of my scrutiny whispered, "You figure a microscope would be of any help in solving this riddle, sugar?"

I swallowed.

No, it wasn't possible. Uh-uh, it couldn't be.

Oh, dear. Was it *her*?

"Yoo hoo, yes, it's true." Fingers lifted to wiggle as the burnt umber mouth let loose an overblown

Texas twang, totally confusing me. "Well, good mornin' to you, too, sunshine. What's with the bug eyes? Don't you like the ensemble? Why, sweetie, it's the new me. Though I've got to give a lot of credit to Mary Kay and Mrs. Coogan."

Mary Kay Cosmetics—*that*, I understood— since it appeared she had enough goods on her face to fill the trunk of a pink Caddy.

But Mrs. Coogan?

She was the retired drama teacher from Hockaday, formerly the director of our school plays, mistress of sets and wardrobe.

"Oh, no," I breathed.

"Oh, yes," she assured me.

This woman . . . my mother . . . they were one and the same.

I felt like a guest on *Rickie Lake*, and I'd always wondered where they found their continual supply of weirdoes. Turns out, I need only have looked in the mirror.

"Andrea, sugar, don't swoon on me now." The exaggerated drawl settled back into the soft, cultivated strains I knew so well, confirming my worst fears.

My dignified Mummy Dearest had morphed into a combination of Mr. Magoo and Peg Bundy.

Clearly, Armageddon was near.

Chapter 10

I staggered against Annabelle's desk, grappling for something solid to clutch, because my knees were caving in. I caught her pencil holder and sent it soaring to the floor, scattering pens and No. 2 lead tips in a dozen different directions.

Holy Mother of Pearl!

"Oh, honey, did I really startle you like that?" Cissy said, her familiar voice coming from this other woman's exterior. "I didn't know how you'd react, but it's nice to see I had you fooled. Because I did, didn't I? I'll bet you didn't know I took a few drama courses back in college, did you?"

She sounded so pleased with herself.

I wanted to puke, but that would be redundant since I'd been there and done that yesterday afternoon. I saw no need for an encore.

My jaw moved, but aphasia set in, depriving me of any response whatsoever. So I dropped to the carpet to clean up the mess I'd made, my heart and stomach changing places, as I fought to make sense of this upside-down situation.

Could it be an early Halloween prank?

A segment for *Candid Camera*?

Until I remembered Alan Funt was pushing up daisies, so no chance of him jumping out from behind a piece of furniture.

There were so many danged reality shows these days, it could be anything, I decided. Were they shooting a pilot titled *My Deranged Mother*? Only I didn't see any cameras or a TV crew. Maybe they were hidden in a secret room behind the bookshelves.

"Andrea, come up off your knees and sit down, so Annabelle and I can explain this to you."

Explain?

How could there possibly be a logical explanation for my dyed-in-the-wool couture-wearing mummy to be dressed up as someone else . . . someone with a diametrically opposed fashion sense? A made-up person named Miriam Amanda Wallace Ferguson, for Pete's sake.

Snap, crackle, pop.

My synapses fired again.

On shaky legs, I rose and plunked the pencil holder back on Annabelle's desk, more or less intact.

"Ma Wallace aka Miriam Amanda Wallace Ferguson," I said, voice shaking, as it all came back to me, and I stared at my mother in costume. "The first woman governor of Texas and nearly as big a crook as her husband, Jim, also a former governor, who got himself impeached. It's in every textbook in every school across the state." I shook my head, incredulous. "So you're impersonating a dead politician and moving into Bebe Kent's place with a carry-on bag. Just what the heck are you trying to pull here? And, please, tell me it's not what I'm thinking."

Annabelle and Cissy shared a glance.

"Well, that depends," my certifiable mother quipped. "What exactly are you thinking, sweetie?"

"Besides the fact that at least one of us is clearly on the verge of a nervous breakdown?"

"Oh, don't be silly," Cissy chided.

"Do have a seat Andy," my old campmate jumped in. "Let us fill you in on what you missed."

"I was only late by fifteen minutes!"

How on earth could I have skipped enough to amount to . . . *this*?

"Ah, but your mother was early, and she knew exactly what she wished to say . . . and do." Annabelle picked up a silver pen that had rolled across her desk and tapped it in the air, toward the empty wing chair. "Sit," she said again.

So I sat.

"We've figured out a compromise," Annabelle announced, though such an agreement seemed hard to fathom. Rather like selling one's soul to the devil, which was lose-lose any way you looked at it.

"And it involved her wearing a costume?" I balked.

"Well, I am going undercover, darling," Cissy said, as if her over-the-top attire wasn't indication enough of that. "Which means having a *cover* to hide *under*, you see. And it's not like you haven't done it before, so why can't I do it, too?"

"Um, because you're a grown-up?" I itched to scream at the top of my lungs.

But I couldn't, not when she'd thrown my own act of lunacy in my face. Lord knows I'd like to forget pulling a Nancy Drew to help a friend, a sacrifice that had involved wearing lavender hot pants and a stuffed bra. Hey, at least Mother was more covered up than I'd been.

Do as I say, not as I do. That's what I needed to get across in this crucial moment.

"What I've done in the past has no bearing on this," I insisted, but Mother's look of dismissal had me quickly turning to Annabelle. "You're really and truly letting her into Belle Meade, dressed like *that*, so she can play snoop? *Hello?* What's wrong with this picture? Because I'm thinking along the lines of Picasso on acid. It's so surreal it's laughable," I said and guffawed to show I meant it.

I didn't sway Annabelle, either. "It's her call, Andy."

"Because she's twisting your arm?" I knew how frightened Annabelle was about Mother going to the media with her suspicions about murder. Still, this scheme of theirs seemed entirely too risky. "Seriously, you *cannot* do this. Call in a private investigator if you must, but don't go through with this charade. I beg you. Someone could get hurt, or very seriously annoyed."

The Woman Formerly Known As Cissy ignored my concerns, recrossing her legs and lifting a shiny black cowboy boot loaded with rhinestones so she could study it with great intensity.

Annabelle rapped her desk with the pen to get

my attention. "Listen up, Andy, and listen good. The last thing I want is a private eye poking around, asking questions and making everyone nervous. I don't know that the lawyers for the corporation would be any too happy about it, either, and I don't want to bring them into this. Besides, what harm can your Mother do in a few days' time, if that's what it takes to put her mind at ease?"

How do I count the ways? I mused, but didn't interrupt.

"If she hasn't found whatever she's looking for by next Sunday, she's agreed to move out and drop her accusations. She'll also politely decline further invitations to play with the Wednesday bridge group, and she'll return Bebe's borrowed passkey."

"That's your compromise?" I scoffed openly. "She'll pretend to be Jessica Fletcher for a week and then fade away like an old soldier?"

"I think it's bloody *marvelous* that Annabelle would give me such an opportunity!" my nut-ball Mother crowed, as if she'd been offered the part of Auntie Mame on Broadway.

Marvelous was not the word I would have chosen to describe the situation.

"She initially wanted to stay through the end of the month," Annabelle explained, and I groaned, because a week seemed too long as it was; three weeks would have been unfathomable. "But I agreed to have Finch order some blood tests on Mrs. Sewell. Whenever the results return negative—and they will—the jig is up. So Miss Cissy's excellent adventure could very well be cut short if the lab works fast." She pressed her palms together, prayerful. "Until then, the staff will know *nothing* except we have a new resident on Magnolia, and Cissy has vowed not to call any of her contacts at the papers or in the mayor's office. So, you see, this solution is a happy medium for all of us."

Medium meant average, which implied normal, and I didn't detect an iota of that here. As for the "happy" part, I certainly wasn't smiling, although my mother seemed unduly perky.

I cocked my head, squinting hard at Cissy in the wig and vintage glasses, deciding I'd have to be extremely drunk to find this amusing.

If I'd had any sense, I would've booked her a room at the loony bin. Instead, I continued to pursue the matter, asking them, "What if Bebe Kent's surviving relatives want to dispose of her townhouse, so another qualifying Belle Meade resident can assume the lease, or however that's done? What if they'd like to get rid of her furniture in an estate sale? You can't just move into the home of a dead woman without some kind of . . . I don't know . . . legal maneuvering"—I swiveled toward Annabelle—"can she?"

But Annabelle was beaten to the punch.

"Oh, I can and I will, because Bebe's cousins agreed to let me do it." Mother patted the arms of her chair, her bracelets clanging like the bells of Notre Dame. "When I got home yesterday, I phoned Jillie's cell before she and Stella flew back across the pond. Since Bebe had paid her monthly fees through September, the surviving family members have an option to serve out her month's occupancy, as per her contract. They've spoken to Bebe's lawyers about appointing me some kind of guardian of her property, if need be, so I can help sort through her clothing and personal effects, weeding out whatever the cousins don't want to keep. Most of the furniture will stay, as her upfront fee was for a furnished residence."

"Stella and Jillie . . . you didn't tell them you thought Bebe was murdered, did you? Please, say you didn't mention wanting to stay over at Mrs. Kent's so you could hunt down her killer?"

Annabelle twirled a hank of hair around her finger.

"No, Andrea, of course I didn't." Mother looked indignant. "I merely suggested I could be of assistance, since I'm here and they're out of the country. They won't have to leave the town-house vacant while Bebe's things are still there, and I'll keep on top of things until the contents can be properly dealt with. The cousins were delighted and Jillie called Annabelle this morning to make the arrangements. So, she's stuck with me, whether she likes it or not." Her cat's-eye glasses fixed on Annabelle, who was busy unraveling her finger from her hair. "Isn't that right, dear girl?"

"Stu-uck," I heard Annabelle drawl.

"So, as long as I'm at Bebe's, I'll make a list of Bea's possessions that remain, mostly her clothing and less valuable baubles, which I'll donate to charity, as Jillie and Stella suggested. Oh, and I've promised to hand over any mail that arrives while I'm the occupant."

"Clothes and mail," I said.

"That's right." Mother seemed suddenly less garrulous as she fiddled with a chunky gold watch on her wrist, one that would've looked eminently suitable on a middle-aged man with a comb-over, an open-necked polyester shirt, and a hairy chest covered with chains.

"That's not all you're going to do, is it? Because it seems a mite over the top to dress up in animal prints and the Wig That Ate Cleveland in order to clean out Bebe's stuff for her cousins and fetch the mail for her attorneys."

Annabelle had a brief coughing fit.

Cissy shifted in her chair. "Well, perhaps I've left out a few minor details."

Much as I figured. "Do fill me in."

"Well, if you must know, Sarah Lee's sister Margery asked me to supervise the packing of Sarah's personal belongings before they're shipped off to South Dakota, which will afford the opportunity to compare crime scenes before Annabelle sends the housekeeping crew in to get things shipshape for the next person on the waiting list."

I stuck a finger in my ear and wiggled, to make sure I'd heard correctly.

Did she say "compare crime scenes"?

Why didn't she just throw on a trench coat, mash on a cigar, and call herself Columbo?

Annabelle's face reddened, as if she were no more pleased with Cissy's use of those words than I was.

"Let me get this straight. You're staying at Bebe Kent's place," I reiterated, "and you'll be going through her things, ditto Sarah Lee Sewell's, playing the part of a new Belle Meade denizen, using a crooked governor's name, and trying to solve two alleged murders before church next Sunday morning, or until the blood tests on Mrs. Sewell return, whichever comes first. Have I got that right?"

The black wig bobbed. "I'd say that about covers it, yes."

"And you're really going along with this?" I turned on Annabelle. "You don't mind her flitting around like Angela Lansbury dressed for Halloween and potentially disturbing the peace and quiet of this lovely community?"

Annabelle squirmed in her seat, fiddling with her hair again. "You know the situation, Andy. Like it or not, I'm at the mercy of your mother for the next few days. I feel a lot like Martha Stewart when she did her stint at Camp Cupcake." She thrust her forearms toward me, wrists pressed together in invisible shackles. "Someone whip up a puff pastry stuffed with a nail file, and make it quick!"

Cissy chuckled.

I was not amused. "You're both raging lunatics."

This was beyond nuts. It was a freaking disaster waiting to happen. Was I the only one here who could see that?

"Won't the Wednesday bridge players recognize you?" I threw the question at my mother in a last ditch attempt to derail this train.

"*You* didn't even know who I was, so how will they?" She wrinkled her nose, and pushed at the bridge of her pointed specs. "The group's not meeting this week, anyway, not after losing two players. And, believe me, I won't seek them out. But if they see me around Belle Meade dressed like this"—fingers stacked with cubic zirconium fluttered from her head to her toes—"well, they won't recognize me any more than you did. And the rest of the residents won't give a lick who I am."

"But people saw you at the reception . . ."

"Not decked out like a refugee from a Tunica Casino shuttle." She primped at her frothy black beehive. "Besides, I didn't stay in the dining hall long. I went looking for Sarah Lee right after I gave you the slip."

"Dr. Finch and Patsy saw us both at Mrs. Sewell's," I reminded her.

Annabelle waved that one off. "Don't worry. I'll take care of it. I'll make something up about Miriam being a distant relative."

"I'm wondering if they shouldn't be in on it. The security guards, too. What if Mother gets in a jam"—but Annabelle made short work of my protest.

"If your mother wants to do this, she has to fly under the radar and not disrupt the staff or the residents. That's part of the pact."

"You worry too much, Andrea," my mother said.

"Can you blame me?" I tried to stare her down, but I was no competition for her, not with those freakily magnified eyes.

Then it hit me. The Mother of All Wrenches to toss in their plan.

What if—and I'm talking a *Big* "what if"—there really was a killer?

Not that I believed it for a minute. Well, I highly doubted it, anyway. But, say, there was a one-in-a-million shot he existed and had gotten away with two murders so far; until "Miriam Ferguson" moved in and started acting like a very grown-up and badly dressed Nancy Drew, threatening to blow the lid on him.

All right, all right, I told myself. *You have something there. Go with it. Stick 'em hard and burst their bubble!*

I fixed a grim stare on my Mother. "Okay, Miss Marple, let's assume for a moment that there's a dangerous assassin running around Belle Meade, targeting lonely widows. What if he catches on to you, huh? You won't have anyone watching your back. What if you get yourself in trouble and need assistance? Who will you turn to? Annabelle? Sam and Bob, the security guards from Mayberry?" I recalled how long it had taken the one to appear in his golf cart after being summoned to the Sewell house. "By the way, Barney and Andy might not see through your costume, but surely they have your plate numbers from the Lexus and Bentley down pat."

"Which is why I drove Sandy's Buick," Mother said.

"*Who*," I asked again, "will you have on your side during this ruse? Will the rent-a-cops be watching over you every minute?"

"Great balls of fire, no!" Annabelle declared. "They've got enough to do, what with sittin' in the guardhouse and all."

"So you"—I said pointedly, staring straight at her—"aim to play Robin to her Batman?"

"Me? Oh, no." Annabelle threw back her head and chortled, before she very primly pointed at me with the silver pen. "You, Sparky."

I begged to differ. "Now, wait just a cotton-picking minute."

"Yes, sugar, that's where we figured you'd fit in." Mother eagerly scooted toward the edge of her chair, stretching a zebra print arm over the space between us to touch my fingers. "You'll be my backup."

"Your backup?" I nearly choked on the words.

"Oh, I get it. You're not the one in charge, so you don't want to play. Your father was right. You're a stubborn cuss and something of a control freak, which you obviously inherited from his side of the family." She withdrew to her chair and sat ramrod straight—something she'd learned at her Little Miss Manners lessons a generation before I—then she fussed with a thing-a-ma-bob on her earlobe that looked like a seashell awash in beads and glitter.

"I'm not being stubborn, Mother, really." How could she not see how preposterous this was? What a horrible position she was putting me in, not to mention Annabelle? As for inheriting my control freak gene from Daddy's side of the family . . . *puh-leeze*! "I just don't see how I can support this charade. I won't."

"Oh, Andrea, don't be like this. I can't do this by myself, sugar. Every good detective needs a sidekick."

"You're not a good detective, Mother," I reminded her. "You're not even a bad one."

"Please, don't fight me on this. It's something I

must do, but I can't do it alone. You're here, aren't you? That must account for something."

"That I'm in need of a good therapist?"

"Oh, pish, don't be silly. Haven't I helped you out before, sweet pea? Wasn't I there for you when you were playin' dress-up after an old school chum got in trouble? I'm not asking for much, just a short couple of days." She fluttered the spider-leg lashes on her distorted eyes. "Say you'll be there for your poor, old mother who gave you life and hasn't asked for much since."

There she went again, using that break-my-heart drawl that had coerced me into accompanying her to Bebe's service and the reception at Belle Meade. Even if the Wizard of Oz had given me a double dose of courage, it would've been impossible to tell her "no."

I wanted to drop to the floor and cry, pound my fists.

Why did she always win?

"Great balls of fire! Tell her to count you in, Sparky, so she can stop pouting and we can get this over with." Annabelle glanced at her watch. "We've got brunch at eleven, and I'd like to have Cissy . . . er, Miriam settled before the church shuttles start returnin' and this place turns into Grand Central Station."

Coercion was such an ugly thing to witness.

"Okay, what if I agree," I said, coming frighteningly close to relenting. "What am I supposed to do, huh? Follow her around? Like that won't look suspicious. Besides, maybe no one paid attention to Mother at the reception yesterday, but I got cornered by a woman named Mabel, who'd spot me in a pinch."

"Mabel Pinkston?" Annabelle's chin came up.

"Yes, and I mentioned I was at the reception with my mother, so won't she be suspicious if suddenly my 'distant relative' moves in?"

"Why's that suspicious?" she asked, but sounded nervous. "Look, we'll make up a back story to cover your tracks. Something about Miriam being a poor relation from Arkansas whom your mother's taken pity on. So she's your honorary auntie."

"Yes, your auntie," Cissy chimed in.

Why weren't they listening to me?

"What if someone decides to Google the name 'Miriam Amanda Wallace Ferguson,' discovers she was a Texas governor in the nineteen twenties and can't be alive unless she's been resurrected!" I screeched at them, sounding remarkably like a squawking seagull.

"Oh, for heaven's sake, don't be such a chicken," Cissy said, drawing a lipstick from an oversized rhinestone-encrusted purse and touching up her burnt-umber lips. "It's not like folks haven't been named after dead people for centuries. Besides, every good Southern family has crazy aunts they hide in their attics. No one will think twice about where Miriam hails from."

"But what about Mabel . . ."

"It's all right, Andy," Annabelle said, though I noted slim furrows of concern between her eyes. "She's been with me for a long time. If she has any questions, she'll come straight to me. Besides, she doesn't live on the grounds. She rents some rooms over a garage in Garland, even though I offered her an apartment here."

"An independent sort, is she?" Mother remarked.

Annabelle nodded, frowning. "She volunteers as much as she works, because she has to watch what she earns, else she'll get kicked off Medicaid"—Annabelle tugged an earlobe, her distress obvious—"but that's her choice, isn't it? She won't let me help her."

"What does she do exactly?" I dared to inquire.

"She's something of a floater, working wherever we need her, delivering meds from the pharmacy, taking books back and forth from our library, sometimes she carries meals to folks who are sick or bedridden."

Speaking of the sick. "What about Dr. Finch and Patsy?" I continued my attack. "They definitely saw me at Sarah Lee Sewell's house with Mother, so they're aware of our connection . . . and the connection between Mother and Sarah Lee."

"Hell's bells, Andy, you're making too much of things." Annabelle tossed the pen down on her desk and leaned back in her chair. "So they saw you with Cissy? Whoop-de-do. That has nothing to do with Miriam Ferguson. Her, they won't know from Eve. Besides, you'll be working here, so you'll have a reason to be on the grounds besides visiting your aunt."

Wait a minute. Back up the bus.

Working? I absolutely hated the sound of that, dreading to hear what else these designing women had cooked up for me. I swallowed before I asked.

"What kind of job did you have in mind for me?"

Without skipping a beat, Annabelle said, "I've arranged for you to volunteer in our library, since you've always been such a bookworm. It's the perfect cover." She picked up an envelope from her desk and shoved it at me, so I reached forward and took it. "Your key's in there, and a name badge, which gives you staff privileges, like access to most everywhere on the grounds."

"What'll that entail, exactly?" I asked as I jammed the envelope into my purse.

"We have a well-stocked library, Andy, full of novels and nonfiction, as well as reference books and online computers." Annabelle glanced at her watch and fidgeted. "Just show up and give Mildred a break now and then. I think you can handle that."

"Of course, she can." Mother added her two cents' worth.

Wow. I was stunned. The pair of them should win the Nobel Sneak Prize for teamwork. I'd been outgunned, and I knew it.

So I figured I might as well grin and bear it.

"That takes care of that, huh?" I said, playing along. "You all have an answer to everything, don't you? You think you've got this all figured out, except for one very important thing."

"What thing, Andy?" Annabelle looked suspicious.

"What did we miss, darling?"

Heck, if I couldn't beat them, I might as well do a running cannonball and jump right in.

"How about some very vital stuff, like do I get a fake name?" I commented. "And what about a disguise? Shouldn't I have more of a cover than saying I'm Miriam Amanda Wallace Ferguson's honorary niece? Can't I call myself something like Arletha Lynn or Daisy Duke and dress in platform boots and have fake body piercings?"

"No!" they cried in unison.

I sank back in my chair, giving them as dirty a look as I could muster. "Geez, always the bridesmaid, aren't I?"

"Does that mean we can count on you, Sparky?" Annabelle asked, wide-eyed, ready to get this over with.

I glanced at Mother, peering beyond her outlandish getup, and reading the hopefulness in her face, and I realized the choice wasn't mine to make. "I'm in," I said, much as it pained me.

Cissy's lips shaped the words, "Thank you."

I blushed and glanced down at the floor and my green-painted toes.

"Good, then it's settled," Annabelle said, slapping a palm on her desk as a judge would a gavel. "And just in the nick of time, because I've got some paperwork to finish before brunch. So if you wouldn't mind . . ."

"Yes, we'll get out of your hair," I said, taking the supersized hint. "You ready, Moth . . . er, Aunt Miriam?"

"Ready as I'll ever be." My mother stood, giving me my first full-length view of her new persona from wigged-out head to her black lizard boots loaded with rhinestones, more blinding than her beaded sweat suit.

Good grief, I mused and realized this would take some getting used to.

Annabelle seemed to be doing her best to ignore us, rifling through the papers atop her blotter, opening and closing the desk drawers.

I slowly pulled myself up from the wing chair, as Mother sashayed her way toward the door, calling over her shoulder in Miriam's deeply twanged tone, "Do grab my suitcase for me, would you, sugar? I'll meet you out at the car and lead you over to Bebe's."

Like I had anything better to do.

From the sound of things, for the next few days, I'd be babysitting her.

"Right behind you," I said.

As she disappeared from the room, I went for the Tumi and clutched its raised handle, barely dragging it two feet before Annabelle came whipping round her desk, lunged in front of me and slammed the door before I could reach it. She flung her curvy, pink cashmere-draped body against the wood panels, clasping something dark against the ropes of pearls at her full bosom. And then I recognized my black shoes.

"Geez, AB, what's with you?"

"Well," she said, catching her breath, "I didn't want you to forget anything."

"You could have just handed them over. Blocking my exit was a wee bit overly dramatic, don't you think?" Although everything that had happened in the last twenty minutes had bordered on histrionics, so it fit with the program.

"Okay, okay, I needed to talk to you. *In private*," she whispered, though no one could hear us unless her office was bugged.

I set the suitcase upright and reached out for the

shoes, which she promptly turned over. I crammed them down into my oversized purse, praying it wouldn't split down the seams.

"So talk," I said, hoping this wouldn't take long, not with Mother on her way out to the parking lot, antsy to start this undercover operation of hers.

Annabelle did a bit of chewing on her lower lip before she started with, "I'm getting a weird feeling about this, Andy. I was up all night thinking about Bebe and Sarah Lee, and wondering if maybe your mother's not so crazy after all." I noticed the puffiness beneath her eyes that even her makeup didn't quite cover from this close a distance.

"What do you mean, 'if' my mother's not so crazy? Did you see her in that costume? She's wearing enough carats of CZ to strangle Bugs Bunny, and I thought she was allergic. Maybe her skin will turn green."

"I'm serious, Andy."

"So am I."

She tipped her head, her features screwed up with confusion. "I thought she was nuts, asking me all those questions after Bebe died. But then Sarah Lee passed so close behind, and I couldn't help connecting them."

"Connecting them how?" Annabelle had been freaking out about Mother's wild accusations when she'd called the night before, so it was hard to believe she'd had a sudden change of heart. "Don't tell me Cissy's gotten to you?"

"No," she said, "It's something else. I'm only saying this because I trust you, Andy. I haven't spoken a word of it to anyone."

"Why the mystery?" I said. She was making me nervous. "What's going on, Annabelle?" My stomach flip-flopped frantically, like Mary Lou Retton on meth.

"Maybe I'm seeing things that aren't there, like your mother, but I want your opinion. You always see things so clearly."

I do? That was news to me. "Spit it out, AB."

She nodded, wiping her palms on her pink and gray plaid skirt. Sweat shone on her upper lip, despite the constant hum of the air conditioner. "It all started a few months ago, when Mrs. Sewell moved in, and she and Bebe hooked up through the bridge group on Wednesday. They were nice ladies, I'm not saying they weren't, but"—her chin came up, and her brown eyes pled for my understanding—"they were *so* hard to please, Andy. They were like Goldilocks with OCD. Nothing was ever just right. They didn't like the color of paint on their walls, so we changed it. They hated the carpeting, so we replaced it. The thermostat wasn't accurate, the house was too hot or too cold, or the trash trucks were too noisy and came too early. Every time I picked up the phone, they were calling to bitch. It went on for weeks."

Yep, sounded like Mother's demanding friends, I thought, nearly asking Annabelle what she'd expected when she'd marketed Belle Meade to the aging Dallas jet set; but I could see she wasn't in the mood for teasing. She was using the sleeve of her pink cashmere sweater to blot her damp forehead.

"You want to sit down?" I suggested, because she had that "Oh, Rhett, I'm about to swoon" paleness to her cheeks.

She tipped her head back against the door and rolled it side to side. "No, I'm fine. I'm almost finished."

If Annabelle fell over in the forest and no one heard her, would she still be fine?

Sometimes I hated that word for being so benign.

Just in case, I braced my legs and kept my arms loose, ready to catch her if she started to topple.

She drew in a deep breath and slowly exhaled, before she continued. "I tried so hard to pacify those women, really I did. They had the staff working overtime, everyone going nuts, and I finally told each of them that they could leave if they didn't like it here. We have plenty of names on the waiting list of people who'd love to reside at Belle Meade, and who wouldn't make noise about every last thing. I'd begun to wish they'd never moved in."

"How'd they take it when you threatened to kick them out?"

She paused to tuck her brown tresses carefully behind her ears, and I caught the tremor in her hands. "They threatened to sue me, and they were dead serious."

"Lawsuits? You're kidding, right?"

"I wish." She stubbed the toe of a shiny patent leather pump against the carpet. "I was hoping it wouldn't come to that. That we could keep the lawyers out of it." She wet her lips. "But then, I don't have to worry any more, do I?"

"Not unless they can file a suit from beyond the grave," I said quietly, considering Bebe Kent was six feet under at the Sparkman Hillcrest cemetery, and Sarah Lee Sewell was next in line.

"They sure saved us all a lot of trouble by, um, dying." She gnawed on her lip again.

I honestly thought she was making too much of this, but asked anyway, "Who knew about their threats, Annabelle?"

"The lawyers for the corporation, of course. Some of the staff I worked most closely with, like Patsy and Arnold Finch." She shifted from one foot to the other. "I might've told a few others, but only because they smelled trouble. They've been with me from the beginning. Belle Meade means as much to them as it does to me."

From the beginning?

"The Finches worked with you in Austin, Annabelle?"

"Yes, Andy, but they're not the only ones. I couldn't have opened in Dallas without their help . . . them and Mabel, of course . . . and Donna Morgan, our fitness director . . . Alice Ann Carpenter, our head physical therapist . . . Rory Flynn, our program director. They came at my request," she assured me. "It's not like they had anything to do with"—she paused—"what happened."

She was making about as much sense as my mother. "Then why did you tell me any of this? You don't think one of them could have . . ."

"No, I don't," she stated firmly, though her gaze fluttered up to the ceiling

Hmm, so why not look me in the eye?

This was nuts. I hoped I still had Tums in my purse.

"You didn't share this with my mother, did you?"

Annabelle brought her gaze back down from

the light fixture and vigorously shook her head. "Oh, no, not a word. It would only have set her off worse."

Like a rocket, I mused.

"I couldn't keep it from you, though. I thought you should know. But, please, keep it to yourself. It's nothing, I'm sure, just more coincidences."

Why was I her sounding board? I was hardly a good judge of the situation, considering my own flesh and blood wanted to pin the tail on the murderer.

"Annabelle, if you have any doubts about this . . . if any part of you believes that someone on your staff would harm two people to protect Belle Meade from lawsuits, I think we should call the police right this minute . . ."

She fell away from the door, hands clasped beneath her chin, pearls swinging from her neck. "No, Andy, no! I would trust anyone on my staff with my life . . . really, I would! They wouldn't hurt anyone any more than I could."

All right. That was more like it.

"Besides," she reminded me, "there were no signs of struggle. No bruises on the bodies. Nothing. It wouldn't make sense unless they died in their sleep, just like Finch said."

That's what I'd been telling Mother, and what I'd firmly believed from the get-go. No evidence, no crime. If those police officers had seen anything suspicious at Sarah Lee Sewell's, they'd be investigating. Right?

To think otherwise meant I'd be jumping on Cissy's bandwagon, buying her conspiracy theory, when I needed to stay calm and be the voice of reason, and not just for Mother's sake. Annabelle was hardly acting like the Rock of Gibraltar . . . or any other rock, for that matter. She used to bend with the breeze, and she was doing it again.

"You still don't believe it was murder, do you?" Annabelle practically stood on tiptoe, so obviously waiting for me to say something. Her fingers worked her pearls like a rosary.

"No, I don't," I reassured her, and maybe myself as well. "Whatever connections you think there may be—that my mother thinks she sees—they're coincidence. They have to be. You run retirement communities, Annabelle, so losing people now and then has to be expected, because human beings don't live forever, much as we'd wish some of them could. I'm sure you've had others complain, and they haven't ended up dead, have they?"

"Not all of them, no," she said, brightening.

"Well, there you go," I replied, because it was logical and rational. "You can't start looking for nefarious explanations where none exist, or you'll drive yourself bonkers."

And end up dressing in a wig and lizard boots with rhinestones, pretending to be someone you weren't.

After a pause and much blinking, Annabelle let out a weighty sigh, ruffling my bangs as well as hers. "You're right, Andy. You're absolutely right all around. Just like at camp. You were always the one who had explanations for the scary sounds in the woods."

Oh, joy. Now I wouldn't have to come up with my own epitaph.

"Good, I'm glad we're on the same page." I

grabbed hold of the Tumi's handle, wanting to be on my way.

"Thank you, Andy." Relief oozed from her pores like perfume—okay, maybe more like perspiration. "I think I've been talking to your mother too much. I'll put this silliness out of my head. I've got a business to run."

"Speaking of silliness, I've got to chase after Cissy before someone grabs her with a butterfly net."

She leaned forward and gave me a quick hug, the suitcase between us, before she turned and opened the door, allowing my exit.

"You keep an eye on her, Andy," she said as I passed, pulling the Tumi over the threshold. "Because I'd hate for anything to happen to Cissy . . . or to you."

"We'll be fine," I tossed back, doing a solid impression of nonchalant. "We Kendricks women can take care of ourselves. We've been doing a pretty good job of it since Plymouth Rock, so I don't think a few days in a retirement community are gonna kill us."

That finished between us, Annabelle shut her office door, closing me off. I stared ahead at the long hallway, telling myself, *I feel calm, I feel calm, I feel calm.*

Aw, who was I kidding?

The mantra was a crock, and I was far from feeling placid, particularly after hearing Annabelle's tale of two women for whom nothing was ever right. I wondered if the thermostat was working properly, wherever they were now, or if it, perhaps, was a little too hot.

Nuts, I thought again and took off after my mother, knowing that, crazy or not, until this jig was up, I'd be watching her back with a vengeance.

Chapter 11

Bebe Kent's townhouse stood at the end of Magnolia Court, a cul-de-sac several streets over from Sarah Lee Sewell's, sandwiched between the eighteenth hole and a small man-made lake. The two homes were within walking distance, I figured, particularly if you cut through the nature paths that crisscrossed the grounds, snaking between buildings and across the verdant landscape.

Being directionally dysfunctional, I could well have driven in circles had I not been following Mother in Sandy's Buick Century. Plenty of signs appeared at each intersection, pointing toward the golf course, the tennis courts, the pool and spa, the clinic, physical therapy, or the Manor House, which seemed the focal point of the community. Still, my internal map ran more on landmarks than on words or arrows.

Since my grand tour yesterday was aborted, I still didn't have a thorough grasp of the layout of Belle Meade, though it seemed that everything stemmed from the main building, like tentacles on a squid, which made perfect sense.

Keeping my Jeep on the slow-moving bumper of the Buick, I glimpsed more of the residences to the west of the Manor, townhouses and condos, one and two stories, some red brick and others whitewashed with painted shutters and small, tidy yards. It could've been any upscale, gated community in Dallas, letting in only those who could afford to pay the substantial costs.

Within minutes, Mother tooted the horn and parked the Century in a small driveway beside a red brick row house with yellow shutters. I tucked the Wrangler tight against the front curb.

"Home, sweet home," Cissy twanged in her best Dolly Parton, clip-clopping on her rhinestone-studded boots toward the portico. All she needed was a guitar and a boob job, and she might've passed for a Pigeon Holler relation.

As I dragged her Tumi suitcase from my back-seat, I saw her check the mailbox and remove a thick bundle, apparently forgotten since Bebe's death. I guessed that, even if the English cousins and Bebe's attorney had filed a stop order at the post office, it would take a while before delivery really did cease. Regardless, I'd bet the next resident would continue getting bits and pieces of missives addressed to Bebe. My mother still received the occasional junk mail or solicitation addressed to Daddy, a dozen years after his fatal heart attack.

My gaze swept over the place, from ground to rooftop, while I rolled the bag forward, but I saw nothing overtly sinister. A bird twittered from a nearby tree, and a squirrel scurried along the covered gutter.

Perfectly benign, I told myself, coming to stand behind my mother as she unlocked the front door.

Still, a prickle of dread raised the hair on the back of my neck as I followed her inside. I rolled the Tumi to a stop in the foyer and waited as Cissy went around clicking on lights and opening drapes to let in the sunshine. As illumination filled every dark corner, I made myself walk around, trying to forget that a woman had died upstairs a mere four days before.

Found dead on Thursday—I mentally tapped off—buried on Friday, memorialized on Saturday. And Sunday was proving no day of rest for the weary.

At least, not for Chief Inspector Cissy.

What did she expect to find here? I wondered. Notes that Bebe had left behind, stating, "To whom it may concern, if you should find me dead, dressed in a lacy nightgown and tucked into bed, it means I was the victim of homicide and the killer is . . ."

"Andrea?"

"Huh?" I turned to find my mother staring at me—well, squinting, really, in that critical way of hers—plenty frightening enough when she wasn't wearing glasses with lenses that made her eyes as big as half-dollars.

"I asked if you'd come sit with me in the living room so we could chat a spell."

"Only if you take those . . . things off your face"— I waved a finger at her Mr. Magoo spectacles.

"Don't like them, do you, sugar?"

"They scare me to death," I said without thinking of my poor choice of words. "I don't much like any of this."

"I'm still getting used to being Miriam Ferguson myself," she announced but obliged, removing the glasses and sticking them atop her frothy black head.

"You sure they won't get swallowed up?"

"What, you don't like my 'do, either?" She fingered her inky cotton-candy wig and let out a lilting laugh. "If only your father could see me now, he'd think I was stark-staring mad."

Um, ditto.

It hadn't escaped me that she seemed to be enjoying this, and I wasn't sure if that boded well for her emotional state. Wasn't there always laughter before the tears? Smiles and grins before the nuclear meltdown?

She'd hardly done more than get misty-eyed at the church. If she bottled up her grief for too long, she'd surely burst.

But I knew how good she was at holding things in.

That was one trait of hers—one of many—that I had not inherited. I couldn't any more hold my emotions in check than a career politician could stop making promises he couldn't keep.

"Come here, sweet pea," Mother said, sashaying into the heart of the living room and sitting down. She patted a spot on the sofa beside her. "Let's talk, just you and me without interference from Miss Annabelle Meade or anyone else. Sweet as she is, the girl is a tad overemotional, don't you think?"

Talk about the crackpot calling the kettle black.

I crossed toward the sofa, admiring the vastness of space, the cathedral ceilings and tall windows, the furnishings that seemed straight out of the pages of *Architectural Digest*. Lots of earthy tones with splashes of red. Leather chairs mixed with patterned fabrics and glossy woods. It was hard to imagine that Bebe could find anything wrong with this.

The fireplace mantel held a striking silver candelabra and a vase filled with tall strands of sea grass, though it was missing anything personal, an heirloom clock or framed photographs. Ah, surely the cousins had already been here and had pocketed whatever had belonged to Bebe, or had set it aside to be packed and shipped.

After covering the distance between us, I dropped onto the cushion next to Cissy, and she put an arm around my shoulders and squeezed. I breathed in the Joy on her skin, and I nearly remarked that she and Miriam shared the same taste in perfume. Sadly, I couldn't say the same for their choice of wardrobe.

"It seems strange," she said, glancing around us, "to be in this room without Bebe, holding a glass of wine, sharing stories, and listening to those old records of hers. Duke Ellington, Glenn Miller, Artie Shaw. *That*, my dear, was music." She sighed. "Now it's so still."

"How can you stay here?" I blurted out, worried to think of her alone in this house, not so much because of Bebe's ghost; but because, much as I hated to admit it, I still wasn't 100 percent convinced someone hadn't harmed her friend. "Won't it . . . creep you out?" An indelicate question, yes, but well intentioned.

She looked toward the stairwell, and I saw apprehension tighten her jaw. "I won't stay in her room, of course," she told me. "But there's a guest room and a pull-out sofa in her study." She faced me again. "I was really hoping, sugar, that you'd move in with me. Surely Mr. Malone wouldn't mind if I borrowed you for a few days. You said he was working on a big case?"

"Yeah, big and out of town," I grumbled. "Gone until Wednesday," I blurted out before I realized what I'd done.

"Ah, well, then he's out of the equation, isn't he? It's up to you, pumpkin." She pounced. "Would you stay here with me? Pretty please?"

Had I fallen right into that one, or what?

I'd been waiting for another shoe to drop—besides the slides Annabelle had returned—and this one beaned me with a resounding *thunk*.

Daddy had always called me "pumpkin," and I had a soft spot for that term of endearment, beyond all others. Hearing it now made my heart skip a beat. She wasn't playing fair, and she knew it. It also made me realize how dad-gummed determined she was, how much she needed me around to act like Superglue and hold her together.

Quicksand.

I felt it sucking at my feet.

Move into Bebe's? That would mean sacrificing my normal routine for Mother's cuckoo scheme. Not an appealing option by any measure.

Oh, boy.

Why had I assumed that my part in this operation would involve no more than a few afternoons, keeping an eye on Cissy while she peered into closets, looking for skeletons, until I went home for supper?

I had my own life to live, a job to do, so why was I even considering this?

"No way, José," came to mind, as I wanted desperately to decline, but my mouth wouldn't cooperate. Something about what Annabelle had told me in confidence had unnerved me, more than I wanted to acknowledge.

"Andrea? Will you do it or not?"

I felt that pang in my chest again, and I knew what the answer was, no matter how I fought it.

Despite our differences, I loved my mother beyond rhyme or reason. I wanted to protect her and, however much I wished she wouldn't do this, there was no stopping her, short of sedation.

If I walked away and she was hurt—or worse—I could never forgive myself.

Never.

"I know this is an imposition on you," she said, pressing her cheek against mine, a rare intimate gesture. "But you have to realize how important this is to me. Can you understand what it means, getting to the truth of what happened? Making sure there's justice served, if need be?"

"I think I do," I told her.

"Truly?" She drew back, blinking with disbelief. "You're not just humoring me, Andrea Blevins Kendricks? Or coddling me because you think I'm particularly vulnerable after losing two of my dearest friends?" Her arm slid away.

Caution: land mines ahead!

I wet my lips and composed my thoughts, determined to avoid commenting on her emotional state or her sanity. What I did want to do was convince her that I knew all too well about loyalty and doing right by the people you love. It had everything to do with why I was sitting next to her.

"It's not like I haven't jumped through a few hoops myself to help someone I once cared about, have I?"

And, as she'd pointed out in Annabelle's office, I had stuffed my sports bra and shoehorned my butt into hot pants to do it.

Enough said.

"You most surely have gone out on a limb for an old friend, haven't you, sugar? I saw it for myself, and I thought you were crazy to do it. Before I realized how determined you were to see it through to the end, so I supported you as best I could, didn't I?"

Dang it. "You did."

She gazed warmly at me, with her extremely made-over face and unsuitable black tresses. The pale blue of her irises seemed so soft in that harsh palette, making me already miss the way she was B.M. (Before Miriam): the blond hair and pink mouth, the pale colors and pearls. The absence of leopard print.

"Sometimes you have to go with your heart," I said, and she nodded. "Even when it seems illogical to everyone around you."

"That's it precisely. I can't ignore my own instincts, not when everything inside"—she tapped the cheetah-spotted patch over the center of her chest—"tells me something is seriously rotten in Denmark." She paused, and her orange-brown lips pulled taut, her expression turned pensive. "If I don't try to find out what really happened to Sarah and Bebe, I'm letting them down. I have to be sure, or what kind of friend am I?" Her chin gave a quiver.

I had never seen my mother so open about her feelings, not with me, anyway. I didn't want to put a damper on this moment of empathy between us. Still, I found it impossible not to share my own misgivings.

"But what if"—I began softly—"you don't find anything? What if this is a wild goose chase you're on, and Bebe and Sarah Lee truly died natural deaths? Will you really be able to let it go in a week or even a few days, if you can't let go now?"

Because, that's what worried me most: that she wouldn't be able to drop this so easily when it was over, however it ended. I didn't want the loss of her friends to become a true obsession.

If it wasn't already.

"That won't happen, I promise you." She sniffed and raised her chin, gestures so typical of her that anyone who really knew her would've seen through the wig and the makeup and the unsuitable clothing. "Besides, I've already found proof that I'm on the right track."

Yeah, yeah.

"I know, the nightgown and the worn-off lipstick," I said, hating to be the purveyor of gloom.

"But those things wouldn't be evidence enough for an arrest warrant, much less a conviction." Hey, I watched *CSI*. "You need witnesses, fingerprints, blood stains, something tangible."

"Oh, this is tangible, all right," Mother said and rose from the sofa, gesturing that I follow. "Housekeeping hasn't yet touched this place and won't until Bebe's things have been removed. Bear that in mind. Bebe's cousins didn't want anyone from the cleaning crew in here until the smaller, most priceless pieces had been properly dispensed with. They were afraid things might be misplaced."

Translation: the cousins didn't want to risk anyone palming an expensive brooch until they had the chance to comb through the townhouse for whatever wasn't in Bebe's safe-deposit box, so they could pack it up and take it back to merry old England.

"Andrea, are you coming?"

Reluctantly, I pushed to my feet and trudged after her, through the opened archway that led to the kitchen, much the same layout as Sarah Lee Sewell's townhouse.

Other aspects were similar as well: the granite-topped center island, ample space for a table and chairs, plenty of cabinets, and racks for pots and pans. A butler's pantry and utility room off to the side. Though no copper-bottomed cookware hung from the ceiling, just empty hooks. Moving boxes sat in one corner, marked with a UK address, so I figured Jillie or Stella had decided to keep some of Bebe's nicer culinary doodads. The shiny surfaces looked remarkably bare. I wondered if the fine china and silver had already been wrapped and shipped?

I found myself thinking of what Mabel Pinkston had said about Bebe at the reception:

"I didn't think she had anybody left in the world besides her lawyers and a couple of long-lost cousins from across the puddle who didn't give a hoot or holler about her until she dropped dead."

"Over here," Mother was saying, and I stopped my inventory of the room to join her by the sink. "This is what I'm talking about, Andrea." She gestured at a dishtowel that had been folded in half, upon which sat two wine glasses, turned upside down. "Just *look* at this, would you?"

Humor her, I reminded myself, the same advice I'd given Annabelle, although I hadn't realized then that Annabelle would take it to such an extreme.

"Okay." I leaned over, peering at the glasses closely, noting a scratch on one and a slight chip in the base of the other. "Yeah, I see what you mean. The quality's not great and . . . yuck . . . they're spotty as heck. What kind of dishwashing liquid does she use? Is it something generic? Probably not biodegradable, either."

Mother snorted rather indelicately. Though maybe that was part of her newly adopted, less graceful persona of Rhinestone Cowgirl. "For heaven's sake, it has nothing to do with the dishwashing liquid! Doesn't this remind you of anything?" She swung her hand back and forth over the goblets, as if she were David Copperfield, preparing to pull a rabbit out of their stems.

Here we go again.

I squinted fiercely, willing my amazing powers of observation to kick in. But they still looked like ordinary glasses. Nothing fancy or expensive, just the kind you could get in a six-pack at Target. Obviously, Stella and Jillie had left them for the trash bin, and I couldn't blame them.

Straightening up, I gave my best guess. "Er, someone drank wine recently." I stated the obvious.

"Yes, yes," Mother said, head bobbing, encouraging me to continue. "And, what else?"

"Um, well, afterward, somebody washed the goblets and left them to drain."

Double duh.

"Go on, go on." Her eyes took on an unnatural glint.

What else was there?

"Well, er, they didn't put them in the dishwasher with the Jet Dry, which would have rinsed off the spots and made them squeaky clean." My voice went up as I finished the sentence, because I had no idea where the heck I was supposed to go with this.

Definitely not where Cissy had intended.

"No, no, no!" She scowled at me, doubly menacing with her frown outlined with a brown lip pencil. Her false-lashed eyes blinked repeatedly, looking like bats trying to take flight and failing miserably. "Don't you see? The way the pieces fit together so neatly?"

What pieces?

I shrugged, no clue what she meant. "No, I don't." Not even a little.

She crossed her arms, and I felt a lecture en

route. "Have you ever known me to rinse out a glass in the sink?"

That was easy. "Not if your life depended on it."

Dried her hands out, you see, plus that's why she had something called "staff."

"Would I ever set glasses on a dishtowel to dry?"

"God forbid." *How gauche was that?*

I liked these questions. They were easy.

"Bebe Kent and I were cut from the same cloth, Andrea," she said. "Which tells you what?"

"That the cloth was pure Chinese silk woven by the emperor's most prized caterpillars?" I guessed, figuring she was throwing me a curveball.

"For heaven's sake, this is serious." Mother blew a puff of air that ruffled the line of her fake bangs. "The fact of the matter is that Bebe Kent would no more have washed out a pair of wine glasses than I would. At most, she would've stuck them in the dishwasher and waited for someone from Housekeeping to run the contraption and empty it for her. Don't you recall Annabelle sayin' that Elvira didn't clean last Thursday morning because she discovered Bebe in bed and got hysterical?" She tipped her head toward me. "So the dishwasher was never run, was it? And the glasses would indicate . . . what?"

Why was she doing this? Couldn't she just stay home and bake pies like normal mothers did on TV sitcoms?

She waited for my answer, so I cleared my throat and punted one for the Gipper. "You said that you and Bebe used to come back here, sip wine and listen to golden oldies after bridge on Wednesdays. So, if those are your goblets, someone came in and cleaned up after you."

"Wrong."

"Why?"

"First of all, I didn't have time for a visit with Bebe, not last Wednesday." Cissy proceeded to explain where my theory went awry. "I had an emergency board meeting for the Battered Women's Calf Fry, so I had to scoot. Secondly, Bebe never poured a drink for an invited guest into anything less than her Waterford crystal. Those"—a flick toward the offending objects—"were part of a set of glassware she won in a cross-town bridge tournament at the Richardson Junior League." Mother wrinkled her nose. "She only used them for people she didn't particularly care for."

Ah, silly me. And I just had one set of glasses that worked for everybody.

"So Bebe shared her Merlot with someone other than you." That seemed a no-brainer. "Maybe a lowly neighbor who dropped by and didn't rate the Waterford. Big freaking deal."

"I wish you wouldn't curse like that, Andrea."

"Sorry."

Mother fiddled with the enormous CZ rings on her fingers. "But you're getting warmer this time."

"How about that Henry fellow who wears Day-Glo golf pants? I heard he's a hot commodity around here. Could be he popped over to do a little horizontal mambo with Ms. Bea?" I offered, considering that Mabel Pinkston described him as a Viagra-fed rooster let loose in the henhouse. Perhaps Bebe didn't mind sharing her worm with other hungry chicks.

"Henry Brooks Churchill? That old coot?" She rolled her eyes. "Sorry, darlin', but you're cold as ice. Beatrice had much better taste in men. Homer was in a class by himself. Come on now. Use your imagination and give it another whirl. I have faith in you."

Another whirl? This was worse than twenty questions.

I was starting to feel like the dumbest guy on *Jeopardy!*

Plumb out of guesses, I scratched my chin. "I'll take 'My Mother Is Off Her Rocker' for a thousand, Alex."

"You're giving up so soon?" Cissy tapped a rhinestone-studded boot on the tiled floor, itchy as a flea-bitten hound. "Maybe it's a good thing you didn't apply to the *real* Columbia," she murmured. "Even with your SATs, they might not've let you in with that dismal attitude."

I pretended not to hear her.

"All right." She relented. "Here's another hint. Bebe had some kind of plans for that evening, a late supper with, to quote her, 'someone you don't know,' but she wouldn't say who."

"Well, why didn't you mention that before?" I crabbed, because she wasn't playing fair. "Someone you don't know, huh? Sounds like Bebe had a date, and maybe he came by for drinks after. She was of legal age"—and then some—"so big whoop. What does that have to do with anything?"

"Ah, but what if this mystery date is the last one who saw Bebe alive?"

"Oh, no, don't say it," I begged, because I should've realized where she was headed five minutes ago.

"All right, I won't."

So I did. "You think he killed her."

"It's a definite possibility, sugar."

"You figure he drugged her wine, then dressed her in her nightgown and put her to bed, before slinking off into the night? That he fooled Dr. Finch into thinking Bebe died a natural death?"

"By George, I think she's got it!" She clapped as giddily as she had at my first—and last—piano recital when I was eight.

"He must be a very clever fellow to do what he did without leaving any tracks," I added with unbridled sarcasm. "Maybe he's invisible."

Cissy seemed oblivious to my tone of voice. "Ah, but he did leave tracks," she said. "They're just very subtle."

"The two rinsed-out goblets?"

"Elementary, my dear, Watson."

I wanted to smack myself in the head.

Arrrgh.

Those glasses were hooey, I sullenly mused. The folks on *CSI* would not be happy with such a pathetic offering of evidence. For crud's sake, they'd had been washed out and wiped down, so there weren't even any fingerprints.

"We're not done yet. Think, Andrea." She egged me on. "Where else did we see a similar scene? A pair of cups drying on a dishtowel."

"In half the houses in Dallas?" I offered snippily.

"*Think*," she repeated.

Did they let patients play bridge in the loony bin? I wondered. Because I was reconsidering paging Dr. Freud and having Mother picked up ASAP.

I resisted tearing out my hair and silently cried "uncle."

"Yesterday," she hinted. "In another kitchen, just a couple streets away from here."

Ostensibly, she was pointing me toward Sarah Lee Sewell's, so I focused on that. I'd puked in the bushes, gone back inside, grabbed the copper-bottomed pot to clang for attention. After Mother had stormed out, I'd stayed to talk to Annabelle, had gone to the sink, and offered her a glass of water.

Click.

On went the light bulb.

There'd been two mugs set upside down on a dishtowel, hadn't there?

Drat, she was right.

My eyes widened, and I saw Cissy's satisfied smile as she picked up on it.

"Yes, at Sarah Lee's," she said before I could. "You saw them, too, and it's no coincidence. There's only one logical explanation."

Logical? On what planet?

I winced as Mother nattered on: "Whoever killed Bebe killed Sarah Lee, too." She rubbed her hands together, positively gleeful, as worked up as she'd been when she returned from Paris with a trunk full of vintage Valentino. "Now it's up to us to find out who this mystery man is, and we only have six days to do it."

Bloody brilliant, Chief Inspector! Let's put out an APB, send out a BOLO, slip on our regulation Manolos, and hit the pavement!

I felt a persistent throb begin at my temples.

No doubt, the cops will pin the murders on the first homicidal maniac they catch who doesn't know enough to put his murder weapons into the dishwasher. The poor sod probably still has his hands full of Palmolive residue. Instead of a lineup, we'll just run the old "Madge" test to see whose skin is the softest.

Insanity, thy name is Cissy.

To think I had whole days of this ahead of me.

Would anyone blame me if I ran away from the old folks' home and never came back?

Chapter 12

I left Mother happily ensconced at the kitchen table with a letter opener and three days' worth of Beatrice Kent's unopened mail. She'd propped the Mr. Magoo glasses back on her nose, which she said was rather like reading through a magnifying lens.

Quelle surprise!

She did promise not to leave the house until I returned, and I had to trust she hadn't crossed her bejeweled fingers behind her back. Oh, what I wouldn't give to implant a chip in her fanny so I could track her with a GPS.

On my way out of Belle Meade, I spotted a golf cart parked near the eighteenth hole, while three gentlemen in ultrabright clothing waited for a fourth man—in knickers—to putt. Though I was only traveling at ten miles per hour, a twinge below the posted limit, I passed a posse of residents on four-wheeled scooters, heading toward the Manor House, presumably for brunch. Which reminded me I'd only eaten a couple of breath mints for breakfast and needed real nourishment soon.

After waving at Bob—or maybe was it Sam—in place at the guardhouse, I headed off the grounds and onto the traffic of Forest Lane, feeling a weight leave my chest as I pointed the Jeep toward home.

My cell phone rang opportunistically as I stopped at a red light, and I stabbed my hand into my overstuffed bag to find it.

"Yo," I answered, knowing it was Sandy by the digits on the screen.

"How is Cissy? *Where* is she?"

"She's at Belle Meade, and she's, um, her usual spunky self," I said, deliberating on whether or not to spill all the beans. If I told her about Mother's alter ego Miriam Amanda Wallace Ferguson and her plan to smoke out a phantom killer, it would only worry her to distraction, maybe more than it worried me. Because I'm not sure she'd comprehend *why*, not the way I was beginning to, having done something awfully similar (and equally foolish).

"When's she coming home?"

The light turned green, so I tucked the phone under my chin to free both hands, though I had to be careful not to move my jaw much when I spoke.

"Um, it might be a few days, Sandy. She promised Bebe Kent's cousins she'd stick around and pack up the clothing to donate to charity, make sure they hadn't left any personal effects behind, things they can't do because they live so far away." Well, it was the truth, just not the *whole* truth so help me God.

"And that's all it is? You're not hiding anything from me?"

Geez, and I thought I'd sounded convincing. "Would I keep secrets from you, Sandy?" No better way to avoid a question than with another question. "Look, I'm going home now to get some things, then I'll be moving into Bebe's with her."

"Why on earth are you doing that?"

"Because she asked me." No lie either. It was the prototypical KISS answer learned by every teenager who'd ever missed a curfew (keep it simple, stupid).

"Oh, well . . . hmm, I imagine that's a good thing, Andy. Real good. You just stay in close touch. Promise me?"

"Cross my heart and hope to die." Well, the first part, anyway.

"And if she could use another hand, I could go on over . . ."

"No, no, not necessary," I cut her off, before that idea could take root in her head. "Four hands are plenty, actually more than enough."

"If you're sure."

"I'm sure."

Good God, I couldn't imagine what would transpire if Sandy were to see Mother all dudded up in animal prints and faux glitter. It might change her mind about whether or not Cissy had come unhinged.

Something I still wasn't so all-fired sure about myself.

"Talk to you soon," I said, snapping the phone

closed and letting it fall to my lap, thankful when it didn't ring again the rest of the way to my condo. I didn't need the added distraction.

Besides, the only other person whose voice I wanted to hear at that moment was Malone's, and yet I knew I couldn't share the latest developments with him, either, for fear that he'd cut his business trip short and hurry back; despite the fact that he couldn't do anything except fret unnecessarily and lecture me about how unhealthy it was to support my mother's grief-borne delusions.

So, much as I was tempted to ring his Galveston hotel room and describe Cissy's new getup and my gig as her wingman, I couldn't do it.

I'd call that a Catch-22. (In other words, I was screwed.)

I was going to have to keep Brian in the dark, as well as Sandy. I'd appointed myself Mother's keeper for the next few days. She was my responsibility, and I was in charge of making sure this vaudeville act didn't go any farther than it should.

I just had to figure out exactly where "too far" was located. (How about north of nutty and south of woo-woo?)

One last stoplight and then the Jeep bumped around a corner, rolling onto familiar turf. I let out a huge breath, and my heart fairly sang with relief.

My home, sweet home.

Though I'd just been away a night, when I finally pulled into the parking lot at my North Dallas complex, it seemed like I'd been gone forever. I didn't even mind that my next-door neighbor's daughter had bedded down her shiny Z3 convertible in the spot that was usually mine.

As I parked the Jeep in an empty slot farther down, I sat for a moment and gazed ahead at the two-story building where I'd lived for the past eight years, since I'd come back after art school in Chicago. Cut into four units, two upstairs and two down, the whitewashed brick sported black shutters and dark green doors, each with a tiny portico and wooden railings. Prickly holly bushes sprouted beneath the windows to keep away the peeping Toms. (That had actually been a selling point when the realtor showed me the unit.) Someone's wind chimes tinkled in the soft breeze, and, in the distance, I heard the squawk of geese from a nearby pond.

Hello, pad o' mine, I thought, tempted to blow it a kiss. It was the first place that had ever belonged to me . . . and me alone.

Almost made me teary-eyed to think I'd ever leave, that someday I'd want something larger, roomy enough for a husband and a family. A house with a fence and a backyard big enough for a swing set.

Somebody, stop me! I was sounding like my prep school chums, who'd been full of plans for catching a man and settling down, even when they were mere teens.

I'd always wanted to live my life differently, to strike out a path that was unique, where I surrounded myself only with the closest of friends, those I could trust, forever following my passion, unconcerned with what others thought of me. It had taken much of my (nearly) thirty-one years for me to form my own identity outside of my family, and I couldn't fathom forsaking that for anyone or anything.

Even for Malone?

Hmmm.

Were love and independence incompatible? I wondered, thinking that didn't seem right or fair. I felt uneasy with the idea of giving up even part of myself, when getting to where I was had been such a struggle. Which is why, after three months with Brian, I still hadn't offered him a key to my condo. The idea of letting go of that control made my pulse race. My own personal fear factor.

Would I ever be able to do it? Would I be able to share enough of myself to be able "to have and to hold, until death do us part"?

My mother had married when she was just twenty-one and straight out of SMU. She'd never known what it was like to be alone until my father had died. And that was hardly the same as starting out that way, leaving college and having only yourself to account for.

By and large, no one constantly asked me, "Where've you been?" Or demanded that I play my music lower, or change the TV channel to *Monday Night Football*. Every choice was mine to make. I had plenty of personal space, and I didn't want to lose it.

I thought of Bebe Kent and Sarah Lee Sewell, women of my mother's generation who had wed so young, too, and I felt a sudden rage in my belly that they had died right at the point where, as Mother had put it, they were coming into their own.

What if someone had deliberately stolen that from them?

What if Cissy wasn't delusional? What if she was right about everything, and the rest of us were in denial?

If that was the case, how could I even think of preventing her from learning the truth? No matter how silly or crazy I thought she was for doing it.

The answer was easy. *I couldn't.*

I dropped my forehead to the steering wheel and banged it gently, wondering what I was getting myself into and hoping I wasn't doing my mother harm by supporting her crusade instead of refusing.

Tap, tap, tap.

I jumped at the sound of knuckles rapping the window and jerked my head around to find Charlie Tompkins smiling at me through the glass. As I caught my breath, I shut off the ignition and pulled my key out. Charlie stepped back, so I could open the door and hop down, drawing my satchel out after me.

His daughter's Beamer was pulling out of my space, and my neighbor nodded in that direction. "I told her not to park there, Andy, but you know how young women are. Woo doggie, but they don't listen to nobody. Particularly to us menfolk."

"No problem," I assured him, rolling the window down a crack before I shut and locked the door.

"You need some help?" he asked, though he had a leash caught in one hand, his elderly beagle tugging on the cord gently as he sniffed my Wrangler's tires. I could only hope he'd save his business for the grass.

"I'm good, Charlie, thanks," I assured him and smiled back. I stepped up the curb onto the sidewalk, and he followed.

"You young women got a thing for doing things your own selves, don't ya?" He tugged on the lead, and his potbellied canine followed him onto the small patch of lawn. "Bet you don't even let a fellow open a door for ya."

"Well, you'd lose that bet," I said, and he laughed.

He had one of those great faces, chiseled with lines that he'd earned working oil rigs most of his life and capped with white hair, twisted onto his brow by a stubborn cowlick. His grizzled twang was the real thing, not the cheap imitation my mother kept taking a stab at as her alias, Miriam.

Charlie and his low-rider beagle walked me to my door, which was right next to his. We reached the portico, when I stopped and turned to him.

"Oh, hey, I have to leave for a few days," I said.

"Business?"

"More like a minor family crisis. Still, if you could keep an eye on things, Charlie, and make sure my mail doesn't overflow the box while I'm gone. I'm hoping I might get home some in-between"—*In between what? Chasing my mother around a retirement facility*—"but I may not be able to slip away so easily."

"No trouble a'tall, sweetheart," he drawled and patted his pants pocket, eliciting a jingle. "Got your spare right on my ring. So I'll go ahead and take your mail inside when it's delivered."

Yep, the eighty-year-old retiree next door had my key, but my boyfriend did not. How was that for having my priorities in order?

"You got any plants to water?" he asked.

"Just this one out front, thanks, Charlie," I said and bent to lay a pat on his doggie's back, when the critter decided to lift his leg and pee on the pot of chrysanthemums sitting on the front steps.

Nothing like the smell of fresh piddle in the morning.

"Oops, sorry, Andy. Guess ol' Bubba figured he'd water 'em for ya."

The story of my life.

"It's okay, Charlie. They were gonna die sometime anyway."

"Happens to all of us, sooner or later," he remarked and pinched a kerchief from his shirt pocket to dab at his slick forehead.

"Dying?" I asked, a topic that was much on my mind of late.

"Well, that, too." He let out a throaty chuckle. "But I meant getting pissed on."

"Oh, yeah, of course."

There was nothing so blunt as the straight-shooting philosophy of a native Texan.

Bubba set to sniffing my foot, so I gave Charlie a smile and a "see you later," before I stuck my key in the lock, escaping inside before the beagle could get a leg up on me, so to speak.

The first thing I did when I got past the front

door was to drop my bulging tote bag on the ground and drink in the familiar surroundings. I took a loving whiff of air, inhaling a pinch of vanilla candle, a smidge of lime from Malone's aftershave, and the faint bouquet of burnt toast. My gaze embraced the walls that wrapped around me, wearing treasured artwork I'd rescued from flea markets and garage sales, mixed amongst my own creations: blurry watercolors mimicking Monet's *Garden in Giverny* and not a few acrylic landscapes paying homage to Cezanne.

Mimicking. Homage.

I was a copycat, wasn't I? Getting my inspiration elsewhere.

The reason I'd gone into Web design, forsaking a more Bohemian lifestyle, was because I'd known early on that my style of art was . . . well, not exactly my own. But I hadn't given up uncovering my creative core, and my latest attempt on canvas was propped on a slim easel near the best-lit window, in the room's far corner. A density of brooding color, heavy on texture and brushstrokes, more emotion than precision.

It was my first real attempt in a long while to put myself out there, to forget who I was *supposed* to be and paint like the real Andy.

"Have no fear of perfection, you'll never reach it."

Hello, Dali, I mused, as his quote came to mind. *I'm trying, Salvador. I'm trying.*

But first things first.

I blew out a rough breath—one that sorely needed a hit of Listerine—and I headed straight for the bathroom. In my haste to catch up to Mother this morning, I'd barely had time to brush my teeth.

Once I had my pearly whites polished, I stepped into the shower, scrubbing skin, shampooing hair and shaving my legs smooth as a whistle. Then I let the water pelt my shoulders as I stood there, chin down, closing my eyes and willing myself not to think of much of anything. I could've stayed there forever, until I'd shriveled to the size of a raisin.

Only I couldn't. I had things to do, no matter how ambivalent I felt about doing them.

After dressing in a clean pair of jeans and a T-shirt, I padded to the kitchen to whip up a peanut butter and jelly sandwich on wheat, throwing in a few pretzel sticks and a big glass of chocolate soy milk on the side.

My definition of a gourmet meal.

I sat down on the couch to eat, pulling the envelope Annabelle had given me from my bag and laying out the papers beside my sandwich plate. Without more than a cursory glance at the slick brochures for Belle Meade—with a fold-out map where she'd highlighted the library—and a groan when I saw my "Volunteer" badge had an awful old photo laminated on it, one Mother must've provided to Annabelle. I looked like a full-grown chipmunk: big teeth, big cheeks.

The card key for Belle Meade slipped out as I gave the envelope a final shake to empty it, and I hesitated before I stuck it into my purse.

Anyone who volunteered or worked at the retirement village got one of those things, as did all the residents. Or anyone the residents put on their "regular visitors" list, like Cissy, who still had one of Bebe's spares.

So how did the place keep tabs on everyone who had access? Not that security did such a swift job of monitoring those who came and went. The guardhouse had been unmanned when I'd driven past it this morning, and Sam—or Bob—had let the Bentley through yesterday with only a cursory nod.

Sure, they had cameras at the entrance and at the front door to the Manor, and I had to figure someone was watching a set of screens somewhere, or at least keeping tapes to view if and when anything unusual happened.

Annabelle had said herself:

"*. . . our security team found no signs of foul play, no indication of a forced entry. Nothing in the house was disturbed or appeared to be missing.*"

So if no one had noticed anything or anyone out of the ordinary on the grounds of Belle Meade the nights Bebe and Sarah Lee had died, did that mean nothing had happened? Or had the killer flown under the radar, as Mother suggested, which would point to an inside job, wouldn't it? Someone who knew the territory and the daily patterns of the residents, then had carefully zeroed in on particular, vulnerable targets.

Like one of the staff members who'd been with Annabelle "from the beginning" and who knew about Bebe and Sarah Lee threatening to sue.

Listen to you, Kendricks. Can you hear yourself?

Oh, Lord, I was channeling Cissy.

I swallowed a thick lump of bread and peanut butter, finished off my pretzels and soymilk, and left the dishes in the sink.

Time to rock and roll.

The clock was ticking, and this sidekick was on duty.

Chapter 13

After I'd emptied my tote bag, put away my black slides, and tossed the dirty clothes into the hamper, I caught the phone as it was ringing.

"Andy!"

The voice that squawked my name belonged to none other than Janet Graham, my redheaded pal who knew enough about my youthful indiscretions to write a book called, *When Good Debs Go Bad*. Though she preferred to pen stories about the snooty social set for the *Park Cities Press*. Lucky for me.

"You never returned my call," she reprimanded. "I even left my cell on vibrate during the Kappa Kappa Gamma Tablescapes benefit at the country club in case you buzzed back."

"Oh, poo, I'm sorry. It completely slipped my mind. I was actually at my mother's last night." I slid onto the sofa with my old Princess phone. "It's just been a maddening couple of days."

"How is Cissy? I know she and Bebe were tight

as ticks, and she looked less than her usual *über*-composed self at the service yesterday morning. Don't tell me she's questioning the meaning of life and has shucked her Chanel for a potato sack?"

For an instant, I panicked, thinking she knew something about Cissy's crazy crusade at Belle Meade, because Janet had a way of finding out about everything—or nearly—if it involved the Dallas elite.

"She's coping in her own unique fashion," I said carefully. "But, you're right, it's been tough for her to lose two friends like that."

"*Two* friends?" Janet echoed, and I winced. Guess she hadn't heard about Sarah Lee Sewell yet, and I wasn't about to fill her in. "Someone else from Cissy's circle passed?"

"Um, maybe I misspoke"—there went my foot-in-mouth disease again—"How's your tribute to Mrs. Kent going?" I tried to steer the subject away from serial dead blue bloods as fast as I could.

"I just sent that sucker to my editor, as a matter of fact. It'll go in Tuesday's edition, along with a profile of Bethany Entwhistle. Do you know her, Andy? She's a former Symphony Deb taking over the reigns of the Art for AIDS Foundation."

"Little blonde who sounds like she swallowed helium?" I'd met her at a fundraiser for local children's charities that Mother had dragged me to last year."

"That's the one," Janet drawled. "Get this"—she cleared her throat—"when I asked what three historical figures she'd like most to have dinner with, she answered, 'Jesus Christ, Mother Teresa, and Britney Spears.' "

"No way!"

"It's true, I swear." I could imagine Janet, sitting at her cubicle in the *Press* offices, her orange-red hair stuck up with chopsticks or butterfly clips, trying hard not to giggle as she interviewed the simpleminded Ms. Entwhistle. "And how about this, Andy. Her favorite animals are her Chihuahuas, Neiman and Marcus, whom she apparently loves to dress up in tailor-made outfits. We got a shot of them wearing black leather Gucci jackets and matching biker caps."

I couldn't speak; I was guffawing so loudly.

"I thought you'd appreciate that one."

I wiped tears from my eyes. "Oh, God, and that's the kind of girl my mother always dreamed I'd become."

"Wait, sweetie, I didn't even tell you the best part. Guess who she'd want to play her if a movie was ever made of her life?" To which Janet added the aside, "*As if.*"

"If it's not Julia Roberts then it's gotta be . . ."

"*Reese Witherspoon,*" we ended up saying in unison.

"Stop," I groaned, "or I'll pee in my pants."

"Wouldn't want that to happen."

As I caught my breath, I realized I had something to ask her. "Um, Janet, can you help me with something?"

"Shoot."

I scooted to the edge of the sofa, twisting the cord around my fingers. "You wrote a piece on Belle Meade when it opened, didn't you?" I remember Mother telling me just that—actually, chastising me for not having read it.

"The swanky retirement village where Bebe Kent lived?"

"I'd like a copy, if I could."

"Didn't you see it when it came out six months ago?" She sounded disappointed. "It was nearly the whole front page of the Society section."

"It's important, Janet."

"Oh, no!" She gasped. "Don't tell me Cissy's looking into the place? I can't imagine her living anywhere but Beverly."

"No, she's not moving. It's not that. I'm more interested in the staff," I said. "I went to summer camp with Annabelle Meade."

"Ah, good ol' Camp Longhorn, the retreat of choice for spoiled kiddies like you, Anna la belle, George W, and every other blue-blooded brat in the state whose first words were 'charge it.' "

"Very funny."

"Okay, I just pulled up the piece from the archives and hit 'send,' so it should be in your email box pretty quick. You want to see some of the clippings I used for background? Most of 'em are from the *Austin American Statesman*, even going back six years to that terrible fire. You know about that?"

"Annabelle's parents were killed," I said. "Yeah, she told me."

"Well, my Austin contacts knew the family fairly well." Janet's voice went down a pitch. "And I was informed, confidentially, of course, that the Meades were rather nasty people. Hard on their daughter and tight with a buck, so Annabelle didn't come into their millions until they were ashes. They didn't leave a penny to anyone but her and the Elk Lodge."

"Nasty people, huh?" I cringed, not at the choice of words, but because I realized how little I really knew about Annabelle's home life. "Her au pair used to put her on the bus for camp," I said quietly. "I never met her mother or father." No wonder Annabelle had always been an insecure, crying mess.

"The Meades apparently didn't socialize much with anyone. Just stayed to themselves and occasionally wrote a check to charity, probably for the tax deduction and not because it made them feel warm and fuzzy."

"Ouch."

"Wish I could gab forever, dear heart, but I've got to hit the road and attend the grand opening of a chi-chi hair salon on Greenville."

"Thanks, Janet, for the article, I mean."

"Lunch next week?" she asked.

"Call me," I told her, afraid to look too far ahead.

We said our goodbyes, and I hung up, but I didn't move anywhere too quickly. I sat where I was for a long moment after, feeling sorry for poor Annabelle and hoping nothing Mother or I did would muck things up for her. She deserved some happiness in her life after such a crappy growing-up.

"The fire investigators ruled it was an accident. They said a burner had been left on the stove, and a potholder or dishtowel must've been lying too close.

Their smoke alarms must not have gone off. Dad was always forgetting to replace the batteries."

If your parents were jerks, did you miss them when they were gone? I wondered. Or were you relieved and, if so, did that make you feel guilty?

I rubbed my temples, not wanting to think about it.

My place was so quiet. I wished I could curl into a ball, right there on the sofa, and not move until Malone returned.

Instead, I dragged myself up and headed into the bedroom, removing a small nylon suitcase from my closet and layering clean clothes, a Def Leppard CD, and my headphones, toiletries, and sneakers into its zippered midsection.

What to pack for several days of sleuthing? I mused, not wanting to forget anything important.

For an instant, I considered bringing my pepper spray, but I had a knack for self-defense backfiring on me. Clumsy should have been my middle name. Heck, I wouldn't even allow steak knives in my house for fear I'd cut off a finger. Wisely, I decided to leave the mace in my kitchen drawer, along with the sharp objects.

I contemplated taking that danged self-help book, too, for something to read with one eye while watching Mother with the other; but the suggestions for de-tensing my life seemed not to be working. The only benefit I could imagine from bringing along *Stress and the Single Girl* would be if I needed a paperweight. And I didn't. So I left it on the nightstand and zipped the suitcase shut. (If Malone hadn't given it to me, it would've ended up in the garbage.)

My luggage ready, I tackled the rest of my mental "to-do" list.

Figuring Malone might try to phone here in my absence, I rerouted calls from my home number to my cell, and I even made my bed and put my lunch dishes in the dishwasher so Charlie Tompkins wouldn't pop in with the mail, poke his nose around, and see a mess.

I sat down at my computer long enough to read emails and notify a few clients that I had a family emergency and would be away from my desk for a few days. No one would mind, I knew, since they were getting my services for free (or close to it).

Before I shut down the hard drive, I retrieved the e-mail from Janet, downloaded the attachment and printed off a copy, putting the pages in my bag without looking at them. I'd save them for later.

Then I took a last look around—at my big, comfy sofa with its crocheted throw, the unfinished canvas that beckoned, the hand-me-down hope chest that served as my coffee table—and I breathed in the quiet, before I picked up my bags and walked out the door.

I wanted to believe this would be over with in a few days, so I'd be home again, Brian would return from Galveston, Mother would go back to her committee work, and all would be right with the world.

Couldn't come any too soon.

On the way back to Belle Meade, I stopped for gas and a car wash, so the gunmetal gray of my Wrangler gleamed beneath the late afternoon sun, the WASH ME plea gone from the rear window.

When I slowed at the guardhouse on my way in,

a white-topped head poked out, giving my car a cursory glance.

I could've waved and kept going, because he didn't seem any too intent on having me stop. But I figured it wouldn't hurt to see if Bebe had any noteworthy guests that stood out. So I idled the Jeep beside the guardhouse window while Bob eyed me curiously, probably wondering what the hell I was doing. Oh, and it was Bob—not Sam—because he had his name embroidered on his chest pocket.

"Hi, there," I said, smiling brightly. "I'm Andrea Kendricks, an old friend of Annabelle Meade's. My aunt Miriam, just moved into a house on Magnolia Court . . . Bebe Kent's old place? What a tragedy . . . Mrs. Kent, I mean. The poor woman. Did you know her well?"

The skin around his eyes sagged, giving him a perpetual squint. "We had words now and then."

What did that mean? They'd argued? Or they'd conversed?

"I'll bet she had lots of friends dropping by to visit."

He shrugged. "Some."

"Hmm, well, she was attractive, wasn't she? I saw her photos at the reception yesterday, in the dining room. She probably had plenty of beaus swinging by to wine and dine her."

"Nope." Bob scratched his bulbous nose. "Would've had to put those names on the visitors' list, and she didn't."

Another car pulled up behind me, so I gave him my best Princess Di wave and lurched onward.

Bumping along the brick path, I backtracked

the route I'd taken earlier when I'd left, winding through the streets that led to Magnolia, finding slightly more activity outdoors than when I'd left. A handful of folks were on the walking path, a few outside with brimmed hats in the gardens, and others heading toward the main building on scooters or in golf carts. The day was mid-eighties, typical almost-fall weather. Rather like Florida without the palm trees, beach, or killer hurricanes.

Entering Belle Meade was akin to driving onto a movie set, a really upscale Mayberry. The place had such a small-town atmosphere despite being tucked right in the midst of a city as big as Dallas.

I had no trouble believing the waiting list to get in was a mile long.

Annabelle mentioned plans to build her retirement villages elsewhere, with the backing of eager investors, and I figured she'd make a fortune if nothing got in her way. Like dissatisfied socialites filing lawsuits . . . or a nosy woman crying, "Murder!"

I gnawed on the inside of my cheek.

Creeping along no faster than a slug, I came around the bend by the golf course and ended up on Magnolia Court, right where I wanted to be. I was elated that I hadn't gotten lost, and even more so to see the silver Century still sitting in the driveway, exactly where it had been when I'd left.

Mother had kept one promise, anyway.

Just to be safe, I pulled the Jeep in behind it.

Clever girl, I told myself, as I hitched my purse around my shoulder and lugged my suitcase out, trudging toward the portico.

When I got to the door, I rang the bell, wishing I'd thought to ask for a spare key. I waited a minute, suitcase getting heavy in my hand, and pressed that sucker again.

Where was she? I thought, swallowing a rising sense of worry, but figuring she couldn't have gone far, not without the car.

For Pete's sake. I raised my free hand to knock on the door, quickly giving up and wrapping my fingers around the knob. A simple twist, and the door pushed inward.

Good God, hadn't she locked herself in?

The moment I stepped inside, I dumped my bags, feeling a rerun of yesterday coming on, of calling for Mother and seeing Sarah Lee's unmoving legs stretched out on her sofa.

I blinked, clearing the vision, reminding myself this was a different house (albeit one where a woman had croaked) and that Cissy had been in no danger when I'd taken off for home. Though that had been several long hours ago.

Why hadn't I stayed? I chastised myself. *What if something went wrong?*

Leaving Cissy to her own devices when her emotions ran so high was a lot like tossing a lit match onto dry tinder and hoping it wouldn't ignite. Disaster could strike in the blink of an eye.

"Mother?" I called out and hurried toward the kitchen, where I'd last seen her poring over Bebe's mail.

Neat piles of letters, postcards, junk mail, and envelopes had been arranged on the table, but Cissy wasn't there. Although the clunky black leather handbag with glitter and buckles had been deposited under a chair.

So she had to be around somewhere, I reassured myself, knowing that a Kendricks and her purse were seldom parted.

Maybe she went out for some fresh air.

I scrambled to the sink to peer through the window overlooking the backyard. The cedar-stained patio furniture sat empty. Even the birdbath surrounded by planted peonies supported nary a feathered friend.

"Mother, it's Andrea! I'm baaaack!"

I jogged through the living room and past the formal dining room filled with reproduction Chippendale; ducked into a nice-sized den with a plasma screen television and leather-bound books that I figured had been bought by the yard to suit the decorator; and finally peered into a full bath downstairs that oozed black marble.

I would've paged her on her cell phone, but she refused to turn it on unless she needed it for "emergencies only." Said she couldn't stand them always going off during plays or at the symphony, and she hated drivers who yakked on them while swerving through traffic expecting everyone else to stay out of their way.

So I had to track her down on foot.

I told myself not to worry as I raced up the stairs, pausing on the second-floor landing where flattened cardboard boxes leaned, awaiting someone to pop them into three-dimension. A rolled-up woven rug, tied with string, had been pushed against the wall. Guess the cousins had separated a few more of Bebe's personal effects from what belonged to Belle Meade.

There were two doors on the left side of the hallway and two on the right.

Three were wide open.

I tried the closed one first and found myself breathing in the odor of a cedar closet full of linens. So I turned in a half-circle.

"Cissy Blevins Kendricks? Are you up here?"

Had she fallen and couldn't get up? Developed a debilitating attack of laryngitis so she couldn't answer?

Or was she playing hide and seek to test my sleuthing skills (or, at least, my patience)?

I poked my head in the nearest opened door, and a rush of Laura Ashley assaulted my senses: a pattern of yellow-and-sage covered windows and walls and smothered a plump double bed with a fabric headboard. Only an oak chest of drawers and mirrored bureau had been spared the floral print, but were painted a coordinating yellow.

I thought that look had gone out with the eighties, along with Duran Duran, Ronald Reagan, and culottes.

Seeking refuge, I ducked into a connecting bath where embroidered finger towels hanging from a silver rack and untouched shell-shaped soaps sat on the rim on the sink.

The far door opened into another room, but this time I found myself surrounded by a desk with computer, fax, small-sized copier, scanner, and phones. Georgia O'Keeffe prints brightened beige walls.

This had to be Bebe's office.

Drawers sat half-opened, most of them emptied, a clear sign that Bebe's lawyers had already given the place a thorough once-over. I wondered if Mother had come up to poke around, too.

Out into the hallway I stepped, calling louder, "Come out, come out, wherever you are!" I held still for a moment after, straining to catch the slightest whispered, "Help me," but I didn't pick up on anything.

The last opened door yielded another bedroom, this one taking up nearly the entire length of the house and dominated by an enormous sleigh bed, now stripped.

I edged my way around it, thinking *that's where Bebe bit the dust.*

Or at least where she'd been found.

It got me spooked.

Not wanting to shout for Mother so close to the deathbed, for fear of disrespecting the late Mrs. Kent, I hightailed it into her massive master bath, full of veined marble and mirrors that watched my every move, rather like a carnival fun house.

"Mu-ther," I tried again, my voice raspy, my arms packed with goose pimples.

Could a kid ground a parent? I wondered, because I was sorely tempted to send Cissy to her room without supper, after I found her, that is.

All that was left was a dressing room and the closet beyond, so I headed in, winding past an elaborate vanity, matching stool, and fringed settee and striding into what looked like a mini-department store with racks of shoes and hats and wall-to-wall clothing in every color under the sun.

And there, beneath a row of ball gowns, sprouting tulle and chiffon, sat my Mummy Dearest, head down, kneeling on the carpet in her rhinestone-studded sweat suit. She was digging through hat-boxes, papers strewn around her. She didn't even look up, so patently was she ignoring me.

I took a few steps farther in, coming around her side, though she didn't seem to notice.

She had on those Mr. Magoo glasses and the black wig from which a wire dangled to a pair of headphones in her ears, which in turn connected to a Discman resting on the floor that I knew wasn't hers. She must've "borrowed" it from Bebe.

I shook my head. Would she never learn? To date, she'd swiped another person's mail, a dead governor's name, and my CD player.

What was next? Hot-wiring cars? Pyramid scams? Insider trading?

"Mother," I said, enunciating each syllable as crisply and calmly as a contestant in a spelling bee.

She didn't even twitch.

For Pete's sake, how loud did she have the music turned up so that she couldn't hear me from six feet away?

Enough was enough.

I walked right up behind her and tapped her on the back.

Her head jerked up so fast I thought the wig might spill onto the floor. Her distorted eyes blinked, but that was all the surprise she emoted. Instead, she smiled up at me as she tugged the headphones from her ears and switched off the CD.

"There you are," she said, as though she'd been the one hunting for me, rather than the other way around.

"Rock and roll?" I said dryly, toeing the Discman.

"Rachmaninoff," she told me. "One of Bebe's."

"Think you had it up a little loud, missy?"

She arched her darkened eyebrows so they disappeared beneath the sharp line of her bangs. "Excuse me?"

"What the heck are you doing?" I started in, even as she reached up a hand and I helped her to her feet. "I've been looking all over for you for the past ten minutes, and you might've heard me hollering if you didn't have those *things* on."

"Well, I've been right here for the last hour, doing exactly what I intended, and I apologize that I missed all the yelling. There's nothing more soothing to a mother's ears than a daughter who's screeching like a banshee."

Wisenheimer.

I gestured at the racks of clothing around us. "Snooping in Bebe's closet? You think the bad guy wore one of her ball gowns? You figure he's a serial killer *and* a cross-dresser, too?"

"No, Andrea, for heaven's sakes. Don't be ludicrous. Not many men could wear women's couture, and Bebe was tiny." She pushed at the froth of black on her head and nudged at glasses fallen slightly askew. "For your information, sugar, while you went gallivanting off to God knows where . . ."

"I went home, Mother, to get my toothbrush."

"All afternoon?"

"I had to take care of the next few days in a matter of hours," I told her, hating the whiny rise of my voice, "so I could be here for you."

She sucked in her cheeks, and I waited, part of me almost hoping she'd come at me with more criticism. It would give me an excuse to turn tail and burn rubber back to the condo, if that's what I'd wanted to do.

Instead, she delicately cleared her throat. "As I was sayin', while you were gone, I've been doing some reconnaissance, and I do believe I've found a few more pieces to the puzzle." She shuffled papers from her left hand to her right and shook them in my face so I couldn't miss them. "Ta da!" she said.

"What are those?" I asked. "Insurance payouts? Blackmail notes? Death threats?"

"Not even close." She smiled a superior smile with her burnt-umber mouth, clutching the pages to her chest. "These, my dear, are Cupid's arrows."

Silly me.

And I thought she was looking for a killer, not a love connection.

Chapter 14

TWO HEARTS, INC.

That was the name on the letterhead along with an embossed gold logo showing a pair of Valentine hearts intertwined. Mother explained that it was apparently a dating service for wealthy widows, which I would've figured out soon enough on my own if I'd read the motto laid out in fancy script at the bottom of the page:

"Matchmaking At Its Most Discreet—For Discerning Women Over Sixty."

From the sum that Beatrice Kent had paid for a one-year membership—$20,000—I'd say "discerning" translated into "filthy freaking rich."

Business must have been good, because they had offices in Dallas, Austin, Chicago, L.A., New York, and London, according to the gilded letterhead.

My eyes skimmed through the details of the contract, noting that the $20,000 annual fee was for local matches only. Should the client request a nationwide search, the fee went up to $75,000. In the case of an international hunt for the perfect dude, the cost was a staggering $150,000.

Woo doggie.

I would've fixed up Bebe with Charlie Tompkins for free.

"I had a feeling I'd find something incriminating in Bebe's personal files," Mother told me as we settled in the kitchen, dusk falling outside the window. "We used to joke that anything we didn't want our husbands to come across we could stow away in our closets, a place they would never dare to venture."

"You hid things from Daddy?"

She patted my hand and said, with a sigh and a heavy dose of condescension, "Dear, dear Andrea. You always were one for fairy tales."

So I liked to imagine there was a "happily ever after." Was that a crime? And Mother and Daddy's marriage had seemed straight out of a storybook, at least to this child's eyes.

Call me naïve, but I'd never dreamed I'd hear her all but confess to keeping secrets from my father. I had figured they'd shared absolutely everything, and learning otherwise gave me a funny feeling. It's not that I was wide-eyed enough to believe couples didn't keep secrets— please, it was my usual M.O.—but I'd thought my parents were different. Sure, there were things I held back from Malone. In fact, we'd made a pact not to discuss past relationships, for starters. But Brian and I were still in the fetal stage of our partnership. Mother and Daddy had always seemed to operate as one, at least in my selective memory.

"Yoo hoo, Andrea?" She waved her fingers in front of my face. "Pay attention when I'm talking to you."

"The papers from the dating service," I said, remembering where we'd left off, despite the momentary distraction. "You found them in her closet."

"Well, I checked Bebe's office first, though there wasn't much left of her paperwork. But I was fairly certain they hadn't dug into her hatboxes, and I was right." Cissy spread the pages relating to Two Hearts across the table, having pushed aside the pile of mail she'd bundled up for Bebe's lawyer—the junk mail had gone in the trash. "I had to believe there was more of a connection than the glasses by the sink, and my instincts were on target."

Where did I hit "Rewind"? She'd already lost me for the second time within a couple of minutes.

"Connection? Right about what? Did Bebe tell you that she'd paid big bucks for someone to find her a man?"

Mother slipped off her pointy specs, setting them on the table. She rubbed her eyes, her drawl slow with fatigue as she responded, "No, Bebe never uttered a word about it. I knew she was itching to socialize more, and I don't mean lunching with the ladies or chairing committees. She missed Homer tremendously, and I sensed she didn't want to live out the rest of her life alone. She'd made comments about how hard it was for women of our ilk to find suitable men, but she never uttered a word about signing up with a matchmaker. Perhaps she'd thought I'd disapprove." She pursed her lips, shook her head. "I'm not surprised she kept it to herself, because Sarah Lee didn't tell me, either."

"Sarah Lee?" That had to be the connection I'd missed, but I was still short of putting two and two together. "What did Mrs. Sewell have to do with this Two Hearts business?"

"Oh, drat, I must've forgotten to show you another bit of correspondence," she said—hardly the first instance she'd held something back from me—retrieving her faux leather purse and rooting around inside it. "I guess it slipped my mind, what with all the excitement this morning in Annabelle's office."

Why did it seem there was a steady stream of things she "forgot to mention"? Wasn't Batman supposed to fill in Robin before they slid down the Bat-pole and raced off for Gotham?

I was beginning to think ours was a seriously unequal partnership. More the Road Runner and Wile E. Coyote than the Caped Crusaders, and I was the one that the anvil kept flattening.

"Ah, here it is. It was among the mail in Sarah Lee's box yesterday."

The purloined letters, I thought.

She pushed a business-size envelope toward me, which I dutifully picked up, the flap already opened. It was addressed to Sarah Lee Sewell and postmarked that Thursday. The return address read only: T.H., INC.

Discreet, as promised, I thought, noting the company was located on Turtle Creek. Posh real estate, to be sure.

I eased out a folded set of papers and flattened them, carefully looking them over.

There again was the Two Hearts letterhead with the gold logo and the now-familiar motto about discreet fix-ups for discerning women over sixty. Though this was no contract. It appeared to be a customer-satisfaction survey, asking questions like, "Did you find your match(es) well suited to your educational background, cultural interests, and socioeconomic standing?" and "Did your match(es) approach your social engagement in an appropriate way (i.e., respecting any suggestions you made, behaving in a respectful manner)?"

My own heart clip-clopped merrily, thinking this Two Hearts business was the perfect distraction for Cissy. If she poked her nose into her friends' love lives, it surely couldn't hurt anyone, and it would keep her busy until Dr. Finch got the results of Sarah Lee's blood tests, at which point we could both pack up and go home, even if Cissy felt disappointed by the outcome.

I refolded the pages and slipped them back in the envelope, trying hard not to smile. "Wow, so neither one ever said anything to you about this?"

"Not a peep." Cissy pouted and plucked at her nylon pants.

I could tell she was upset at being left out. She knew Bebe slept in the buff and that Sarah Lee didn't leave the house without her lipstick intact, but she wasn't privy to the fact that her friends had started dating again after all those years.

"Maybe they were too embarrassed to let anyone in on it," I said to make her feel better. "I mean, they were both in their early seventies, right? Why would anyone want to hook up at that age, anyhow? It's hard enough when you're young and gravity hasn't started dragging things toward the floor."

"What did you say?" Cissy's chin snapped up, her eyes narrowed like a Disney villain. The kohl-pencil lines had smudged into gray-black bruises, adding to her angry look. I braced myself for the rant that was sure to follow, uncertain of what I'd done until she rubbed my nose in it.

"The wrong thing?" I offered, as it was obvious.
Gulp.

"For heaven's sake, Andrea, just because Bebe and Sarah weren't twenty-five doesn't mean they didn't have the same feelings younger women do. We all want to be loved by someone, don't we? We appreciate a warm word and gentle touch now and then, even if our parts aren't so pert as they used to be."

"I didn't mean that older women don't deserve to find love again." I scrambled for an apology, cursing my propensity toward verbal diarrhea. "It's just that Bebe and Sarah Lee were both married for *so* long before their husbands died. Isn't that more than most of us ever get? Shouldn't that be enough?"

"So you think losing a spouse should turn us into nuns?"

Hail, Mary! Had I said anything about nuns?

I stared at my mother, less surprised that she was twisting everything I said into something critical and more astonished by her use of the word "us," wondering what that implied . . . if it implied anything at all. I couldn't imagine her being less than faithful to my father. She still wore her engagement ring and wedding band. In fact, I'd never seen her without them in the dozen years since his death.

But she didn't elaborate, and I didn't ask.

Accepting that she'd kept things from Daddy was one thing. But I sure as shooting did *not* want to know about her love life, if she even had one. I preferred to believe she'd stayed true to my father, particularly considering the way she got on my case about being a "good girl" with Malone. Or did the rules not apply beyond a certain age? I'd have to brush up on Amy Vanderbilt, see if she had a chapter on double standards.

"I'm sorry," I told her. "You're right. Everyone's entitled to seek a soul mate, at any stage of life."

"Apology accepted."

And, thankfully, that was that.

"I wonder"—Mother tapped her fingers on the Two Hearts contract—"if there's a way to find out what gentlemen they'd gone out with and when? If Bebe had a dinner engagement on Wednesday, and if Sarah Lee had dressed up for a tête-à-tête on Friday evening, then it seems likely each had plans to meet with someone the nights they died. Perhaps, whoever called on them was the last to see them alive." She reached across the table, grabbing my hand. "What if it's the same person, and he's the one who killed them?"

A heartwarming thought, indeed.

If Mother had her way, Two Hearts, Inc., might want to go with a plug from Jack the Ripper.

"I saw a computer in Bebe's office," I said, recalling the PC on the desk upstairs. "She may have used some kind of calendar software for her appointments. If she doesn't have a password, I can get in and see what's there. I can check out the Two Hearts Web site while I'm at it."

"Perfect!" Mother smiled. "Annabelle has asked Housekeeping to let me into Sarah Lee's tomorrow, so I'll search for a schedule or day planner and any further correspondence with Two Hearts. We'll get to the bottom of this in no time, Andrea, I know it!"

I started to get up, but she waved me back into my seat.

"Andrea, darlin', where's the fire?" she drawled, a subtle warning that I wasn't going anywhere.

"Don't you want me to check out Bebe's computer files?"

"Isn't it a little late for that? Surely it can wait until morning."

Though the window to the backyard revealed a purple sky and the crescent of a rising moon, the clock on the wall showed only half-past seven. That was still plenty early in my book.

"Sure, it can wait," I told her. Heck, this wasn't *my* Sherlock Holmes fantasy; it was hers.

"I'm suddenly ravenous, and I imagine you are, too, aren't you, sugar?"

My definition of "ravenous" was entirely different from Cissy's. To me, it meant, "I'm so hungry, I could eat a horse!" To my mother, it implied, "I'm so hungry I could eat a dinner salad with dressing on the side!"

Actually, a salad wasn't a bad idea.

"I could go for something," I admitted. It had been a while since that peanut butter and jelly sandwich. "You didn't skip lunch did you?"

"Heavens, no." She scooted out of her chair and stood behind it, gripping the head-rail so that the bling on her fingers winked. "As a matter of fact, I went on over to the Manor for the tail-end of brunch, so I could practice bein' the new me!" She let go of the chair and did a little "ta-da" pose. "I was fabulous, if I must say so myself. Academy Award performance."

"Great, I'll tell Spielberg you're free when this gig is over in a few days." I rolled my eyes. "Did Dr. Finch and Patsy see you?"

"I didn't even see them."

"What about your bridge pals?"

She shrugged. "I strolled right past two of them, and they didn't bat an eyelash. Believe me, I did nothing to draw attention to myself."

Except donning an animal-print sweat suit, rhinestone studded boots, and a wig that could've belonged to Little Richard.

"I did meet your friend Mabel Pinkston," she said.

"My friend?" I laughed, thinking of the lady in pink who thought she was Dr. Ruth. "I hardly know her."

"Well, I feel like we're on the road to becoming best buddies," Mother gloated. "She latched onto me the moment her radar detected fresh meat, as

though she were my personal welcoming committee. She sat and talked my ear off while I ate, asking was I widowed, did I have children, and on
and on."

"I'm afraid to hear what you told her," I said,
wondering what kind of history she'd given
Miriam Ferguson.

"I mixed truth with a few minor fibs, telling her
I was widowed, though unfortunately I'd been
barren and unable to conceive my own child, despite painful attempts at fertility treatments."

Those were minor fibs? I thought and rolled my
eyes. *Oh, Lordy.*

"But," she continued, "I did say I had a distant
branch from my family tree here in Dallas, which
is what lured me from the backwoods of Podunk,
Arkansas, in order to live out my Golden Years in
surroundings more pleasant than the tarpaper
shack I used to call home."

"Lovely image."

"I aim to please." Her drawl turned thick, in
what I'd begun to think of as "the voice of
Miriam." "Oh, and I mentioned my sweet little
niece who was helping me move in."

"That's me!" I perked up at the mention.

"Though a distant relation, taken to my bosom
like the closest of kin, particularly since you so
eerily resemble my dead baby sister, Bonita, may
she rest in peace."

Bonita? I nearly choked. Where did that come
from?

"How did she die?" I couldn't resist inquiring.

"Runaway cable car in San Francisco. Lord, but

it was ugly," she said and clicked tongue against teeth, even throwing in a convincing flinch.

"Um, Mother, I think you've been watching too many soaps."

"It's our cover, sweetie. All good detectives have them. It's not the same as telling *real* lies," she assured me.

I'm sure the pastor at Highland Park Presbyterian might disagree with her on that one, but I'm no expert on morality.

"Anything else I should know?" I asked, wondering how I was going to remember all these tall tales Cissy was pulling out of her hat. Or out of her "teased to within an inch of its life" wig, as the case may be.

"Let me think . . . well, as best I can, what with my tummy howling." She wandered over to the refrigerator and peered in, shaking her head at the meager contents and obviously getting sidetracked. "We're gonna have to call over to Simon David and have them deliver. Bebe must've never eaten in. Which reminds me." She shut the fridge door and turned around, flattening her palm against her chest. "The fresh salmon at brunch was to die for, Andrea. As pink as a grapefruit and so tender. If I'd had a baggie, I would've brought some back for you."

"Thanks, anyway," I said, not a big fan of salmon, thinking this persona of Miriam was starting to take over my mother's body, as I could never imagine the Cissy who'd groomed me for deb-dom so much as contemplating bringing home a doggie bag. Not for a human being much less for Fido.

"Oh"—she clapped—"I did ask Mabel to keep her eyes open, in case any of the residents had eligible grandsons, since my adorable citified niece was on the market."

For crud's sake.

"I have a boyfriend, Mother." As if she'd forgotten.

"But do you have one of *these*?" She pointed at her third left finger, to the emerald-cut diamond engagement ring that glittered there and nestled against her wedding band—the real stuff that Daddy had given her, not any of her borrowed pieces from QVC.

Moo, I thought, unbought cow that I'd become.

"No," she said, when I didn't respond, "I didn't think you did."

Tempted as I was to stick out my tongue, I refrained.

Here I was ditching my real-life to play sidekick to the Tacky Sleuth, and she was taking potshots at my relationship with Brian? Who could blame me if I came out swinging?

Batter up!

I smacked my palms on the table, getting her full attention. "Since I have no intentions of getting myself fixed up with anyone's grandson, I'll just have to tell Mabel Pinkston all the sordid bits you left out, including why I'm actually unavailable."

She screwed up her face. "What on earth are you talkin' about? What sordid bits?"

"The fact that you, my wacky, backwoods, oh-so-distant Aunt Miriam, must've had one of your recurring blackouts, resulting from all those years of drinking booze from your homemade still, as you obviously forgot that I'm already promised to the son of an Alabama farmer to whom you traded me for a pregnant sow, not only because you have a serious sorghum craving but because you felt so guilty at pushing your baby sister onto the cable car tracks that you can hardly bear to have me around and see Bonita's likeness in my eyes."

Ha! I finished, out of breath, and slightly buzzed. Maybe I should write a romance novel.

"Well, I never!" Mother stared at me for a long moment after. "Blackouts? Homemade liquor? Traded for a sow? Sorghum craving?" She shook a finger. "You, Andrea Blevins Kendricks, are very, very naughty."

"I learned from the master."

"Ah, you must mean your father. He had a gift for gab, among other things." She smiled, but it was a wobbly effort—heck, she pretty much wobbled all over—and I shot to my feet.

"Mother?" I caught her arm to steady her, and she sighed.

"Must be a dip in my blood sugar," she told me. All right. Playtime was over.

"What say we order in something to eat and then get to bed early? It's been a long day for us both." She poked at her wig, making a face. "My head's hurtin' from the bobby pins besides, and I'd sure love to wash my face and get out of this outfit. I do believe I'm getting a rash from all this nylon."

Beneath the layers of Mary Kay, she looked plumb tuckered out, and I wasn't feeling very chipper either.

"Food, then rest," I agreed, knowing we would live to sleuth another day, God willing.

I followed her upstairs, lugging her suitcase, to get her settled in the guest room with the double bed. It was a no-brainer that I'd take the foldout sofa in Bebe's office, which meant we'd share the connecting bath.

Oh, goody, I'd get to experience a glimpse of the sorority life I'd missed by going to art school in Chicago.

Not surprisingly, neither of us wanted to sleep in Bebe's gargantuan sleigh bed, even with clean linens.

As I headed back downstairs to order salads from Chef Jean's kitchen—one of the perks of living at Belle Meade was twenty-four-hour "room" service—I heard the rush of water as Mother hit the shower. By the time she had scrubbed the coats of paint off her God-given face and had her salon-given blond hair wrapped in a towel, I'd have arranged for something to eat.

Using instructions tacked to the refrigerator with a magnet, I phoned the dining hall at the Manor House and placed an order with a woman who carefully asked about food allergies before she suggested the spinach salad with strawberries. Sounded good to me. She mentioned a chocolate bread pudding that was the featured dessert of the day, and I figured Mother and I could both use a shot of sugar in our systems. After repeating the address on Magnolia Court, she told me to expect the food in about fifteen minutes.

No wonder there was a waiting list to move in

here. I couldn't even get Pizza Hut to deliver that quickly.

While I waited, I scrounged around Bebe's kitchen, retrieving a couple place mats and enough flatware to set the table. Though the fridge didn't have much in it, there was bottled water, half a gallon of fortified orange juice, and a nearly dry carton of soymilk with an expiration date of last week (sort of like Bebe).

For some reason, I'd expected to find the remains of a bottle of wine, though perhaps I was looking in the wrong place.

If Mother was right about a mysterious visitor showing up at Bebe's house on Wednesday evening and sharing a glass of wine, then where was that particular bottle o' *vino*? I didn't see anything open in the fridge.

Pulling wide the cabinet underneath the sink, I slid out the wastebasket, gingerly probing past an empty cereal box, wadded paper towels, and assorted discards. But no bottle.

I trekked outside, located Bebe's garbage-can-on-wheels, and plucked off the lid. Trash pickup must've been recent, maybe in the days before she'd died, because there was nothing in it except something sticky glued to the bottom. I couldn't find a recycle bin.

If I put any stock in Mother's theory—and that was debatable—then the missing bottle fit. Perhaps Bebe hadn't lived long enough to toss it, which meant someone else had disposed of it, which implied there was something fishy, some reason not to leave it behind.

Like traces of a poison, I mused. *But what?* Something that couldn't be easily detected, or Dr. Finch would've seen the effects on the corpse and would never have declared Bebe's death to be natural. Ditto Sarah Lee's.

Or would he?

I thought of Arnold Finch and his pompous demeanor, his dark but chilly good looks, and the way he'd avoided shaking my hand. He'd rubbed me wrong from the start, but Annabelle swore he had the Belle Meade ladies swooning over his bedside manner. Still, he'd be in the perfect position to cover up a murder, wouldn't he?

Muhaha! Only the Shadow knows!

Mother was right. It was late, and my mind was spinning into overdrive.

Whistling to ward off the evil spirits, I meandered back into the kitchen, dead-bolting the door behind me. My pulse slowed down as I washed my hands, though I had to hurriedly wipe them dry on my jeans at the chime of the doorbell, knowing it wasn't the Avon lady.

Food, glorious food!

As I started for the door, I heard Mother call out, "I'll get it, sugar."

My initial reaction: be my guest.

On second thought: what if someone from the Belle Meade staff should see her looking like Cissy and not Miriam? It could send Mother's plans up in flames right from the get-go.

What to do, what to do?

Only one thing came to mind fast enough.

I pulled an Annabelle.

"Nooo," I cried and raced from the kitchen, jetting through the living room and into the foyer, catching Mother just as she twisted the doorknob and pulled.

I threw myself between her and the door in a body block, shutting it hard with my booty before any damage was done.

Cissy jumped back and tugged at the lapels of her pale pink bathrobe, matching slippers on her feet, and a towel fastened turban-like around her head. Devoid of the thick layers of makeup, her skin had a pearly sheen, her puzzled blue eyes blinking at me below perfectly arched brows.

"Andrea, my word, are you on drugs?"

"For Pete's sake, Mother," I snapped and turned to peer out the peephole, spotting Mabel Pinkston standing on the porch with several foil containers in hand. I swung around, pressing my back against the door panels, as Mabel punched the bell again, trilling, "Hello? Is everything all right in there? I've brought your dinner!"

Cissy stood scowling at me, her hands on her hips. "She has food, Andrea. Aren't you going to let her in?"

"Do you realize how you look, *Miriam*?" I hissed, drawing out the name like an accusation.

"Well, forgive me for not donning something more formal . . . wait a second. Miriam, did you say? Oh . . . ah . . . oops." She put her hands up to the twist of towel on her head, felt for the missing glasses on her nose.

"Mind ducking into the kitchen?" I suggested,

unless she wanted to pull a *Mrs. Doubtfire* and stuff her face into the meringue of a pie—if we'd had a pie with meringue, that is.

"Gotcha, partner," she said, giving me a wink and pulling the imaginary trigger of a gun shaped like her fingers.

At least she didn't tell me to just put my lips together and blow.

I waited until she'd slipped out of sight, all the while Mabel banged on the door with her fist, calling, "Yoo hoo? I know you're in there."

Drawing in a deep breath, I composed myself, before I flipped the deadbolt and swept open the door. "Hello." I smiled with all the sincerity of a used-car salesman. "Mrs. Pinkston, right? So lovely to see you again."

"You do look familiar, child." She squinted at me as she held a stack of aluminum boxes in her arms.

"We spoke yesterday," I reminded her, "at the reception for Bebe Kent. I didn't properly introduce myself." I stuck out my hand. "I'm Andrea Kendricks. My aunt Miriam Ferguson just moved in today. Well, she's not actually my aunt," I babbled on. "She's a second cousin once removed or something like that, but we're related just the same. I'll be visiting for a bit, until she's settled in."

"Miriam Ferguson, yes, of course. I had the nicest chat with her at brunch this afternoon. Snappy dresser." Mabel made an "mmm" sound. "Ah, sure, I remember you, sister. Warned you off the oysters, didn't I?" She looked me over quite thoroughly, penciled brows knitted. "But didn't you say you'd come to Belle Meade with your mother? Where is she in all this?"

"My mother?" *Think, Andy, think!* "Well, you see, she felt compassionate enough about Miriam's circumstances down in Arkansas to want to move her to Belle Meade, but she's not exactly on good terms with the Ferguson side of the family, if you get my drift." I leaned in conspiratorily. "A long-standing feud over my grandpappy's will. Set everyone off like the Hatfields and McCoys."

"Oh, sister, if I had a nickel for every time I've heard that one," Mabel said, craning her neck to peer around me into the house, obviously waiting for an invitation to come in.

Which she was not going to get.

"Geez, what am I thinking? Let me get those," I offered, indicating the foil containers she held. She reluctantly unloaded them into my hands. "And thanks so much for bringing them over, Mrs. Pinkston. It's nearly eight o'clock. Isn't that awfully late for a part-timer to be working? Annabelle . . . Ms. Meade . . . she mentioned that you lived off the grounds."

"I do at that." She crossed her arms and shrugged. "But it's no problem going back and forth. I love my work. I'd do anything for Annabelle. I don't mind sticking around after I've punched out on the clock. Besides, when I get home, it's to empty rooms. And it's not much fun talking to yourself, is it? Sometimes even the plants don't care a fig what you have to say."

"Maybe you need different plants."

"Hell, I end up killing 'em all anyway, so they get theirs," she said and forced a smile, rocking on her tiptoes to peek past my shoulder.

Could I have felt any guiltier for not asking her to join us? But I couldn't, not with Mother out of disguise in the kitchen.

"Look, Mabel, I'd invite you inside, but we've had such a tiring day," I finally admitted, because I didn't know how else to get rid of her. "I'm sure we'll be seeing you around plenty. I'll be working in the library a little while I'm here, big ol' book-worm that I am."

"All right then, I'll see you around, sister," she said with a jerk of her chin. "I'm here rain or shine." She stood on the stoop for a minute after, the moonlight deepening the lines in her face, and I wanted to reach out to her, to drag her in where she had people to talk to, not plants.

But I didn't move.

She turned and stepped off the porch, though I didn't see a car parked in front.

"Do you need a lift home?" I shouted after her.

"No, thanks, child," she called over her shoulder and gave me a finger wiggle. "I take the bus. Know the routes like the back of my hand."

Well, okay.

I nudged the door closed with my shoulder, shifting the food containers to slip the deadbolt and reset the lock on the knob.

Phew. That was close.

"Did she catch me?" Mother asked as I brought the containers into the kitchen, and I shook my head, telling her, "No." At least, I didn't think so.

After Cissy's delighted "ooh" when she glimpsed our order, we ate in relative silence. We were both too pooped and talked-out to find much more to say. Besides, the spinach salad with strawberries (and strips of Gouda, pecans, and lime juice) was beyond amazing, as was the chocolate bread pudding. If that wasn't a well-balanced meal, I didn't know what was.

By the time we'd finished, Mother's turbaned head had dropped perilously close to her plate, so I promised to take care of the trash if she'd go up-stairs, dry her hair, and hit the sack.

"Sleep tight, don't let the bed bugs bite."

"Thanks, sugar," she said and brushed a strand of mousy-brown from my face, tucking it behind my ear. "For seeing my side of things."

I scrounged up a smile for her benefit, so pleased to be looking at her again and not her alter ego, Miriam. Made me forget all the times when I'd wished for another mother, someone who wasn't so perfect and who didn't expect so much from me, since I was decidedly imperfect (and al-ways would be).

"Goodnight, Andrea."

" 'Night."

Then she was gone, the kitchen suddenly so still without her. Not even a dripping faucet or ticking clock to distract me.

I sank back down into the chair and set my chin in my hands.

My head ached, saturated as it was with Mother's accusations about rinsed-out glasses, missing lipstick, frilly nightgowns, and an up-scale matchmaking service that may have hooked up her friends with a killer date.

I chewed on my lower lip, wishing Malone were there, so we could hash over things.

This was going to be trickier than I'd imagined.

Looming ahead were at least several days of pretending to be Miriam Ferguson and her distantly related niece; acting out a real-life version of *Clue* and trying to find out who offed Mrs. Peacock in the library with a candlestick.

Boy, oh, boy.

I made myself stand and gather up the remnants of our dinner, disposing of the foil containers in the trash and saving the water bottles to recycle. Before I turned out the lights, I picked up the documents relating to Two Hearts, retrieved my suitcase from the foyer, and hauled everything upstairs to Bebe's office, where I'd be hanging my hat temporarily.

I had a few things to do before I could rest, despite Mother's advice to let it wait until morning. We were staying in a strange house where a woman had recently died. I figured sleep wouldn't come easily that night.

As exhausted as I was, I could still feel the tingle of adrenaline, the prickle of "what ifs" raising goose bumps on my arms.

Trying to pin the tail on a possible, potential, maybe, could-be killer was a nerve-wracking business.

Had Nancy Drew ever needed Ambien to catch a few winks when she was working on a case? I had a feeling even Miss Marple put something stronger than lemon in her chamomile tea. Philip Marlowe and Sam Spade would've gone for the whiskey, no question.

As for me, I tied back my hair, splashed my face with cold water, and slipped out of my jeans and into sweatpants and an oversized Tee. I propped a pillow behind my back and sat Indian-style in Bebe's desk chair, put the keyboard in my lap, and cracked my knuckles, like a soloist preparing for a piano concerto.

Then I booted up Bebe's computer and tried not to feel guilty for whatever sins I was about to commit, starting with *Thou shalt not hack*.

Chapter 15

I woke up with my face in a puddle of drool.

Something pressed into my cheek, but I was too bleary to know—or care—what it was. Groaning, I raised my head, ever so slowly, the crick in my neck making it impossible to move my chin from right to left without a lot of wincing involved. I'd fallen asleep with my contacts in, and they stuck uncomfortably to my corneas, my vision hazy until I blinked a couple dozen times and loosened things up.

The computer tower at my feet still whirred quietly, and shooting stars zipped across the screensaver. I couldn't remember if I'd dreamed, though I had a vague recollection of glimpsing my mother in that hideous wig and scary eyeglasses leaning over me.

It's a wonder I hadn't awakened screaming.

I wiped the slobber from my chin and glanced across the keyboard to the spot where I'd reclined my head atop a legal pad before I'd nodded off. An uncapped marker lay across my nearly illegible scribbles, and I raised a hand gingerly to my cheek, afraid of what I'd see on my skin when I made it to the bathroom mirror.

Bugger, I thought. *Please, don't let that marker be permanent.*

I'd stayed up well into the wee hours, digging into the files on Bebe's computer and sorting through scattered pieces of her thoroughly organized life. Skipping some much-needed shut-eye had been worth it and would save Mother a trip to the dating service (and the $20,000 membership fee).

Once I'd unlocked the user password—kept in Bebe's desktop Rolodex under *P*—I'd gone straight for the downloaded files and hit pay dirt immediately.

Bebe had stored plenty of Two Hearts-related files on her hard drive, including several PDF newsletters touting their success rate ("Over 60 percent of Two Hearts' matches have resulted in wedded bliss for discerning clients"), a couple of postdate surveys like the one Mother had found in Sarah Lee's mail, and a copy of Bebe's membership questionnaire, an encyclopedic collection of her likes and dislikes, personal history, and romantic expectations that ran on and on for twenty-one pages.

As my neighbor Charlie would've said, "*Woo doggie.*"

Also stored in her shared files was a letter from Two Hearts, which I'd printed out and read again for at least the tenth time.

"Dear Mrs. Kent,

After comparing your questionnaire with those

provided by the gentlemen in our database, we have selected those whose answers most closely reflected your own. Photographs of each gentleman have been attached as JPEG files, and contact information is being given to you, so that the ultimate decision on whether or not to pursue a particular prospective match is placed squarely in your hands.

It is our most heartfelt wish that you find someone who can fill your life with the joy and companionship you desire . . . *blah blah blah.*"

My eyes skimmed down to the names of Bebe's proposed beaus, though I pretty much had the whole thing memorized at that point:

- Tom Walcher, 69, a retired engineering consultant and part-owner of a winery in Grapevine, Texas, who enjoyed crime fiction, liked to travel to mystery conventions, and ultimately dreamed of taking a whale-watching cruise to Alaska with a special someone;
- Reed Andrews, 71, Plano, TX, a former Dallas Cowboys player, retired insurance broker, and founder of a charitable organization called "Touchdowns for Teachers" that raised money for school supplies, books, and scholarships, seeking a companion who enjoyed dining out and attending sporting events;
- Stephen Lloyd Howard, 62, an Iowa farm boy, retired Naval officer, Vietnam War veteran, and former agent for the IRS who loved fishing and hunting, had three

grown children and a sister in Nebraska, and hoped to meet an old-fashioned, low-maintenance woman.

A low-maintenance woman like Bebe Kent? *Ha!* Now that was hilarious.

Still, they were quite an interesting trio, I thought, and fumbled beneath the legal pad to retrieve the pictures of Tom, Reed, and Stephen.

Tom, the wine-loving mystery fan, had a full head of dark hair, aviator glasses, a square jaw, and a warmhearted grin that revealed a slight gap between his front teeth, à la David Letterman. He wore a jacket, crisp-collared shirt and tie, looking every bit the retired engineer (minus the pocket protector). Hey, some women liked the button-down type, though I'd bet Tom donned his jeans when he was out and about his vineyard, inspecting his harvest.

Bachelor Number Two, aka Reed, sported sideburns straight out of the sixties, maybe to make up for the lack of hair on his cue-ball-smooth crown. He had puppy-dog eyes, a wide nose, and the thickest neck I'd seen this side of Warren Sapp. He balanced a meerschaum pipe on calloused fingertips, as if he were about to shove it between his sulky lips. Ah, this guy would make a worthy opponent to James Bond. We could call him *R*.

The third of Bebe's matches, Stephen, had a sun-kissed, outdoorsy appearance, with faded ginger-colored hair, a solid jaw, and broad grin that set his blue eyes atwinkle. He had his arms crossed in a way that said, "I'm dependable as a Chevy," and I noticed a wedding band on his left hand. This was surely a man with a great love in his past that he wasn't quite willing to give up just yet. Maybe not until he met that easy-to-maintain gal worthy of sharing his heart again.

I only had one major problem with the fellas.

A vintner with dreams of watching whales frolic in Alaska? An ex-pigskin pro who bought school supplies for classrooms? A Navy veteran cum farmboy who still wore his wedding band?

Come on. Really.

Not a Charlie Manson among them, so far as I could tell, which meant no carvings on their foreheads or visible tattoos of demons. None of them looked remotely like a killer. Okay, except the football player, a little.

Which actually put my mind at ease. If my mother were going to pursue these bachelors on her wild goose chase, I figured she'd be safe enough as any single woman in Big D. As long as she armed herself with Altoids and a good excuse for leaving early, she'd be prepared for anything.

I yawned, glancing at my terrible penmanship on the legal pad. I'd jotted down a few dates from Bebe's online calendar marked "Dinner" with a time and restaurant but no name, the most recent on Wednesday evening.

While Mother occupied herself with the riddle of "who was with Bebe last," I wanted to do a little fishing of my own. I hadn't yet gotten to the articles Janet had emailed about Belle Meade and the fire at the Meades' lake house. I figured I'd take them with me to the library in the afternoon, where I'd have some peace.

Jiggling the mouse, I brought up the desktop on the computer and checked the clock: twenty past eight.

Geez, I felt positively slothful.

I shuffled together the photos and the copy of the Two Hearts letter, ready to share them with Cissy. The door to the connecting bath was closed on my end, so I knocked and leaned an ear against it, twisting the knob when I heard zilch.

I went straight ahead, passing through a lingering cloud of Joy, but saw no sign of her when I stuck my head into the room where she'd slept.

The bed was neatly made, and Mother's borrowed black wig was no longer draped over a lampshade, where I'd seen it the night before.

This time, I didn't panic. My Jeep boxed in the Buick, so she couldn't have gone far on foot, not in those ugly rhinestone boots.

I put aside the photographs and letter, and I gave myself permission to take a long, hot shower in Bebe's guest bath. When I finally emerged from the steam and cleared a spot on the mirror, I could only make out a vague squiggle of black on my cheek from sleeping on the marker. It looked a little like the mark of Zorro.

Great.

After I'd dried and dressed in jeans and a clean T-shirt, I headed down to the kitchen and dropped the photographs on the table. The place echoed like a tomb. It didn't take a huge leap to realize Cissy had skipped out, and I found the answer as to where when I saw a note stuck to the refrigerator:

"Got up early and went over to Sarah Lee's so Elvira could let me in while they cleaned. I called Sandy and asked her to have Simon David deliver whatever she usually orders and to put it on my tab. They'll deliver this morning so don't move! See you soon. Love, M."

Stick around. Poo.

I crumpled the paper in my fist as I considered walking to Sarah Lee Sewell's instead of waiting for the danged groceries. With my luck, they wouldn't arrive for hours, like the AC guy who always promised to come sometime between eight and five and showed up at 4:40.

Well, I had nothing better to do, did I?

The doorbell took that instant to chime, putting a quick end to my internal grumbling.

When I opened up, I saw the Simon David truck parked at the curb. On the stoop stood two pimple-faced young men, balancing carton stacked upon carton so they had to peek around the cardboard corners to see ahead of them.

"Order for, um, Mrs. Ferguson?" one asked, his voice strained, and I hoped he wouldn't get a hernia.

"Come on in," I said and waved them in. "Follow me."

I led the way into the kitchen so they could deposit their loads on the center island. *Geez, Louise, but Sandy's order would feed a family of five for a month!* I wasn't even sure the fridge would hold everything.

The delivery boys began unpacking, but I put a halt to that, telling them I'd do it myself, thank you very much. When I herded them to the front door, they lingered on the stoop, hanging back with expectant smiles, and I realized they wanted a tip. If Mother had been around, she could've peeled a Benjamin off the stack in her wallet. I, on the other hand, rarely had more than a few bucks to spare.

I muttered an apology and gave them the last three dollar bills from my purse, which had them glancing at each other and frowning. I could almost read their minds: "She expects us to split this? Cheap frickin' chick."

I'd barely shut the door on them, when the bell rang again.

"Guys, that's all there is"—I started off, only to clamp my mouth shut when I saw who it was.

Patsy Finch.

The doctor's wife had her fair hair pulled back with a blue headband to match the blue shirt beneath her white lab coat.

What the heck was she doing here? Was it a professional visit?

I didn't see a welcome basket loaded with prescriptions in her hand, just a large manila envelope.

"Good morning . . . Andrea, isn't it?" she said, watching me carefully (or maybe I was paranoid). "Is Mrs. Ferguson in?"

"Well, hi, Patsy. Call me Andy, and, no, my aunt Miriam has gone out for a bit." I ushered her in. "If you wouldn't mind coming into the kitchen, I've got a mess of groceries to unload. I think my dear aunt aimed to feed everyone on the block, or she's hoarding in case we're quarantined with the bird flu."

"Some people are like squirrels storing nuts for the winter, eh? Arnold finds that often in children of parents who lived through the Great Depression."

"Right, like squirrels," I said, though it was more like a Highland Park matron used to having someone else keep the pantry stocked and panicking when she found it lacking. *"What, no water crackers? No Brie? How am I supposed to live in such deprivation?"*

"Go ahead and have a seat," I instructed, gesturing in the general direction of the table and chairs. "Would you like something to drink? There's bottled water and orange juice, at least."

"I'm fine." She glanced at the watch on her wrist. "I need to get to the clinic in a few minutes besides so I can open up the pharmacy at nine."

"Was there a particular reason you wanted to see Miriam?" I asked and began to rummage through the contents of the boxes, withdrawing plastic bags containing fruits and vegetables in every color of the rainbow. Bread, bagels, cheeses, and eggs soon followed. I pulled a bagel from its wrapping and took as big a bite as I could fit in my mouth. Didn't offer one to Patsy, though. Rude of me, wasn't it?

"As a matter of fact," Patsy lectured, "your aunt never filled out the medical questionnaire that Annabelle always requires of our residents before they move in. We like to have copies of physicians' records, and a list of medications and allergies for any newcomers, as well as their health insurance information so we can get them into the system right away. We have a centralized database for all

that. As I'm in charge of the pharmacy, I'll coordi-
nate their prescriptions to make sure everything's
proper and all refills are promptly dispensed."

She waved the manila envelope at me until I
looked over. "I've brought the standard packet, including a release to send her primary care doctor
so that we can get her record up-to-date as soon as
possible. Arnold will want to set up an appointment, too, for an initial consultation since he'll be
assuming her basic care, and he'll want to ask her
if she has a DNR order on the books, just in case."

"DNR?" Was that like a DUI? Which Mother
most certainly did not have on or off the books.
Or maybe it was like the DAR, of which she was
a proud member.

"It means Do Not Resuscitate," Patsy explained,
and I swallowed hard, not liking the sound of that,
especially on an empty stomach. "It lets us know
not to go to medical extremes to revive her, should
she stop breathing."

*What a delightful thought, Dr. Kervorkian, thanks so
much for sharing.*

"I'll make sure she gets the paperwork." I uttered yet another fib. Because I knew Mother was
never going to fill out any forms or provide her
medical records.

"I could wait a bit, eh? I was hoping to take care
of it myself," Patsy suggested, and I busied myself,
stuffing food willy-nilly in the fridge.

"No need," I assured her, putting away a key
lime pie in the freezer. *Key lime pie?* Was that a
sugar staple in Mother's house, like Ding-Dongs
were in mine? "I don't know when she'll be back.
It may be hours."

"Did she go to Jazzercise? That's a popular class at this time of the morning. Girl who teaches it, Wendi, has a big following. I could track her down there."

"Jazzercise?" *Mother working up a sweat?* Not in this lifetime. "Could be, Patsy, I don't really know. She was gone when I woke up, which wasn't all that long ago." I wasn't about to tell her that "Miriam" was really at Sarah Lee Sewell's, poking around in her drawers.

"Well, hello, boys!" I heard Patsy chirp.

Too much coffee this morning? Or did Patsy see dead people?

"Mind if I ask what these are for?" she asked, and I realized she'd spread out the photos of the three men from Two Hearts that Bebe had downloaded. "Nice-looking fellows. Are they friends of your aunt's?"

Rats.

I'd forgotten about those, what with the delivery boys showing up. I figured it wouldn't look good to race across the room and snatch them from under her nose, would it?

"Oh, yeah, those fellows"—I cleared my throat—"well, actually, I found the pictures in a folder for one of Bebe's charities. They're part of a calendar called, uh, 'Prime Tenderloin' that Bebe was putting together to, um, raise money for the . . . er, Cattle Ranchers for PETA fund," I made up as I went along, finding the lies came easier the more I told them.

"I get it, like those 'Calendar Girls' from Britain. Even had a movie made about them."

"Yes, just like that." My armpits felt damp.

Maybe I wasn't cut out for deceit. Mother made it look so easy. "Um, by any chance, Patsy, do you recognize them? Ever see them around Belle Meade? I was wondering if they were residents. I'd sure like to hook one of them up with my aunty. She's more than a wee bit lonely after all those years in the backwoods of Arkansas with only her still and a banjo."

She studied the faces, tipping her head this way and that. "No, sorry." She glanced up with a shrug. "I can't say that I have, and I'd remember them, I think. Considering the dearth of eligible fellows around here, except for poor Henry."

"Oh, I heard 'poor Henry' does all right for himself."

Patsy Finch giggled, her cheeks a bright pink, so she looked positively girlish and about as guile-less as a Girl Scout. Until she got up from the table and approached, slapping down her brown enve-lope and planting her palms flat on the granite is-land, looking as long-faced as Mr. Ed.

"Mind if I ask you something rather personal, Andy?" she said.

"How personal?" I flinched.

"You weren't with your aunt at Mrs. Sewell's yesterday, you were with your mother, right? If I'm not mistaken, she's the pretty blonde who called the police and had such a row with Annabelle in Sarah Lee's kitchen. Though I heard something about a family feud. So your mother and aunt aren't speaking?"

"That's right, which is why I volunteered to get Miriam settled and Mother wants nothing more to do with her." I had picked up the bagel to take another bite, but quickly set it down and wiped my hands on my pants.

"I see." Patsy stepped away from the center island and stuck her hands in the pockets of her lab coat. Small as they were, they disappeared entirely. "It's just odd, that's all."

"What's odd?" My heart skidded along my ribcage. "My relatives?" I laughed nervously. "Because I'd have to agree with you there."

She shook her head. "It's not that, Andy. It's something more practical. Annabelle must have told you that we've got a lengthy waiting list of suitable candidates who applied months ago to live here, even before we opened this location. When a resident . . . vacates the premises," she put it diplomatically, "whoever's at the top of the list gets first crack at the opening. Only I looked at the database this morning and didn't see Miriam Ferguson's name anywhere on it."

Is that all? More fibs, coming up!

"Well, Annabelle had a hand in that, you see," I rattled off. "She did it as a favor, seeing as how we go way back."

"To when you were campmates, right?"

"Yes."

She drew a hand from a coat pocket to scratch her chin. "That's what Annabelle said, more or less. Well, she claims she had some kind of pact with your family to take care of Mrs. Ferguson as long as she's upright."

"Annabelle's good at keeping her word." At least, I hoped so. My response seemed to satisfy Patsy, if the slow bob of her chin was any indication.

"Yes, she's very loyal, isn't she? Arnie and me . . . we'd do anything for her, for Belle Meade." Patsy lowered her voice to a whisper, adding, "Don't be upset with Annabelle, but she confessed to us both that Miriam has a rather spotty past in politics, and her late husband was in terrible trouble with the government, the poor dear. So it's understandable she's prone to acting strangely, what with all that stress she's had to live with."

Holy guacamole, Annabelle was at it, too, spinning tales that wove the real-life Miriam Amanda Wallace Ferguson's background into the fake Miriam's. Pretty soon, between, Mother, AB, and me, we'd have created enough manure to fertilize all sixty-six acres at the Dallas Arboretum.

"Miriam's, er, problems have definitely affected her more above the neck than below," I said, fighting to keep a straight face, because Patsy looked so earnest.

"Don't worry, Andy. Your aunt is in good hands here."

"What a relief."

Another peek at her wrist and then, "Ach, look at the time! I've got to get back to the clinic and open up the pharmacy. Just have Miriam drop this off as soon as she's able, then she can set up a consult with the doctor, and we'll get everything squared away."

"Great."

I walked her to the door and followed her out to the porch.

She started down the steps, before hesitating. She turned around, a finger raised to the air as if testing the wind.

"Oops, one more thing, Andy, if you wouldn't mind. Could you collect Mrs. Kent's prescription medications for me, if they haven't been thrown away? Just put them in a shoebox and drop them off at the clinic, or I can pick them up later."

"Sure," I told her. "I'll see what I can find."

I'd put "go through dead woman's medicine cabinet" on my to-do list, right after "baby-sit Mother" and "stick eyes with hot pokers."

"Thanks a bunch. We usually collect the meds ourselves and dispose of them for the family, but we've never had anyone move into the residence of a decedent so"—she hesitated—"well, fast."

"I understand." I did not want to get into another discussion with her about why the rules had been bent for Miriam.

She nodded, tipping her head and squinting at me through the brilliant morning light so I felt sure I had a hunk of bagel stuck between my teeth. "Your cheek," she said and pointed. "Bruise?" she asked.

It took a second for my brain to register what she meant.

"Oh, this?" I lifted my fingers to the spot where I'd slept on the marker. "I fell asleep at the computer and had a run-in with a pen. Looks like a Z, doesn't it? For Zorro." I pantomimed carving the letter into the air.

"Um, more like an L actually."

For loser, I thought, dropping my sword arm to my side. How fitting.

"Don't worry, I'm sure it'll wash off in a few days."

Hurrah.

"Gosh, I'd better run," she said, and she did.

I watched as she dashed across the lawn toward a three-wheeled cycle parked at the curb, behind where the Simon David truck had stopped earlier. The thing was rigged with baskets and a bell, too, I realized, as she jangled it several times before pedaling down the street and out of my line of vision.

Nice enough lady, I thought, wondering why there was something about her I didn't trust, much the same way I didn't trust her husband.

"The Finches worked with you in Austin, Annabelle?"

"Yes, but they're not the only ones. I couldn't have opened in Dallas without their help . . . It's not like they had anything to do with what happened."

They knew about the threatened lawsuits, and Patsy herself brought up loyalty and how they'd "do anything for" Annabelle.

I wondered if that included murder.

Chapter 16

 If I were writing an official report on my undercover work as Mother's sidekick, I would have summed up the rest of the morning something like this:

9:15 a.m. Ate two bagels with raspberry cream cheese, chased down with a glass of fresh-squeezed juice from Simon David.

9:40 a.m. Brushed teeth, gathered up the bachelor photos from Two Hearts and the articles Janet had e-mailed, stuffed in purse.

9:50 a.m. Emptied the contents of Bebe's medicine cabinet into a gallon-sized plastic baggie (don't ask if that had felt creepy), also stuffed into purse.

10:00 a.m. Locked up the house but couldn't deadbolt the front door (still no key) and drove over to Sarah Lee Sewell's.

Trés exciting, no?

Well, no. In fact, it sounded positively boh-ring.

If my initial twenty-four-hours at Belle Meade had provided me with a peek into the *Lifestyles of the Chic and Shamus*, then I'm glad my guidance counselor at Hockaday had steered me toward art and graphics. Besides, I don't think I had the right equipment to be a real private dick.

After only one wrong turn, my Jeep sniffed out the route to Sarah Lee Sewell's place. The front door stood wide open, accommodating a fat black hose that emanated from the rear end of a bright yellow van marked, AAAA CARPET SERVICE, parked in the driveway. A white Ford Escort sat at the curb and had graceful curly-cued letters identifying it as BELLE MEADE HOUSEKEEPING.

I was relieved that Mother hadn't been at Sarah Lee's house without adult supervision. She still had me worried, and that nagging concern for her mental health wouldn't abate until she was back home on Beverly Drive, with Sandy Beck hovering over her (the usual routine).

The powerful whir of the carpet cleaner hit my ears full blast as I stepped through the front door. A woman in a bright yellow T-shirt and cap—to match the van, of course—propelled the machine around the living room, the furniture pushed to the fringes, some pieces stacked atop others. If I had yelled bloody murder, she wouldn't have noticed.

A glance into the kitchen revealed another woman at work in blue jeans and a white T-shirt, hair tucked under a kerchief and headphones plugged into her ears. Her compact body swayed as she mopped the tiled floor with great vigor.

Elvira, from Belle Meade's Housekeeping department, I figured, by sheer process of elimination.

I began to tiptoe across the slick tiles, trying to

get her attention, when she saw me and threw up a hand like a traffic cop.

So I stopped, where I was, but I was far enough into the room to earn a disapproving frown.

She peeled off the headphones, leaned on the mop, and shouted above the carpet machine's din, "What d'you want? You looking for someone?"

"Woman with black hair and glasses," I yelled back. "Her name is Miriam."

"Who?"

"*Miriam Ferguson*," I bellowed.

"Ah!" She hooked a thumb. "Upstairs!"

I nodded, started to say, "Thank you," but she put her headphones back on and resumed attacking the floor with her O-Cedar.

The cap-wearing carpet cleaner didn't even glance at me as I raced up the steps, eager to escape the din.

I found Cissy quite easily this time without having to stick my nose into any strange bathrooms or closets. After spotting her from the hallway, I slipped into the room she occupied and shut the door behind me, noting only the vague hum of machinery beyond. It was blissful. I could finally hear myself think.

Cissy didn't look up as I entered, neither did she flinch as the door clicked closed. She seemed to be somewhere else entirely (as she had a lot these past few days).

She stood in the center of the master bedroom, surrounded by brown packing boxes; chin hanging down, she crushed a black dress against a garish—doubtless, borrowed—cheetah-print blouse, holding on for dear life.

"Mother," I said, so as not to startle her. "Can I help?"

As soon as she lifted her head with that black bouffant wig and saw me through her cat's-eye specs, she quickly composed herself and carefully folded the dress, setting it down in the nearest box.

"Good morning, sweetie. No, no, I'm making good progress. Just packing up Sarah Lee's things for her sister. She wants them shipped to South Dakota. Annabelle said she'd send a volunteer to help. There's so much more to do than I thought when I promised Margery."

"So much for detecting, huh?" I teased.

"Well, I did bag up those mugs from her kitchen before Elvira could get to them," she informed me. "So that evidence is safe in my satchel."

"Good thinking." Though I wondered how she thought anyone would get prints or residue off them when they'd been washed already.

"I just never imagined how large Sarah Lee's wardrobe would be, when she donated a truckload to the Welfare to Work program before she moved into Belle Meade. I wonder what her sister will do with it all."

I watched her lift a shimmering beaded gown on its hanger from atop a pile on the bed. "Oh, how she loved this Bob Mackie"—Mother smiled, as if remembering a private moment—"said it made her feel like a showgirl."

"Can't imagine Mrs. Fleck will have much cause to wear Bob Mackie in Sioux Falls."

"It's Flax, sweetie, and she lives in Bison, not Sioux Falls."

"My point exactly."

"It's just a shame. It really is." She sighed, adding the gown to the box she'd been working on. Then she put her hands on hips wrapped snug inside a pair of black jeans. The denim cuffs were tucked into those awful lizard boots littered with rhinestones. Had my old drama teacher Mrs. Coogan found those at Tammy Faye Bakker's yard sale?

Egads.

Stranger still, was seeing my mother in denim. I can't remember her ever donning a pair before, and I had a feeling I wouldn't ever again after this. I wish I'd brought my camera. I could always use the photos as leverage the next time she tried to twist my arm into doing something I didn't want to do.

"Did you find anything else about Mrs. Sewell's involvement with Two Hearts?" I asked to distract her.

"I'm sorry, Andrea," she apologized, "but I haven't yet had a moment to look for any papers. I've been so preoccupied with *this*." She indicated the mess around her. It did look as though a bomb filled with couture had exploded. "Thank heavens Sarah's good jewelry and her best silver were stored in a safe deposit box at the bank. I'd hate to be responsible for that, too."

"Don't worry about Sarah Lee's papers from the matchmaker," I told her. "I don't think it matters."

"How do you mean?"

"Because of what I found on Bebe's hard drive"—I drew my bag off my shoulder and sifted through the contents to find what I needed—

"check out this." Once I dislodged the photos and letter I'd printed off Bebe's computer, I wove through the maze of boxes to hand them over.

The closer I got, the more she tipped her head and got squinty. "Darling, what's that on your face?" She actually wet her thumb and reached out to rub my cheek.

Gross, a spit bath!

Did she think I was three years old or something?

"It's ink, geez! It'll come off in a few days." I brushed away her touch, pushing the papers at her. "There were only three matches for Mrs. Kent that I could find. It should be easy enough to figure out if any one of them saw Mrs. Sewell as well. Their phone numbers are right on that letter. See?"

"Brilliant!" she said, forgetting about the smudge on my face as she took the pages and went back to the bed, sitting down amidst the contents of Sarah Lee's emptied closet. "Oh, my, oh, my," she murmured, and I watched the expressions shift on her face as she read the men's biographies. She chuckled softly when she got to the photographs. "I can't believe Bebe dated this one"—she pointed to the bald Mr. Andrews who used to play football—"he looks like her old butler, Nigel, who eloped to Vegas with the cook not long after Homer died. Bebe wanted to strangle him for stealing away the best personal chef she'd ever had."

"Ah, a case where the butler *did* do it," I said to myself.

Mother blinked. "What's that, sweetie?"

"Nothing." I felt like Mrs. Pinkston talking to

her plants. "Look, I'll leave the *tres hombres* to you, all right? I've got a few things to look into this afternoon."

"You do?" She blinked her magnified eyes, seeming pleased by my statement. "Well, that's wonderful, darling. Yes, I'll take charge of investigating our suspects, once I've gotten help sorting through the rest of Sarah Lee's closet."

Our suspects, huh?

Whatever made her happy.

I wasn't about to admit that I didn't think any of the Three Hearts bachelors had a fig to do with her friends' deaths and send her high hopes crashing like the *Hindenberg*. It was good to see her smile, so what did it hurt?

"How about I meet you back at Bebe's house for lunch?" I suggested. "One o'clock all right? I don't have a key to the place, so you'll have to let me in."

"Oh, sweetie, get one from Annabelle this morning." She removed the black glasses to rub the bridge of her nose. "Because I might be here all day," she told me. "Depending on what gets done. I know I should be focused on my undercover work, but I did promise Sarah Lee's sister, and I can't go back on my word."

"Why don't you call my cell whenever you're ready to take a break. I can come pick you up." I didn't want her wandering around the grounds alone, but I wasn't about to say that to her.

Cissy nodded. "Yes, I'll call you when I'm ready."

"Then I'm off to the library," I said, grabbing my purse and hearing the rattle of pills in tiny bottles—the bag from Bebe's house—that I'd promised to drop off later at the pharmacy. Which got me to thinking I should pick up Sarah Lee's leftovers as long as I was here, save Patsy the trip. "Does Mrs. Flax want her sister's prescription meds?" I asked Mother. "Because Dr. Finch's wife, who's the pharmacist, usually collects them. She was by Bebe's this morning and brought up the subject."

Among other things.

"No, I'm sure Margery doesn't care what happens to Sarah Lee's old drugs. The only things she'd like from the bath are the linens." Mother slipped her glasses back on. "Go ahead and take them."

So I stepped over to Mrs. Sewell's bathroom and switched on the lights. As I tentatively approached the marble-topped vanity, I caught a whiff of rosewater and talc.

It was disconcerting, the way bits and pieces of a life stayed behind, well after someone had gone. I could still stand in my father's study, draw in a deep breath, and smell his Cuban cigars. Maybe it was a way of reminding us they weren't so far away after all.

Forgive me, Mrs. Sewell, I thought, before I pulled open the mirrored cabinet and added her cache of goodies to Mrs. Kent's. The plastic bag barely held all the labeled vials and bottles, but I managed to zip the thing closed and shove it back in my purse before I shut off the lights and ducked out.

"All right," I told my mother, "I'm off."

I pulled open the door and came face to face with Mabel Pinkston.

Her false-lashed eyes and sagging features cheered when she realized who I was. A grin twitched on her rouged lips.

"Hello, Andy," she said, hands clasped at her belly, below the appliquéd teddy bear on her long-sleeved pink shirt. Pink tennis shoes poked out beneath the hem of her tan slacks. She was really into this "pink for Pinkston" thing. "What a pleasant surprise to see you. Were you helping your aunt? Annabelle sent me over, thinking Miriam was at it all alone."

"I just dropped by for a minute." I glanced back at Cissy, who I saw quickly hiding the papers I'd given her beneath a stack of clothes on the bed. "You caught me leaving," I said, easing myself—and my bulging bag—past her, afraid she'd try to convince me to stick around and pack boxes all the livelong day. "Go on in. You girls have fun," I called in parting, before I left Mabel to Mother.

At least Cissy would have someone with her, which made me feel a whole lot better—and less guilty—about dashing off to the main house.

I took the stairs down two-by-two and skipped over the black tube in the doorway, not decelerating until my butt was in the driver's seat of my Wrangler.

Then I followed a pack of three-wheeled scooters going two miles an hour over to the Manor House. Before I got inside, I remembered to put on my name badge, and I used my keycard to get in without having to intercom Annabelle.

Since I hadn't exactly studied the brochures with the map, I paid careful attention to signs and arrows, managing to make my way to the library without having to ask for help. (Yes, I was proud of myself.)

Set at the end of a wing, near a sunny solarium, Belle Meade's private library was a haven for bibliophiles, with shelves of hardback books spanning the room and paperbacks loaded on spinning turntables. A station with four flat-screen computer monitors benefited from placement in back near a bank of windows, and natural light filtered through sheer fabric shades. Cushioned chairs with ottomans and coffee tables filled with newspapers and periodicals had been tucked into each corner. Only one seat had an occupant.

At least I wouldn't have to deal with an angry mob of bookworms on my "first day." Ha ha.

I approached a woman perched behind a curved wooden desk. Her pink scalp gleamed through white hair, light as down. She was reading the morning paper with a large magnifying glass. I softly cleared my throat, and her pale eyes looked up. The badge at her breast read, MILDRED PIERCE, but she didn't look a thing like Joan Crawford.

"I'll bet you got teased a lot," I said, pointing at her nametag. "Great book and not a bad movie."

She sniffed. "Dear girl, I could tell you stories. The film came out when I was just a girl. I can still see those sordid promotions." She framed a theatre marquee with thick knuckled hands and recited dramatically, *"Don't ever tell anyone what she did . . . A mother's love leads to murder.* Oh, boy, now that's hyperbole." She looked me over. "I'm surprised someone your age even knows about it."

"I love noir film," I confessed, "and James M. Cain."

"What can I help you with?" she asked.

"I'm Andy, a temporary volunteer. I don't know what I'm supposed to do exactly, except show up . . ."

"Oh, perfect timing, dear girl. Yes, lovely of you to relieve me." She smiled and gingerly rose from her seat, picking up the cane that leaned beside it. "If you wouldn't mind—Andy, is it?—why don't you take the desk while I have my break." She patted my hand. "Thank you, dear, I'll be back in thirty minutes."

"You're welcome, Mrs. Pierce."

Although I wasn't exactly sure what I was supposed to do in the meantime.

Her gait slow but steady, she ambled out of there, and I went behind the deserted desk to drop my purse, sitting down in her still-warm chair.

I glanced at the newspaper article she'd been perusing, about the rising costs of Medicare premiums and prescriptions, the square of glass that lay atop it increasing the print to the size of the biggest letters on an eye chart. I could've read the piece from twenty paces.

It made me want to start eating carrots, much as I hated them.

I tapped my fingers, glancing around, wondering if I should at least pretend to be studying the Dewey decimal system. But the only other person in the room—the woman in the easy chair—didn't appear to need volunteer assistance. She had a book in her lap, her head drooped forward, her mouth wide open, soundly snoring.

Well, I wasn't about to do anything that might wake her, which meant doing something quiet.

So I reached for my bag and juggled around the bagful of prescriptions in order to retrieve the folded-up e-mails from Janet Graham. I smoothed the pages and started with her feature on Belle Meade she'd done for the *PCP*.

PARADISE FOR THE PLATINUM YEARS, her headline cried, with the subtitle, BELLE MEADE OPENS ITS DOORS IN DALLAS.

"Forget the golden years," her story began. *"So-called 'retirement villages' are now aiming for the platinum set, men and women in their sixties or better who have no fiscal worries and want to live free of care, in a safe-guarded environment offering all the amenities of Club Med with an on-duty geriatric specialist. After proving so in demand in Austin that the waiting list to move in runs six months to a year, Belle Meade, the apex of luxury living for the aging jet-set, has opened its doors in Dallas . . . and is already filled to the gills."*

Janet went on to describe the "amenities" in great gushing detail, sounding an awful lot like a press release, with plenty of color photos to boot. But then the *PCP* was hardly the *New York Times*. Its hard-hitting pieces covered Highland Park High football games and upping of property taxes. The rest of its pages touted local restaurants and hair salons, home decorating tips, where to get the best bikini waxes, and plenty of photos of the Park Cities glitterati at fundraising galas. They even had a column called "He Said, She Said," with the latest gossip from "field hockey moms" and "polo dads."

I skimmed down to her quotes from Annabelle, whom she described as *"a full-figured Texas beauty with a master's degree in business administration from UT-Austin and a tragic past involving the deaths of her parents, Gretchen and Stanley Meade, of the Austin Meades, in a house fire at Lake Travis."*

I shuffled the papers, sticking Janet's feature beneath the other pages she'd sent, articles from the *Austin American Statesman* about the fire itself, dated six years earlier.

I figured Janet had gleaned her info about the fire from there, and from her reliable sources, rather than from Annabelle, who had to have been reluctant to discuss it. I could see that it had pained her to tell me, and I was her most trusted Camp Longhorn bunkmate.

A two-column article that Janet had marked with a page number and date, noted simply, LONG-TIME LAKE TRAVIS RESIDENTS DIE IN FLAMES and provided sketchy details of the event, revealing only that the fire had been called in by the family's housekeeper, Mrs. Franklin Albright, who lived in the caretaker's cottage with her husband, Franklin, the couple's groundskeeper. Mrs. Albright apparently had suffered burns to her arms while attempting to rescue her employers, but the fire had quickly engulfed the old shingle-style home, built in 1874, reducing it to a pile of rubble.

There was a grainy photo of the Albrights, a heavy-set woman with bandaged hands covering her face, her husband's arm around her. I put the page down and slid the magnifying lens over it, though it merely blew up the pixels, like a Seurat painting made up of tiny dots. Though I could better see a mailbox in the background with MEADE painted upon it.

The next attachment from Janet was the Meades' obit from the *Statesman*, recounting their lives with utmost brevity: the fact that they were born and raised in Austin, both hailing from wealthy families, that each had graduated from UT, and had lived quietly on Lake Travis thereafter. It listed their only surviving child as Annabelle Griffin Meade of Austin. The photo of the Meades showed a grim-faced pair who much resembled the stone-faced, pitch-fork-wielding farmer and his wife in the Grant Wood painting, *American Gothic*.

Ugh. It's no wonder they'd shipped Annabelle off to Dallas to attend boarding school and had a local au pair put her on the bus to Camp Longhorn each summer. They looked like the kind of folks who ate children, not raised them. I wonder if they let her come home for Christmas?

Poor AB.

If I hadn't felt sorry for her before, I did then.

Again, I shuffled the papers, bringing up several smaller follow-up pieces on the fire investigation, one suggesting an accelerant may have been involved, with the police and arson inspectors interviewing several "persons of interest," including the caretaker Albrights and the Meades' daughter, who'd been at the house for dinner the very evening of the tragedy.

I noticed the date between the first article and the last one—stating that all had been cleared in the case and the fire deemed "accidental"—was six months.

Wow. I couldn't imagine Annabelle having to live under suspicion for so long, with people wondering if she'd killed her own parents by torching their house. It's amazing she'd come through as strong as she had. I would have fallen to pieces, no question.

"Thank you, dear girl." A finger poked gently into my shoulder, and I looked up to find Mildred Pierce hovering.

Had it been thirty minutes already? I hadn't even realized how much time had passed; I'd been so deeply absorbed in the articles.

She obviously wanted her chair back, so I quickly put her magnifying lens back atop her newspaper, gathered up the pages I'd been perusing, and grabbed my purse.

"Do you need me to stay for any reason?" I asked her as she settled into her seat and tipped her cane against the desk.

I saw her glance over at the snoozing woman before she smiled at me. "I think I can manage on my own, hon."

No skin off my nose.

I returned her smile, wished her a good day, and headed into the hallway. Instead, of leaving, I took a left toward Annabelle's office. As long as I was there, I had a few questions I wanted to ask her.

The door sat half open, so I poked my head in to find Annabelle on the phone, doing a lot of "uh-huh"-ing. She motioned me in, and I wandered around while she finished up her phone call. I admired the colorful pottery lining a good many shelves, most clearly HECHO EN MÉJICO, but others bore the WELLER or NEWCOMB marks on their bases.

Expensive stuff, I noted, being a fan of *Antiques Roadshow*.

Besides plenty of leather-bound books, I discovered two silver-framed pictures I hadn't seen before. The last time I was in her office, I'd been too distracted by my mother's altered appearance to notice any photographs.

I picked up one that showed a chubby little girl with her dark hair in pigtails stepping into shallow water at lake's edge while a woman in a tent-like sundress with a floppy hat and sunglasses reached out her arms.

"That's my guardian angel," Annabelle said from over my shoulder. I hadn't even heard her hang up the phone. She leaned against her desk, arms crossed, watching me. "I don't know what I would've done without her. She was more of a mother to me than my own mother ever was."

I put the frame back and reached for the other, of Annabelle in cap and gown and the same heavy-set woman at her side, in profile, beaming with pride.

In this one, I could make out enough of the woman to know I had seen her before: in a grainy news photograph.

"Your guardian angel . . . that's got to be Mrs. Albright, right?" I set the picture down and turned to Annabelle.

"Did I tell you about Emmy? I guess I must have. Else how would you know?" She tugged her flowered cardigan closer around her.

"Actually, I saw a photo that ran with an article from the Austin paper."

"What article?" She squinted.

"An old one, about the fire."

"Oh." She began to twirl her hair around her finger, and I knew that it bothered her, thinking I'd looked it up. That I was checking on her past.

"It said that Mrs. Albright and her husband had lived in the caretaker's cottage at your parents' home on Lake Travis. He kept the grounds, and she kept the house."

"Kept the house, waited on my parents hand and foot, and took me under her wing because no one else cared enough to do it." Annabelle ceased fussing with her hair. "Em made me feel like I was worth something, and she protected me. I think my parents sent me off to boarding school to separate us, because it hurt them to see how much Em loved me, and how I loved her. She's the only true family I ever had."

So much for blood being thicker than water.

"What happened to the Albrights, after the investigation?" I asked, gently as I could. "Did you keep in touch with them?"

"Frank passed away," she said and let out a slow breath, wandering over to the nearest window. She adjusted the shutter slats so she could peer into the courtyard. Sunlight slid across her skin, giving it a pearly cast. "The poor man wanted to take Em and get out of Austin after everything, but he never got the chance."

"Heart attack?" I guessed.

"He went to bed one night," she said quietly, "and never woke up again."

Just like Bebe Kent, I thought.

"What happened to Mrs. Albright? Did she leave Austin after losing him? I can't imagine she stuck around."

Annabelle closed the shutters with a snap, and her face closed off as well. "I prefer not to discuss her, Andy, if you don't mind. Not that I wouldn't want to, but she's moved on with her life, and I respect her for that. My parents didn't leave Em or Franklin a penny, would you believe? After all they did for my family." She made a noise of disgust. "I've done as much as I can to help Em out, but she would never take money from me. She always said that a child shouldn't be responsible for a parent."

"Interesting perspective," I said. "Do you keep in contact?"

She frowned. "Can we talk about something else, Andy?"

"Okay," I said, as she looked unsettled by talk of her parents and the Albrights. Though I couldn't blame her. "Any word on the blood tests?"

She shook her head and crossed back to her desk, dropping into her chair. "It's only been a day, right? But I'll let you know as soon as I hear. How's your mother doing with her sleuthing?"

I laughed. "Oh, man, you should see her. She's packing clothes at Mrs. Sewell's, and it's a mess over there." I went to sit in one of the high-backed chairs across from her, hugging my bag in my lap. "Mrs. Pinkston showed up just as I was leaving, about half an hour ago. That should keep her busy and out of trouble, right? Because Mabel doesn't know anything about what Mother's really doing, right, Annabelle?" When she didn't immediately answer, I said again, "Right, Annabelle?"

"Didn't I say I'd keep it hush-hush?" There went her prissy side again, acting all affronted.

She tucked her hair behind her ears and lowered her gaze to her blotter, suddenly finding the papers spread across it far more interesting than anything we were discussing.

Whatever.

I figured it was time to ask for a key to Bebe's house and duck out. But before I could say anything, my cell chirped from my purse, and I had to extricate the bag of prescription vials in order to find it, buried beneath. Finally, I flipped it open, spotting an unfamiliar number. "Yes?" I said warily.

"Andrea? You're not going to believe this! Guess what I've gone and done?"

"Where are you, Mother?" First things first.

"Still at Sarah Sewell's, but I have to leave soon. Mabel said she'd stay and keep working so I can dash back to the house and freshen up."

"Freshen up? For who?"

We'd mentioned having lunch, but surely she wasn't this worked up about eating a sandwich with her daughter.

"What's going on?" I pumped her.

"I've got a lunch date, sweetie . . . actually, two of them, and I haven't much time. So would you rather I go alone, or would you like to come?"

"I have to drop off this stuff for Patsy at the pharmacy first," I told her, "so if you can wait a few minutes . . ."

"Yes, yes, I'll wait, because I'm thinking a chaperone's a good idea," she drawled, "after all, one of the men I'm meeting could very well be a homicidal maniac."

I'm sorry, but I grinned despite myself.

My daddy was right. Life did go in circles. My mother had arranged so many blind dates from hell, fixing me up—often unwittingly—with the loser sons of her rich friends, and now she was finally getting hers, going out with men she thought could be serial killers.

Gas to drive Cissy to restaurant: Around two-fifty a gallon.

Payback: Priceless.

Chapter 17

"How does my hair look, darling?"

"It's not your hair, Mother, it's a wig."

"But is it too big? I teased it up this morning and gave it a little extra oomph." She put a hand to the black mushroom cloud atop her head, which I duly contemplated, figuring there was enough nesting material there for a small hawk to rest comfortably.

But I didn't want her to be self-conscious about it. Besides, this was Texas, where larger than life was the rule, not the exception. I'd seen bigger hair on the cashiers at Tom Thumb. "It looks fine," I said.

"You sure?"

"Positive."

I leaned back against the blue bench at the IHOP on Mockingbird Lane, Cissy across the table, nursing a cup of coffee while we waited for Bachelor Number One to arrive. Cissy had asked the waitress to pull up a chair, so we could keep an eye on the guy without either of us having to sit next to him.

Mother had allotted each gentleman twenty minutes, and it looked as though the first dude was already three minutes late. The way Cissy kept glancing at her watch, she wasn't pleased.

I was merely enjoying the fact that my upscale mama had her butt planted on a bench upholstered in a man-made substance from which syrup and jelly could be easily expunged, a far cry from silk damask. It would likely be the first and last time I'd ever see Cissy Blevins Kendricks in such a plebian haunt. She'd already frowned disapprovingly at a baby in a highchair across the aisle that would spontaneously release the most ear-splitting shrieks. Like that never happened in the dining room at the Four Seasons.

"Who's on first?" I asked to distract her.

"Thomas Walcher," she said and not very happily.

"The whale watcher?"

"Yes."

"Who's on second?"

"My word, Andrea, but you sound like that old comedy sketch."

Well, why not, when I felt like I was *in* a comedy sketch, sitting in the pancake house, playing chaperone to a woman who looked like a downsized Dame Edna.

"So who's after the whale watcher?" I tried again.

"Stephen Lloyd Howard."

"The IRS agent?"

"The *retired* IRS agent," she corrected.

Which left a bachelor unaccounted for.

"What happened to the football player?"

"He declined my invitation for a meeting." Mother sniffed, stirring more cream into her coffee, so I noticed her bare hands, free of all but her wedding and engagement rings. Maybe she'd snagged the QVC jewels on one too many of Sarah Lee's gowns while packing. "Apparently, Mr. Andrews didn't see a need to answer any questions about Bebe Kent, because he swore he'd never even met her. Said she stood him up last Wednesday, and he'd made reservations for dinner at Sevy's Grill."

"Nice," I said, as it was an elegant spot for a blind date.

"Not so nice," Mother finished, "as Mr. Andrews ended up eating his steak alone. He said the wait staff would vouch for him. He was there from eight o'clock until nearly ten, when he finished his apple pecan chimichanga."

I sighed. "You called the restaurant, didn't you?"

"*Mais oui.*" The French phrase seemed so out of place, coming from those burnt-umber lips. "They confirmed what he said. He didn't leave until after dessert."

Oh, boy. I knew where this was going.

I fiddled with the straw in my half-drunk orange juice, wishing I didn't have to say this, but I did. "So you think someone else waylaid Bebe at her townhouse and that she didn't show up for her date with Mr. Andrews because she was already dead, or at least entertaining her killer? Let's not forget, she'd used the cheap wine glasses, so she couldn't have liked whomever it was very much."

"And your father didn't think hiring a tutor for

you when you were three would pay off," Mother said dryly, and I stuck out my tongue.

She reached across the table to gently slap my hand, though I pulled it back fast enough to evade her . . . and in the process knocked the rest of my orange juice straight into my lap.

"Ah, geez." I slid out of the bench, grabbing up the napkins to press them into my crotch, while Mother took a kerchief from her purse and dabbed it in water, offering help that looked almost obscene.

Which was when Bachelor Number One showed up, opportunely.

He cleared his throat, and we both stopped what we were doing.

"I'm Tom Walcher," he said and looked us over, sweat popping out on his broad forehead. "Which one of you is Miriam?"

"She is." I pointed to my bewigged Mother, who awkwardly smiled at her bow-tied suitor. "If you'll excuse me."

I slipped away, dashing off to the ladies' room, where I spent a good ten minutes standing in front of the hand dryer, the warm air aimed at the wet spot on my jeans. It hardly earned me a glance from the two women who entered after.

You didn't need cable TV anymore to see weird things.

By the time I was dry enough and had made my way back to the table, Mother sat alone.

"Where'd he go?"

"Home," she said, matter of fact.

"What'd you do to him?" I asked as I slid back into the bench. "And where'd this come from?"

Mother must've ordered me another juice, because a fresh glass sat at my place, along with a recently delivered stack of pancakes dressed up with chocolate-chip eyes, a whipped-cream smile, and a maraschino-cherry nose.

"I told the waitress my little girl was hungry," she said, explaining the food I hadn't ordered. "As for Mr. Walcher"—her cheetah-printed shoulders shrugged—"he couldn't have killed a fly, much less Bebe and Sarah Lee. When he's not running the winery he co-owns in Grapevine, guess what he does?"

"Mystery conventions," I recalled from his bio.

"Besides that."

"I haven't a clue," I said, adding copious syrup to my fat stack of flapjacks before I shoveled in a forkful and mumbled with my mouth full, "raises orchids?"

She took a sip of coffee, and I wondered if she was working on the same cup she'd started with. "He founded a group that rescues horses about to be sent to the Alpo factory. Puts them out to pasture on some of the acreage he owns that doesn't have soil fit for growing grapes. They call it 'Save a Nag,' " she said.

"Of course they do." Sounded like an organization to spare the lives of desperate housewives.

Mother sighed and did a watch-check. "Anyway, Mr. Howard should be along any moment. Let's hope he shows more promise than the first gentleman."

More promise in the homicidal maniac department, I knew she meant, and I had to fight to keep from snorting orange juice through my nose. When I finally swallowed, I rubbed my sticky fingers on a paper napkin and told her, "Look, Mother, if it were as easy as *CSI*, everyone would be doing it."

That didn't wipe away her frown. "I did talk to Sarah Lee's neighbor this morning. Helen something or other. I asked if she saw anything suspicious on Saturday night. She remembers taking her dog for a walk about eight o'clock, which was her usual routine, but everything was quiet, she said. Didn't see a strange car in front of Sarah Lee's place, or notice anything out of the ordinary."

"Maybe the killer rode a bike and stashed it in the bushes."

"Or else he parked the car elsewhere and walked."

Something tugged at my brain, but I couldn't shake it loose. Whatever it was, I'd realize it sooner or later. Usually later, like in the middle of the night when I'd shoot up in bed and find my answer. Only it was too late to ever share with anyone . . . except a barely conscious Malone.

"Oh, sweetie." She sighed. "What if I'm on the wrong track?"

"You thinking about calling it quits?" I said, setting down my fork and sitting up straighter, feeling strangely ambivalent. "If you're ready to go home, I'm sure Annabelle would understand."

Hell, she'd be grateful as all get-out.

"That's not what I meant!" The pointed toe of her boot nudged my shin. "I'll just have to broaden my scope, consider other suspects, like the mailman or Elvira . . ."

"The housekeeper?"

"Well, she has a key to the residences, doesn't

she? And so many of those chemicals she cleans with could be lethal." Her magnified eyes didn't reveal fanaticism so much as desperation, which almost worried me more. "There's always the meter reader and the exterminator."

"The exterminator?"

How apropos.

I think she would've listed the carpet cleaner and the chimney sweep next if the tall, ginger-haired gentleman with the easy smile hadn't come around the corner and made her lose her train of thought.

"Mrs. Ferguson?" he said, his eyes on Cissy. "I'm Stephen Howard. Your one o'clock appointment."

He extended his hand, and she lifted hers, rather limply, I thought, as if she expected him to bend over and kiss it rather than shake it. Though shake it, he did.

"I'm Andrea," I volunteered and stuck out my hand, too. His grip was firm and dry, which scored him at least a point. How I hated sweaty palms. "I'm Mrs. Ferguson's, er, niece."

"Is that right? Well, I'm pleased to meet you both." Without prompting, he took a seat in the extra chair and drew it up to the table.

The waitress passed behind him, and he flagged her down. "Start me off with an iced tea, if you would." He turned to Mother first, then to *moi*. "Can I offer either of you anything?"

I shook my head. "I'm good."

Cissy slipped the black-rims from her nose and batted her overpainted eyes at him. "Why, since you're takin' charge, Mr. Howard, I'd appreciate an iced tea as well."

The waitress waddled off, scribbling on her pad, and I settled back to watch Mother put her Mata Hari *mojo* into action.

She started off engaging him in pleasantries, with talk of the weather—"well, it's the usual Indian summer, isn't it?"—and how traffic had been coming over—"did you hit any of that awful construction driving in from Plano?"—all the while, surreptitiously scrutinizing the cut of his jib and the fit of his clothes.

The man wasn't holding up too badly for a sixty-two-year-old, I had to admit, though gray had crept into his red hair and lines of age carved his sun-freckled skin.

If I didn't know that "Miriam" was merely on the prowl for a killer, I'd say my mother found Stephen Howard attractive, the way she leaned toward him and smiled coyly, laughing a little too loudly when he joked about the sad state of his golf swing.

"I'm more into hunting and fishing than whacking a tiny ball around eighteen holes," he confessed, which Mother seemed to find charming, judging by the google-eyed look on her face.

I, however, remained unimpressed, particularly when he went into a narrative about his last deer-hunting trip.

Killing Bambi for sport?

Blech.

My father had only shot at clay pigeons, and I had respected him for that. No real man needed to kill a living creature to prove he was macho.

So why was my mother acting all goofy over Stephen Howard's meandering tale of the misad-

ventures of tying a fourteen-point buck to the grill
of a truck? Unless it was part of her plot to nail
him for murdering Bebe and Sarah Lee, I certainly
didn't get it.

"So how big did you say your shotgun was, Mr.
Howard?"

"Call me Stephen."

"All right"—lashes batting—"Stephen."

If they kept this up, I'd have to order a barf bag.

The tea arrived, and their scintillating discussion moved onto the merits of real sugar versus
Sweet 'N Low.

"Aspartame gives me headaches," Stephen declared, and Mother cooed, "Oh, goodness, me,
too!"

I nearly choked. I'd witnessed my mother
dumping *beaucoups* of Sweet 'N Low into her coffee not twenty minutes before.

Could she behave more like a teenager? I covered
my face with my hands, peeking through my fingers as though I were watching a scary movie. *My
gosh, get to the point*, I wanted to holler.

Finally, Cissy did a quick Texas two step, danc-
ing the conversation toward Bebe Kent and Sarah
Lee Sewell, asking Mr. Howard dead-on about his
meetings with them, when they'd occurred, where
they'd gone, if anything unusual had happened.

She wasn't throwing any Barbara Walters soft-
balls, for sure.

I half-expected her to grab the dude by his col-
lar and demand to know whether or not he'd poisoned the wine he'd shared with Bebe before
sliding her into bed in her nightie . . . and if he'd
done the same with Sarah Lee's tea before she'd

succumbed on her sofa, after leaving her lipstick on the tainted mug (which he'd then washed and left to dry on a dishtowel).

But Cissy didn't get that far before Stephen Howard raised a finger and politely requested to cut in.

"You'd like to hear the details of my dates with your two friends?" he reiterated.

Mother nodded. "Yes, please."

At which point her gentleman caller did a very odd thing.

He sat back in his chair and crossed his arms, a truly enigmatic grin on his face. "Well, before I kiss and tell, I have a question for you, if you don't mind, Mrs. Ferguson."

Mother looked at me, and I shrugged.

"Certainly," she told him.

"Aside from the fact that you somehow got privileged information from the dating service, there's something else that concerns me more." He pulled on his lip, squinting like Clint Eastwood, before he dropped the A-bomb. "I worked for the revenue service for thirty years, ma'am, and I still have plenty of friends there. In fact, I had one of 'em look you up, just to see what I was getting myself into," he said, sounding way too sure of himself. "Or rather, I had 'em look up Miriam Amanda Wallace Ferguson."

Cissy glanced at me again, and I saw the lump go down her throat as she swallowed. "You don't say?"

"Yes, ma'am, I do say, and I found out something you'll find very interesting." He unfolded his arms to scratch his jaw. "It turns out that no such person as Miriam Amanda Wallace Ferguson exists. Not one living, anyway. Last woman by that name died in nineteen and sixty-one. She was the first female governor of this state for a while during Prohibition, though I'm guessing you already know that."

Oh, she knew, all right, because I'd warned her someone else besides me had recalled what they'd learned in Texas History, I wanted to say, but kept my trap shut.

"Really? Hmm, that's all very intriguing, but there must be some mistake," Mother murmured, trying to act nonchalant, slipping her glasses back on, only they were turned upside down. She plucked them off again and stuck them in her purse. "As you can see, I'm as real as it gets."

Real?

This coming from a woman buried beneath an inch of makeup, wearing borrowed clothes, and a wig that looked a lot like Cousin It.

"Oh, there's no mistake." He set his forearms on the table, his gaze shifting between us, not looking at all amused. "So, you mind telling me who you really are and what the heck you're doing?"

"Oh, dear, look at the time!" Cissy grabbed her purse and started to scoot. "Goodness, Andrea, we'd better go. We have that . . . *thing* to do."

"Yes, that thing," I echoed and followed her lead, sliding toward the edge of the booth.

Only Stephen Howard wasn't about to let us go anywhere.

He swiveled in his chair, crossing his legs so they blocked Mother's escape route and planting a hand on the end of my booth, which meant I either had to stay or climb across his shoulder.

I stared at Mother, willing her to get us out of this.

In a pickle, that's what we were, getting shaken down by a Navy veteran who'd served in 'Nam and spent three decades with the IRS.

Another fine mess you've gotten us into.

"Whatever's going on, why don't you tell me the truth? Maybe I can help, if you'll let me," Mr. Howard offered, his masculine tone so earnest, his pale eyes pleading with Mother, wearing her down, as evidenced by the slump of her shoulders.

She glanced over, and I shook my head. Firmly. Decisively. If I'd shouted, "keep your big mouth shut," I couldn't have been any clearer.

And for a whole second or two, she stayed mum.

Then she cracked, faster than Humpty-Dumpty taking a swan dive toward the sidewalk. "I'm Cissy Blevins Kendricks of Beverly Drive in Highland Park, and this is my daughter, Andrea . . . I'm really a blonde, and I do believe I have an allergy to synthetic fabrics. . . ."

Name, rank, serial number, hair color, shoe size.

You name it, she coughed it up to good ol' Stephen, telling him that both Bebe and Sarah were dead—which was news to him, judging by the surprise on his face—and explaining that she was "looking for closure" by finding out as much as she could about the last days of their lives. At least she didn't use the words "undercover" or "serial killer." Though that hardly reassured me.

I imagined a swarm of government agents descending on us, weapons drawn, handcuffs at the ready to arrest us for . . . what exactly? Impersonating a dead governor? Lying to blind dates?

Okay, maybe *that* wasn't going to happen; but, at the very least, he'd think Mother had gone off her medication, and I was aiding and abetting her delusional bender.

I shrank into the booth's corner, waiting for her to finish. If the man had any sense at all, he'd do what the rest of us did on really awful setups: make the usual excuse that he had to use the restroom, then he'd flee like a bat out of hell.

Only this guy didn't seem to be budging.

After Mother finished her sob story about seeking peace by tying up the loose ends in the lives of her two deceased friends, Stephen palmed her hand in his and patted gently, saying things like, "there, there," and offering use of his pickup truck to haul Bebe's and Sarah's packed-up personal effects to FedEx.

By the time I was able to drag Mother out of the IHOP, it was nearly three o'clock. She'd decided to have a chef's salad, while Stephen had ordered a burger, and I'd sat in the corner of the booth munching on a plate of onion rings, debating if I actually had the ability to turn invisible. I felt like it, the way the two of them ignored me so completely for a solid hour.

While Cissy went to use the powder room so Stephen could settle the check at the register (he had insisted, believe it or not), he caught my elbow and reiterated, "If there's anything I can do, Andrea, you let me know. Your mother's a good woman, and I'd like to help her, if I could."

I wasn't as sure as Mother that this Stephen Lloyd Howard could be trusted, but it wasn't because I thought he'd dusted Bebe and Sarah Lee.

My resistance had more to do with Cissy slipping him her unlisted home phone on a napkin (yes, right under my nose). It's not the kind of thing a daughter wanted to see, particularly one who was such a loyal daddy's girl.

Still, I squashed my misgivings, because I had something I could use a hand with, and Stephen Howard seemed the perfect guy for the job. If he could pin down the nonexistence of Miriam Ferguson so quickly, then he could surely find the answer I needed in a snap.

"As a matter of fact, Mr. Howard . . ."

"Stephen, please."

"Okay, Stephen. There is one thing you could do," I said and proceeded to explain, writing down two names on the back of my business card, circling my cell number and asking him to call ASAP.

I had a weird sense that someone else wasn't who she was supposed to be either.

After Mother and Stephen had exchanged "goodbyes" in the parking lot, I put the IHOP in my rearview. I switched on the radio, but Cissy shut it off again, preferring instead to relive each moment of her pancake house encounters with Tom and Stephen, coming to the conclusion that neither could've harmed her friends.

So she was fluctuating between Elvira and the bug spray man.

I considered tossing Colonel Mustard and Miss Scarlet into the mix, but instead I kept my eyes on the road and just drove.

Chapter 18

As far as I was concerned, we couldn't reach the gates of Belle Meade soon enough. After I waved to Bob at the guardhouse, Cissy insisted we go straight to Bebe's place. I wondered if Mrs. Pinkston would be expecting her to return to Sarah Lee's, but Mother didn't seem to care. She wanted to take off her wig for a while and, as she put it, "let my head breathe."

I think she really wanted to lie down and nap.

Which was okay by me.

I wanted her to stick around the house for a while, anyway, until I heard back from Stephen. When my cell phone rang not long after Cissy had ascended the steps to upstairs, I thought it might be him.

Instead it was the doctor's wife, Patsy Finch, who'd gotten my number from Annabelle. She'd had a chance to go through the medications I'd dropped off earlier and claimed I'd left something out.

"I emptied their medicine cabinets, Patsy. There wasn't anything else," I assured her. "What you've got is what they had."

"Are you sure?"

"Yes, I'm sure."

Did she think I'd snatched a vial of pills, or a bottle of Maalox?

For crying out loud.

"I'm not accusing you of anything, Andy, really, that's not it." Still, she sounded worried enough. "But it's . . . odd, that's all. Can you take another look around, see if there's anything you might've overlooked?"

"What's going on, Patsy?" I wanted to know. "What's so odd about missing a few vials?" Both women were gone. It's not like they'd need more pills.

"I've got patients waiting for pickups, but maybe you could come by in thirty minutes. After you give Mrs. Kent's house another pass, okay?"

"All right."

She hung up, and I stood with the phone in hand, staring at it for a minute. That pang of uneasiness settled in my belly again, only it felt stronger than before. Like something was really off, and I just couldn't put my finger on it.

I slapped my cell shut and trudged upstairs to Bebe's bathroom, opening cabinets, rummaging through drawers, even checking out her night tables, merely scoring a metal tin with Bayer aspirin.

Surely, this couldn't be what Patsy had been so concerned about.

I crossed the hall and made my way to the guest bath, where Mother extricated bobby pins from her hair, after having removed the Wig from Hell.

"Is there something you need, darling?" she asked, as I maneuvered around her, searching nooks and crannies, finding extra bars of soap and tiny shampoos stolen from hotels around the world, but little else.

"Patsy Finch said all of Bebe's medications weren't in the bag I dropped off this morning. Have you seen any other prescriptions lying around?"

"No, sweetie, can't say that I have."

Regardless, I went back downstairs, combing through the marble-filled bath off the foyer, tackling the kitchen after that. I managed to add a couple bottles of vitamins to the Bayer, which I dumped in another baggie.

I yelled up to Mother that I'd be back in a bit and please not to go anywhere.

"Where would I go without my hair?" she called down from the top of the steps, holding the black bird's nest in one hand and a brush in the other. "I'd blow my cover."

"I like you better as a blonde," I told her.

"That's what Mabel said this morning."

"Mabel?" Uh-oh. "Why would she say something like that? Did she see you last night when she delivered our dinner?"

"Oh, no, it wasn't that," Cissy assured me. "She merely suggested I'd look better blonde than brunette. That's all. Don't be such a worrywart. The woman is perfectly harmless." She held the wig to her chest and stroked it, as if it were a cat. "I do feel sorry for her, Andy. When she pushed up her sleeves while we were packing, I saw those awful scars on her arms, and I told her I knew a fabulous plastic surgeon who could do wonders for her. But I think she was embarrassed."

"Not everyone believes plastic surgery is a cure-all, Mother."

"And they are so wrong, darling."

I shook my head, and she grinned.

"Keep the door locked," I told her. "And stay put."

I took off in the Jeep for the main house, driving faster than the eleven-mile-an-hour limit. She'd be fine, I told myself, figuring I wouldn't be gone long besides.

The pharmacy was part of the clinic where Dr. Finch saw his patients, in the same wing as the gym, physical therapy, and the salon.

A chime went off softly as I entered, and Patsy peeked through a cutout in the wall.

"Good, you're right on time. The doctor only has a few minutes before his next appointment," she said and gestured that I come around through the door marked PRIVATE, which led to a rear office.

Behind an imposing walnut-stained desk sat Dr. Finch in white lab coat, the dozen or so vials I'd previously delivered spread out before him, along with a pair of patient charts.

"Did you find anything?" Patsy asked, coming in behind me and closing the door, so that I felt a bit like a caged rat.

"Just these." I handed her the baggie with the aspirin and vitamins, which she eyeballed then shook her head.

"That can't be all of it."

"But it *is*," I insisted, as she scurried over to her husband's side, showing him the baggie and eliciting an even deeper frown. "I looked everywhere humanly possible, and there wasn't anything else. So why don't you tell me what's up? Maybe I can do something about it."

"Go on, Arnie," Patsy said and nudged her husband. "She's a smart girl. Maybe she can help."

Dr. Finch cleared his throat. "We seem to be missing the same medication from both Mrs. Kent's supply and from Mrs. Sewell's."

"What if they ran out and didn't get a chance to refill?" I suggested.

They exchanged a glance. Then Finch told me, "No, that's not the case, Miss Kendricks." He tapped the manila folders. "Our records show that refills were delivered to each of the women very recently."

"How recently?"

He cleared his throat again. "Just before the patients died."

Hello!

"What was it? Narcotics, sleeping pills?" I walked up to the desk, gazing at the multitude of vials scattered on the green blotter. "Could they have overdosed?"

I wondered if Mother had been right about her friends dying before their time, only getting the "how" part wrong. Maybe it wasn't murder at all, but suicide.

"It wasn't narcotics or sleeping pills," Patsy said, the grim set of her mouth at odds with her childlike features and sky-blue headband. "What's missing is an antihistamine, Andy, a generic drug called hydroxyzine hydrochloride. Mrs. Kent and Mrs. Sewell both took ten milligrams at bedtime for allergies."

I laughed, despite their serious expressions. "Allergy pills," I repeated. "That's what you're so freaked out about?"

Arnold Finch opened his mouth, but Patsy squeezed his shoulder, and he clamped his lips shut, like a ventriloquist's dummy. "It was hydroxyzine Pamoate, in this case," she said. "It comes in oral suspension, drops that can be mixed with liquids. It's easier to swallow, as some of our patients have trouble taking so many pills."

"Drops, like you give kids."

"Just like that, yes." Patsy nodded. "The drug is very effective for allergic reactions, but they're also used as tranquilizers. Around fifty to one hundred milligrams is often given to patients to sedate them before surgery."

"That sounds dangerous," I said. A little too much of your allergy meds and you were ready for the OR.

"No, no, the medication's safe enough for babies, but at a low dosage. Particularly since geriatric patients may have increased reactions. We warn them not to drive when they're drowsy, and not to use alcohol, which can heighten the drug's effect."

"So this hydroxy—whatever—that's missing. If it's not narcotic, why all the fuss?"

Patsy paused, and I saw her grip tighten on her

husband's shoulder. "The refills delivered to Mrs. Kent and Mrs. Sewell each contained a three-month dosage. We're just concerned that those bottles haven't turned up."

"Three months? Is that enough to knock someone off her feet?"

"Enough to knock a horse off its feet," Arnold Finch said with a snort.

Whoa. That didn't sound good.

Tranquilizer. High sedative effect. Increased reaction.

The words went round and round in my head, and I was putting together a picture that I didn't like at all.

"Okay, I have a question." I wet my lips. "How big a dose would be fatal?"

Arnold worked his tie loose, like he was having trouble getting air. "Unfortunately, Miss Kendricks," he intoned, "the PDR doesn't cite a lethal dose."

"What's the PDR?"

"Physician's Desk Reference," Patsy explained. "Basically, the bible for approved drugs. Which is all to say, we don't know how much is lethal. And it'd be impossible to find out, because there's no way to assay the quantity of the medication in one's system after it's ingested."

"Really?"

"Yes, really."

It was hard to imagine such a thing. I thought all drugs had some kind of limit, a point of no return that everyone agreed was dangerous.

The next thought that popped into my head: What if someone out there knew what that lethal limit was?

I hung on tightly to my purse, fully understanding why the Finches were so rattled. "You said the refills were delivered shortly before each woman passed away." Dr. Finch was avoiding my eyes, so I looked squarely at Patsy. "Did you deliver them yourself?" I could still picture her on the bike, pedaling away from Bebe's that morning. "Was there anything odd about their state of being? Did they seem despondent? Suicidal?"

Dr. Finch rolled his eyes, like I was an idiot.

"If they'd wanted to die by their own hands, Andy, they wouldn't have gone for an overdose of antihistamines." Patsy picked up a vial from the desk and shook it, so I could hear the pills rattle inside. Lots of them. "Not when Bebe Kent had Hydrocodone left over from a hip replacement in the spring, and Sarah Lee Sewell had a regular prescription for Xanax."

"Hydrocodone. That's codeine, right?" And I knew what Xanax was, considering Mother's uptight crowd popped those babies like candy.

"Yes, it's a codeine derivative."

I squeezed my eyes closed then opened them, trying to get a fix on this. "You never answered me, Patsy. Did you deliver those refills? Or was it someone else? Was it Mabel Pinkston?"

Talk about hearing a pin drop.

"Please tell me you didn't send her on any more deliveries today, not with any more of that drug, if she's misplacing things."

"Personnel matters are private, Miss Kendricks, and any conjecture about what happened to the hydroxyzine is best pursued by us. So I'd say we're done here." Dr. Finch shot up from his chair. "This discussion is over. I think you should go."

Bing! A light went on.

"You're afraid, aren't you?" I said. "Of getting sued."

If Mabel Pinkston had anything to do with this mess, then they'd be in deep doo-doo, as would Annabelle and Belle Meade itself.

"Leave now, Miss Kendricks." Dr. Finch had his hand on the telephone. "Or I'll call security."

"You're not going to brush this under the rug, are you?" I looked at Patsy, pleading. "What if the medications were involved in those women's deaths?"

Dr. Finch began punching buttons on his telephone.

"It's all right," Patsy said. "I'll walk Andy out." She came around the desk to take my elbow, forcibly guiding me from Dr. Finch's office.

Lawsuits, missing meds, rinsed-out glasses, two women dead.

"Patsy, talk to me," I begged her, as she ushered me through the "private" door and past several ladies perusing magazines in the waiting room. "You know about the lawsuits, about Bebe and Sarah Lee's threats, so what if there's some connection to the missing meds?"

She practically shoved me through the clinic's doors, murmuring, "I'm sorry, Andy," before she closed them in my face.

Well, I never!

Okay, maybe once or twice.

But still, how rude to throw me out like that

when I'd done them a favor, scrounging through dead people's medicine cabinets.

My cell rang in my purse.

I snatched it up and flipped it open.

"Yes," I snapped, my hackles up, whatever hackles were.

"Andrea?" The voice was tentative. "Andrea Kendricks?"

"Mr. Howard, is that you?" I was heading down the hallway, toward Annabelle's office.

"My friend got what you were looking for. Those names you gave me? They belong to the same person."

"The same?" I stopped, listening as he filled me in.

"You're sure?" I asked when he was done.

"No doubt about it."

"Thanks, Stephen. You've been a big help." I ended the call and dropped the phone in my purse, not certain of what to do.

Oh, dear, oh, dear, oh, dear.

It was starting to make sense, things that were said, gaping omissions. But I hadn't put all of it together before, couldn't have pieced it together until Stephen's call.

And still I wasn't sure.

What came to mind, strangely enough, was Mildred Pierce reciting the promo blurb from the movie posters, all those years ago:

"A mother's love leads to murder."

Maybe it had.

And maybe Annabelle knew it.

I kept walking, passing people and doors and

framed oils on the walls, hardly aware of my surroundings.

When I reached the door to Annabelle's office, it
was shut, but I went in without knocking.

She hung up the phone abruptly as I entered,
eyes wide when she saw who it was.

"Great balls of fire, Andy, I just heard from
Arnold Finch, who said you were in his office,
throwing around words like 'lawsuit' and 'liabil-
ity.' "

"What about murder and missing sedatives?
Did he mention those, too?"

"I'm worried about what being here is doing to
you, Andy. I think you're starting to believe in
Cissy's mixed-up theory." Annabelle chewed her
lip. "You know, perhaps it's best for all concerned
if you and your mother leave Belle Meade tonight.
I'll call you when the blood tests on Mrs. Sewell
return. So could you turn in your keycard and
badge? No hard feelings, right?"

She wanted to kick us out?

Without hearing a word I had to say?

Well, damned if I were going anywhere until
she listened up.

"You asked me before if I thought something
was wrong . . . even *you* had a feeling there might
be something to Mother's suspicions. Well, guess
what? I think so, too. In fact, I'm almost sure of it."
I marched up to her desk, slapping my palms
down hard enough to set her pencil holder rattling. "The worst part about it is what's wrong be-
gins and ends with you."

Her cheeks turned scarlet. "What's that supposed to mean, Andy? You think I'm responsible for what happened to Mrs. Kent and Mrs. Sewell?"

I looked her in the eye without flinching. "What it means, is that I think you know who is."

"You're nuts," she said and laughed. "How can you say such a thing?"

"Two words," I told her, straightening up and holding up a pair of fingers. "Mabel Pinkston."

"What?"

"Oh, wait, you're right. That's not it. Two more words," I said. "Em Albright. Although it's *M*, short for Mabel, not for Emma or Emily, like I originally believed. They're the same person, Annabelle, but then you knew that, didn't you?"

She stared, unblinking. "You're wrong."

"Am I? Then maybe you can explain why Mabel Pinkston Albright files tax returns but no one named Emma or Emily Albright does, huh?" I nodded. "Yeah, a friend of mother's checked it out. So no more lies."

"Don't do this, Andy, I beg you," she whispered, her face pale as an eggshell. "Stop this, before you hurt someone."

Stop? I was just getting started.

I went over to the bookcase with the photos of Annabelle and her so-called guardian angel. "She's lost a bunch of weight since the fire, hasn't she? But it's still Mabel, isn't it?" I faced her. "Why did you hide this, Annabelle? Is it because she's hiding behind you?"

"She's a good woman, and I won't hear you bad mouth her, okay? So don't go dredging up things that can't be changed." Her eyes welled, but I felt no sympathy. "The fire scarred her forever, can't you grasp that?"

"When she pushed up her sleeves while we were packing, I saw those awful scars on her arms, and I told her I knew a fabulous plastic surgeon who could do wonders for her. But I think I embarrassed her."

"The scars, yes." I stared at her. "From the burns that she suffered when she supposedly tried to save your parents. But that's not really what happened, Annabelle, is it?" I was fishing here, but I had a big fat worm on my hook, and she bit.

"It wasn't her fault. She was tired and she was cleaning up dinner and she left a rag too near the burner. So what?" Tears streamed down Annabelle's cheeks. "She never meant for anyone to get hurt. But the smoke alarm didn't work, and they never woke up."

"Was it really an accident, AB?" My heart pounded as I said it. "Or did she do it because she loved you and hated them? Hated how they'd treated you all your life. How they'd treated her."

Annabelle had set the stage.

". . . I was there the day it happened. I had dinner with them both, and it turned into a row, as usual. I can still hear the screaming in my head. God, they could be vicious. The last words I uttered that night before I ran out, slamming the door, were that I hated them. Despised them to the core. 'I wish you'd die!' I told them both. The next morning, they were dead."

Had her guardian angel granted her wish?

I wet my lips. "And what about Mabel's husband? Do you really think he died a natural death, and such a convenient one, too, since he wanted to take her away from that place . . . away from you."

"Frank is dead. The poor man wanted to get out of Austin after everything, but he never got the chance . . . He went to bed one night and never woke up again."

Annabelle rose from the chair on legs so shaky I felt sure she'd fall. She felt her way around the desk, keeping one hand on the edge, then stood but a foot away. I could see the terror in her face.

Was she so scared of what I was saying? Or of what she'd ignored for so long? Two women might be alive if she hadn't put her blinders on.

"Let this alone, Andy, I beg you." Tears splashed down her cheeks, onto the silk of her blouse, leaving splotches that wouldn't go away. "She wouldn't hurt anyone, not even for me."

"She told me herself that she'd do anything for you."

"She wouldn't kill for me, Andy!" She angrily swiped at damp cheeks. "She wouldn't."

"But I think she did," I said softly.

"Who knew about their threats, Annabelle?"

"The lawyers for the corporation, of course. Some of the staff I worked most closely with, like Patsy and Arnold Finch. I might've told a few others . . ."

Mabel knew. Annabelle would never have been able to keep something like that from the woman who'd raised her.

"She delivered the drugs to Mrs. Kent and Mrs. Sewell before they died," I went on, because I had

no doubt it was the truth. The Finches' silence
when I'd posed the question had been more
telling than words.

Had she mixed the drops in tea for Sarah and
wine for Bebe, knocking them cold, once and for
all? Afterward, once they were still and unbreath-
ing, she'd even rinsed out the glasses so there'd be
no trace of a crime.

I suddenly realized my mother wasn't so crazy.

Mabel Pinkston was.

Crazy like a fox.

"Were there others, Annabelle? In Austin, before you brought her here?" I asked, my voice
hoarse, incredibly drained. "Is that why you wondered about connections, because you feared the
worst, but you couldn't make yourself believe it?
You couldn't believe Mabel had killed for you, because then it would be over. You'd lose her forever.
You'd be all alone."

Annabelle shook her head violently. "No, Andy,
no. You're twisting this, seeing things that aren't
there. You're doing this because your mother
wants you to take her side. She's out to get me, like
the others."

"No, AB, that's not it at all . . ."

Then I stopped. Realized what she'd said. And
raw panic struck.

My mother.

Oh, God.

"I like you better as a blonde."

"That's what Mabel said this morning."

My blood iced over.

I grabbed her by the arms, ignoring her wince.
"Did you tell Mrs. Pinkston who Cissy is and

what she's doing here? Did you tell her my mother was out to get you? Please, tell me you didn't."

"She wouldn't hurt her . . . she wouldn't." But there was fear in her eyes behind the tears, and I knew even she wasn't convinced.

"Where is she now? *Where, Annabelle?*" I was shouting, and I didn't care.

"I don't know, I don't know. She said she had some deliveries to make after lunch and then she was going home early. She wasn't feeling well."

"You'd better hope she went home."

I let her go, and she hugged herself, shivering. "She wouldn't harm Cissy. I'm sure of it."

"You'd better be right," I said, backing up toward the door, watching her weep and knowing there was nothing more I could do for Annabelle Meade, not like in our camp days, where it had taken a few words of compassion or cookies from my care pack to make her smile.

I hightailed it to my car, desperately wanting to get back to Bebe's house, collect my things—and my mother—and get as far away from Belle Meade as possible. If I never saw the place again, it would be too soon.

I made a left onto Magnolia and nearly passed Bebe's townhouse altogether. I hit the brakes and did a U-turn, backtracking past the near-identical residences to find the one I'd missed, because my landmark had vanished.

I pulled the Jeep hard against the curb.

The Buick was gone.

It wasn't in the driveway. Wasn't anywhere in sight.

I jumped out and raced up to the house, finding the door unlocked, when I'm sure I'd set the lock when I'd left.

Dammit.

I'm calm, I'm calm, I'm calm as a frigging cucumber.

This had happened before, I reminded myself. Cissy had an irritatingly independent mind of her own. Maybe she was too restless to nap and had gone back to Sarah Lee Sewell's to finish packing.

"Mother!"

I ran up the steps to the guest room, ducking into the connecting bath, noting the absence of the black wig and cat's-eye glasses.

Okay, okay, she must've put them on before she went out.

That implied free will, didn't it? You couldn't force a wig on someone, could you? Then I glanced at the floor on the other side of the bed to see the black leather handbag with the buckles and glitter.

I snatched it up, spilling its contents on the bed. Wallet, coin purse, day planner, compact, lipstick, calling card case, and cell phone. I shook it, upside down, making sure I hadn't missed anything.

Where were the car keys?

Cissy would never take off without her purse much less drive ten feet without her wallet and ID. She was such a stickler for propriety.

Maybe she'd had to go in a hurry, I told myself, as I rushed down the stairs, through the foyer and past the living room into the kitchen, looking for a note, like she'd left that morning, checking the fridge, the table, the countertops, the sink. . . .

Oh, no.

My breath caught in my throat.

There, draining atop a folded dishtowel, were two rinsed-out mugs. A teakettle sat on a back burner of the stove, still warm to the touch, so they couldn't have been gone long.

It was the killer's M.O.

And I'd bet money on Mabel Pinkston.

Which meant the crazy bitch had come and gone . . . and she'd taken Cissy with her.

Chapter 19

I rushed to the Jeep and peeled out of Bebe's street, honking at a pair of helmeted bike riders taking up the middle of the road and finally swerving around them. Going well past the posted eleven-miles-per-hour limit and tires squealing with each turn, I went by Sarah Lee's, two streets over—my only hope—but I didn't spot the Buick there, either.

"Where are you, Ma?" I said out loud and smacked the steering wheel, helpless and afraid.

No use dialing Cissy's cell, since it was back in the bedroom with her purse. She wouldn't have had it turned on, anyway.

What next, what next, what next?

Okay, okay. I retrieved Annabelle's office number from my cell's memory and, one hand on the wheel, used the other to dial it, running over her "hello" with a rushed, "Cissy's gone and so's her car . . . I think Mabel's got her . . . hell, I think she drugged her before she stuffed her in the car . . . dammit, Annabelle, you have to tell me where she lives!"

Click.

She hung up.

Aaargh!

I hit the re-dial and got her again, "Give me her address, Annabelle, or I swear I'll . . ."

Click.

She hung up again.

Four years of sharing a bunk at Camp Longhorn, and it comes down to this? I should've let the mosquitoes eat her alive.

Panic overtook me, and I shook so bad I dropped my cell to my lap. I had to stop before the guardhouse and dig it from between my thighs. I was close to hyperventilating, trying mightily to figure out what to do next and coming up empty.

I saw Bob poke his head through the window of his tiny shack, and I bumped the Jeep forward, rolling the window down. "Did you see my moth . . . Miriam Ferguson leave the grounds in a silver Buick Century, maybe ten, fifteen minutes ago?"

He scratched his jaw, taking his own sweet time. "Matter of fact, she went right by without a wave, but I recognized that dark hair and those glasses. Her blonde friend in the passenger seat must've had a Bloody Mary too many at the Early Bird Happy Hour. Couldn't even hold up her head."

"You said Miriam was driving?"

"Yes, ma'am."

"And a blonde was in the other seat?"

"Potted as a plant."

Wait a danged minute.

Mrs. Pinkston wasn't blonde.

She must've been wearing the wig and glasses, not my mother.

Cissy was the blonde who couldn't hold up her head. So Mabel *had* drugged her, and I had no idea how much, or how long she had until it put her to sleep permanently.

I hauled butt out of Belle Meade, tearing past the Stonehenge posts and into Forest Lane traffic.

How could this be happening?

I didn't even know where to go.

And if I didn't get to her soon, she might not wake up again. Like Bebe and Sarah Lee . . . or Franklin Albright, Mabel's goner of a husband.

What to do, what to do?

Call the police?

Tell them a pyromaniac serial killer with gray hair and pin curls had kidnapped my wig-wearing mother who'd been using a fake name to play Miss Marple at an old folks' home after two ladies from her bridge group had gone boots up?

Oh, yeah, that would go over big.

Think, Andy, think!

I looked up the last number to call me, and I pressed Send, murmuring, "Answer, please, answer," before I heard the now-familiar voice on the other end say, "Andy, is something wrong?" He obviously had CallerID, too.

"Stephen, you've got to help. I think my mother's in big trouble, and I don't know what to do." I told him why, talking as fast as I could, and he didn't laugh, didn't hang up, just put me on hold for what seemed like forever while he made some calls on his landline.

I was on the verge of a crying jag, and I would have let loose right there and then, if I didn't have anything better to do.

But I did.

I had to keep it together.

When he came back on, he gave me an address on Garland Road and added, "I'm heading out the door right now. I'll meet you there myself. Hey, it'll be all right, Andy. We'll find her."

It'll be all right.

I repeated those words over and over again in my head as I made my way to Mockingbird and headed east, toward White Rock Lake and Buckner Boulevard.

Mabel had a good head start, and I kept hitting red light after red light, until I thought my heart would burst from my chest.

Not for the first time in the last two days, I sorely wished Cissy had a chip in her fanny so I could track her with GPS.

Holy Moly! That was it!

Why hadn't I thought of it before?

Sandy's Buick had OnStar with GPS tracking. Maybe we couldn't train a satellite on Mother, but we could get a fix on the Century.

I speed-dialed the house on Beverly and Sandy picked up on the first ring.

Without preamble, I told her to use the landline, call OnStar, tell them a woman had been carjacked in her vehicle and to get in touch with the Dallas police. "Just don't hang up!" I begged, as I wanted to hear everything, to know what was going on and where to drive, so I could get to Cissy first.

I had trouble concentrating on the road, earning

honks that barely registered, clutching my cell to my ear and steering one-handed. Telling myself just to listen and breathe and go forward.

I want my mommy.

A little voice cried in my head, nearly drowning out Sandy as she said, "Andy, they've got the car . . . it's stopped on Garland . . . somewhere near the entrance to the Arboretum . . . they're sending the police . . . please stay with me . . . tell me when you get there. I have to know that she's okay."

I hit the accelerator, weaving around vehicles moving too slowly, rushing through a light as it flipped from yellow to red, my emotions bubbling nearer to the surface as I got closer and closer.

From Mockingbird, I took Buckner, spotting a cop car well ahead, already turning on Garland, and I prayed they were going where I was going, that they'd reach Cissy and she'd be okay.

A speedy two miles on Buckner, and I shot right on Garland, counting the blocks from five to four to three, two, one, until the Arboretum entrance came up on the right.

A siren whirred behind me, and I saw an ambulance in my rearview as I pulled into the main parking lot to spot the blue-and-white stopping behind a car at the far end of the lot, about as far from the ticket booths and visitors pavilion as you could get.

"She's here, and so's the ambulance," I croaked into the cell, telling Sandy before the phone dropped from my hand. I didn't bother to pick it up.

I covered the space between in no time flat,

threw the Jeep into Park, and flung myself out the door, running toward the Buick as one of the uniformed officers leaned into the front seat.

The second officer looked up and came toward me, ready to make a tackle.

The siren on the ambulance screamed as it approached, drowning out my cries as I pushed at the cop who grabbed my arm to stop me.

"She's my mother, Cissy Kendricks," I said breathlessly, because she didn't have her purse, didn't have her ID. "Someone gave her sedative drops back at Belle Meade and drove her here." I gazed around us, at the half-empty parking lot. "Did you see her? Did you see someone fleeing the scene?"

"Take it easy," was all he said. "Take it easy."

The paramedics jogged past us, hauling a gurney piled with equipment, and the cop who restrained me shouted to them that he had "the daughter" and that there was a possible "drug OD of some kind."

I saw them lift her out of the front seat and lay her down gently.

The harder I struggled to get away from the cop, the more tightly he held me.

Through tears, I watched them hook up an IV, take her pulse and her BP, then they raised the gurney and ran it toward the opened doors of the ambulance, passing close enough so I could see her face.

Her eyes were closed, skin paler than pale, but she was breathing.

I think.

I mean, she had to be breathing, didn't she?

"I want to go with her," I cried, but the cop gave me a hard shake, silencing me, and he bent down to look in my eyes.

"They're taking her to the Doctor's ER. You're in no shape to drive. I'll get you there, all right? That your car?"

I nodded numbly, shivering so badly I couldn't have gotten behind the wheel if my life had depended on it. He helped me into the Jeep, and, once inside, picked up my cell and passed it over, before he put the thing in gear and hauled ass.

The hospital sat on Poppy Drive, literally—thankfully—around the corner, and we arrived just after the ambulance. I scrambled out, sprinting after the gurney going through the auto doors.

"Hey, hey!" A nurse in scrubs grabbed me, asked my name and who I was chasing. I opened my mouth and it all spilled out, Cissy's name, her age, what drug I thought she'd been given, and how long ago.

Someone else drew me toward the chairs in the waiting area, where I sat and fought back tears, until Sandy showed up in a matter of minutes and put her arms around me. Together, we waited and waited, for what seemed an eternity.

When finally we were told we could go in, one at a time, Sandy prodded me forward, despite how much I knew she wanted to see Cissy with her own eyes.

I would have snuck her in beside me, if the nurse hadn't stood there, guarding the door like the Secret Service.

"She's had a tube down her throat, so she'll be

hoarse for a while. Her stomach won't feel so great, either," the scrub-wearing bodyguard told us.

But hoarse was far better than dead, so I thanked her profusely.

I entered the room on tiptoe; quiet as a mouse as I crossed toward the bed.

Cissy curled in a fetal position beneath the sheets, the curtain pulled halfway around it to give her privacy.

I went right to her and reached my hand through the side rail. I needed to touch her, feel the warmth of her skin. She didn't have to be awake, just alive.

Gingerly, I curled my fingers around hers, as if she were fragile and might break if I held on too tight.

She opened her eyes, looked up, and grimaced. "Gastric *lavage*," she croaked in a whisper. "It sounds French, but all it means is they suck your guts out. Ugh."

"They had to, Mother," I reminded her. "You had enough sedative in your system to knock a horse off its hooves."

She gestured at the water on the fake wood table beside her, drawing herself up higher on the pillow. I held the cup and straw so she could take a sip. When she was done and settled back, she sighed. "Is Sandy here?"

"Waiting just outside." I hesitated. "Stephen's on his way, too."

I thought maybe that would please her, but she showed no sign of it. She blinked hard, her face fighting her emotions.

I saw her throat work as she swallowed. "Mabel

Pinkston tried to kill me, didn't she? She came to the door after you left, and I let her in. I thought she was a harmless old woman." Her pale eyes glistened. "She put something stronger than honey and lemon in the tea. I was halfway through the cup when it hit me. While I could still stagger, she hustled me out to the car and shoved me in." She stopped, her chin trembling. "Why would she do that, Andy? Why would she want to hurt me? I hardly knew her."

I stroked her hair, as she'd stroked mine when I'd been sick as a child. "She did it because she knew what you were up to."

"How?"

"Annabelle told her you were out to destroy Belle Meade." I debated whether to spill the rest then and there, but she had a right to hear, after what she'd been through. "I think she killed Bebe and Sarah Lee, too. They'd threatened to sue, and Annabelle panicked. Mabel came to her rescue, made things right, as she had Annabelle's whole life."

"She killed Sarah and Bebe?" A feeble moan worked its way through her cracked lips, and she squeezed her eyes shut. Tears streaked out between dark lashes. "So I was right all along. They were murdered."

"You were dead-on."

For a moment, she was quiet, and I heard voices outside the door.

Mother said hoarsely, "I was fooled by a woman I felt sorry for. I underestimated Mabel Pinkston, and she got the better of me. Do you know what that means?" She hiccupped. "I'm a lousy detective, aren't I?"

She looked so despondent, so miserable in the hospital gown, having had a tube down her throat and her stomach pumped; seeing her like that would have broken my heart any other time.

But I was so glad she was okay, and I wanted her to stay that way.

I bent close and whispered against her damp cheek, "I'm only gonna say this once, so listen good. You may be a crummy detective, Cissy Blevins Kendricks, but you're a most amazing woman. Oh, yeah, and you'll play Nancy Drew again over my dead body."

Without the slightest hesitation, she whispered back, "I guess we'll see about that, won't we, Sparky?"

Epilogue

★ If I were to write a final report on *The Case of the Murdering Mabel*, as Mother liked to call it, my conclusions would've amounted to something like this:

Stephen Howard, my new-found hero, ended up nabbing the elusive "Em" as she walked to her rented rooms up Garland Road. She'd ditched the black wig and eyeglasses somewhere en route from the Arboretum, and I hoped Mrs. Coogan wouldn't be too upset when Cissy didn't return them. As I see it, that was the one decent thing Mabel did.

The Dallas police were holding Mabel Pinkston Albright on assorted charges, including kidnapping and attempted murder. Mother's statement and testimony would be the biggest piece of evidence against her.

Okay, maybe the *only* evidence against her.

Much as the D.A.'s office claimed they'd like to investigate the deaths of Bebe Kent and Sarah Lee Sewell, there wasn't much to go on. Particularly since the blood test on Sarah Lee returned negative, showing only traces of all the meds she'd been taking, including the hydroxyzine Pamoate. Like Dr. Finch had told me, there was no way to quantify how much of it was in someone's system once it was ingested; ergo, no one could prove the women were poisoned with their own drugs.

Mabel had been much smarter than anyone had given her credit for.

Annabelle wasn't talking. Big surprise. She was lucky not to be behind bars herself, charged with blind faith and stupidity.

Mum's the word with the Finches, too. (I guess, birds of a feather keep their beaks shut together.)

Anyway, I was out of the detecting business, and Cissy was, too, whether she liked it or not. We just weren't cut out for undercover work. Or out of cover, for that matter.

Case closed.

Qué será, será.

End of report.

Brian Malone returned from Galveston on Wednesday, stopping by my condo on his way to his apartment. Now *that* was a man with his priorities in order.

I kissed him good and hard as soon as I opened the door, and I didn't care a fig that snoopy Penny George was standing on the sidewalk, watching, her mouth hanging open. I was sure she'd rat me out to my mother at their next Bible study, but being with him again was worth every moment.

Malone had the brilliant idea to move it inside and nudged me through the door and toward the bedroom, until I put the kibosh on his reunion plans, at least for the time being.

"Go brush your teeth or whatever else you need to do to freshen up," I told him. "We're meeting Mother and Stephen for a double date."

"A double date?"

"Her words, not mine."

"Who's Stephen?"

"I'll tell you on the way."

"On the way to where? I thought Cissy was taking it easy."

I brushed a lock of brown from his forehead and wiped my lip gloss from his mouth. "Would you believe the Mockingbird IHOP?" I said and shrugged. "Mother has a sudden craving for pancakes with faces on them."

"Is she nuts?"

Ah.

Life was back to normal.

Whatever normal was.

Where High Society Meets The Murder Set

SUSAN McBRIDE's

Debutante Dropout Mysteries

BLUE BLOOD
0-06-056389-3/$6.50 US/$8.99 Can

To the dismay of her high society mother Cissy, Dallas heiress Andrea Kendricks wants no part of the Junior League life—opting instead for a job as a website designer. Now her good friend Molly O'Brien is accused of killing her boss and somehow Andy must find a way to help clear Molly's name.

THE GOOD GIRL'S GUIDE TO MURDER
0-06-056390-7/$6.99 US/$9.99 Can

Andrea is on hand to witness domestic diva Marilee Mabry's new TV studio go up in flames. And when a body turns up in the rubble, the apparent victim of some very foul play, Andy has to hunt down the killer.

THE LONE STAR LONELY HEARTS CLUB
0-06-056408-3/$6.99 US/$9.99 Can

Though doctors declare retired senior Bebe Kent's death totally natural, Cissy Kendricks believes her old friend's demise was hastened—and she enlists her daughter Andrea to join her in a search for the truth.